"IF ... I'LL KILL HIM!"

Orwoz and his assassins had jumped down off the platform and were running up the aisle between the stunned Saltspeakers and us. When they were almost to us, Theshei shoved me away. As I staggered back, he held the Black Stick out parallel to the ground and snapped it like a twig. It split down the long axis, leaving two sharp tapering points.

He stood there for an instant holding the two halves—the knobbed end like a spear and the other like a sword. I stumbled toward him, and Theshei threw the spear end right at my head.

He was too close for me to duck. The point sliced open my forehead as it went past. It would have struck Orwoz in the throat if the knobbed end hadn't hit me in the right forehead like a hammer.

Then I couldn't see anything, and I couldn't think. It was like I vanished. Or the world did.

COSMIC THUNDER

WILLIAM JOHN WATKINS

AVON BOOKS • NEW YORK

COSMIC THUNDER is an original publication of Avon Books. This work has never before appeared in book form. This work is a novel. Any similarity to actual persons or events is purely coincidental.

AVON BOOKS
A division of
The Hearst Corporation
1350 Avenue of the Americas
New York, New York 10019

Copyright © 1996 by William John Watkins
Cover art by Matt Stawicki
Published by arrangement with the author
Library of Congress Catalog Card Number: 96-96021
ISBN: 0-380-78203-0

First AvoNova Printing: July 1996

AVONOVA TRADEMARK REG. U.S. PAT. OFF. AND IN OTHER COUNTRIES, MARCA REGISTRADA, HECHO EN U.S.A.

Printed in the U.S.A.

RA 10 9 8 7 6 5 4 3 2 1

For my son, Wade,
who died unexpectedly of meningitis
at the age of thirty

Everything dances.
Nothing lost.
Nothing gained.
Everything that goes remains.
No good-byes.
And nothing dies.

For my wife, Sandra; my daughter, Tara; and
my son, Chadom, who keep me in the world

CHAPTER
1

IF I'd assassinated Theshei like I was supposed to, things would never have turned out the way they did.

Since the Change, people have pretty much forgotten that things weren't always as good as they are now, and maybe they're right to forget. Is and was don't matter much anymore except to me. I was around pretty much from the beginning. In fact, I went to school with Theshei, although his name was Naster Greatbridge then. He changed it when we got religion and joined the Saltspeakers. That was one of the things you were supposed to do: put away your old name and become a new person, dedicated to Sowing the Salt.

To tell the truth, I think that as far as Theshei was concerned, half the attraction of the Saltspeakers was changing his name. He didn't like his name much. I believe his mother got it from her favorite flower or something, but if so, she should've saved it for the sister he never had, because it shaped his life in ways I'm sure she never intended, although What-Went-By clearly intended them. I guess she imagined him all grown up in some exotic profession where that name would have been an asset, but she overlooked the fact that he was going to have to grow up with it first, and he was going to have to grow up around other kids. Naturally, they called him Nasty.

Generally, there's only two things you can be with a

nickname like that: either a geek or a goon. As always,
Theshei found another alternative. He was both. And
neither. He really didn't have the size to be a goon, and I
don't think he entirely had the temperament either. Not
that he couldn't defend himself; he could and had to.
Some musclehead was always coming up to him and
saying, "OK, Nasty, let's see how nasty you are." But he
learned pretty early that no matter how bad he kicked
somebody's butt, there was going to be another one
along sooner or later, and another one after that. So
when he could avoid a fight, he did.

He was amazingly quick, and he could afford to stand
there dodging punches and trying to use reason. In fact,
he used to win lunch money giving people five punches
for a quarter and double their money back if they hit
him. Hardly anybody ever did. When reason didn't
work, he got it over with as quickly as possible, sometimes by faking an epileptic seizure. While that saved
him a considerable number of beatings, it didn't particularly endear him to other kids, who tended to shun him
like the vice principal's son for a couple weeks after a
really convincing mock convulsion.

But that kind of isolation never lasted very long.
Normally, when you treat a kid like he's a geek for a
couple weeks, he accepts the general consensus and
becomes one. But not Theshei. He was one of those
people who truly don't care what other people think. Not
one of those people who rejects popular opinion about
themselves, but one of those people who just never give
other people's opinion of them a first thought, let alone a
second. And since that's the kind of person every kid
would really like to be, it was pretty hard to keep
shunning him.

But in a lot of ways, it was just as hard to like him.
Even for me, and I was his best friend. For one thing, he
was always wondering about things no normal kid gives
much headroom to, like the meaning of the universe,
death, life after death, and existentialist contradictions.

Speculative philosophy is a scary thing in a person under thirty-five, and theology isn't much better; so asking people whether they thought God was hermaphroditic since both men and women are made in his image tended to drive other kids away.

Taking science courses in high school didn't improve that any. Most kids don't want any part of a guy who asks you if you think the universe is random or homogeneous and if the statistical clumps and voids of a random universe might resolve into apparent order on a local level. Teachers don't even like questions like that. They like answers even less, and Theshei had dozens for every question. I suppose if he didn't write everything backward on his tests, he could have gone off to college on some sort of scholarship if things were the way they once were. But they weren't. So instead, we joined the Saltspeakers.

I guess it had something to do with the turning of the Millennium, but two things came back in vogue as the century went out: drugs and cults. People have forgotten that there ever were such things as the Sugar One-Shot or the Saltspeakers, they seem so ridiculously wrongheaded now. But the end of a century always makes people think it's going to be the end of the world, and things got crazier and crazier as the century dwindled. And, of course, the arrival of the Sandscripti, those luminous ghosts from outer space, didn't help things any.

At least we assumed they were from outer space. They didn't actually have any ships, and the official word on them was that they had "appeared," apparently simultaneously, all over the world. Every country had them, but on the whole there weren't all that many of them. The first six weeks they were here, the Government kept ours secretly confined, but it's hard to confine somebody you can put your hand through, and it's even harder to threaten them. Nobody, not even the hardheads in the military, wanted to see what the Sandscripti would do if they were successfully attacked.

Initially, I think, the military started to shoot at them, but since bullets, bombs, electricity, lasers, magnetic fields, and everything else they tried passed right through the Sandscripti and the Sandscripti didn't seem capable of acting upon anything on earth directly any more than anything here could act directly on them, human beings put up with them.

There was the usual call to nuke 'em, but any chance of that disappeared when they left voluntary confinement and spread out across the country. We'd tried that solution a few years earlier on some other creatures we didn't like, and it didn't work very well. There was no keeping them a secret after that.

After a while, we just got used to them floating around, sort of like luminous ghosts, and we accepted that they were going to haunt our world for as long as they liked, and there was nothing we could do about it. Not that people didn't keep trying. Thousands of psychics, holy men, holy women, priests, rabbis, shamans, witches, and whatnot tried to exorcise them in a dozen different languages, but nobody had any luck. Besides, they were useful. Sort of.

The Sandscripti could communicate by drawing luminous figures in the air with their light wands, and indirectly, they gave us a lot of useful information, but all they really wanted to talk about was the Ribbonverse and its creation. We'd have been glad to talk to them about that, but the Ribbonverse can only be talked about in Sandscripti, and Sandscripti can only be spoken with the light wand, and nobody knew how to use one.

So for a while, it was pretty much a one-way conversation—until they set up their schools and offered free room and board to anyone who wanted to learn how to use the light wand. I suppose they would've stayed in the education business, but the lawyers must have gotten hold of them and told them about the advantages of being a religion. And even though the whole concept of the Ribbonverse sounded a lot more like physics than anything else, since there was no way to know what the Sandscripti were going to teach us about the Ribbon-verse once somebody learned to use the light wand, there was no way to prove it *wasn't* a religion.

So for about three months, the Sandscripti, with no theology at all, were on their way to becoming one of the largest Nontraditional Theological Alternatives. But it turned out the light wand wasn't easy to learn, and human beings who made even small mistakes with it tended to evaporate in a flash of light. After the first hundred vaporizations or so, new converts dropped way off.

In fact, the only converts they got were fanatical physicists and people on the run. The Sandscripti gave sanctuary to anyone willing to try to learn the light wand, and since nobody knew what the Sandscripti could do, nobody dared to violate it. Not even the Government could get you if you were under Sandscripti protection. But it was a last resort, because if you didn't make at least some progress with the light wand, you were back on the street, and the odds were that whoever you were running from would be in the crowd of revenge seekers who always waited outside any Sandscripti temple.

The Government tolerated the Sandscripti mainly because it couldn't do anything else. They were beyond coercion, and they possessed unknown capabilities for retaliation. As long as they weren't a problem, the sensible thing to do was to let them alone. It was one of the few sensible things I ever saw the Government do.

The Sandscripti may have faded into the background after that, but not before their presence added fuel to the Great International Party. About three years before those double zeros came up on the calendar, the Great International Party started spontaneously on all seven continents and didn't burn out until the Change. The media called it the Party on the Eve of Destruction because everybody was expecting some minor country to nuke some other minor country and kick off Armageddon. Plus, places whose names weren't dry on the map yet had strains of sicknesses nobody had any immunity to, and a guy with a suitcase could take out New York City just by opening his contaminated baggage in the subway.

A lot of people thought the ecology was going to collapse, or the ozone hole was finally going to cover all of the Northern Hemisphere, or the earthquakes were going to keep getting bigger and bigger until the continents flipped over. Some people even thought the sun was going to go nova, or the comet that wiped out the dinosaurs was going to come streaking toward the perihelion of its ten-million-year orbit and go crashing through the solar system again. But no matter how much the Partyers disagreed about the way in which the world was going to meet its fate, they all agreed that the Sandscripti were the shiny heralds of the end of the world. All their belief did was make them party harder.

And then, of course, the world economy falling apart didn't help things any. It had been going sour in the United States for a long time. Jobs went south, over the border south; jobs went west, beyond the ocean west; and they never came back. A small jihad in the Middle East tainted a sizable portion of the oil supply, and then the Japanese stock market, which was pretty much a casino anyway, went belly up. The Japanese wanted to cash in their Treasury bills to pay their stock losses, only we didn't have the money. And we couldn't raise it, not quick enough. The Government was on the brink of declaring temporary bankruptcy, only it never got the chance; the whole world economy lost faith in itself, and that's all it took.

It turned out a lot of the world's wealth was just promises anyway, which was fine as long as nobody tried to cash them in all at once. And then somebody did. Then everybody did. Currencies disintegrated. The price of energy soared, and air conditioning became a thing of the past. Building stopped. Factories stopped.

Trade stopped. There just weren't any jobs. Nobody believed it could go down that fast. Ordinary people suddenly discovered we were all two paychecks from the sidewalk, and that's where a lot of us ended up. Especially the young.

There just wasn't any place else to go. Families broke up, like mine did, and went somewhere else, anywhere else, looking for work. Some turned to each other; others turned *on* each other instead, and stories of somebody going crazy with despair and killing their own family got so common the news wouldn't even cover it. You had to kill total strangers, and rich ones at that, if you wanted to get any media attention.

In a few months, half the towns and cities in America looked like those disaster pictures you used to see on TV with people lining up outside tents to get handouts of food. Just like that, we were all living in the Third World, all except ten percent anyway. The middle class was gone almost overnight. Five percent were rich, one percent handled the money of the rich, four percent looked after their lawns and their children, and the rest of us tried to find some work that lasted longer than a day. Americans were stunned. Nobody believed it could happen, and by the time they did, they were too whipped to believe it could change.

I didn't figure that all out for myself. Theshei and I used to talk about it a lot, and he was the one who pieced most of it together. Most of the time there wasn't much to do but lay around in that little shack we made out of cardboard boxes and talk. He'd stopped living with his family a while before because he couldn't get enough odd jobs to keep up his end, and he was just too old to feed if he wasn't bringing anything in. I didn't have much family left by then anyway, but if I had, I'd have been in the same boat. Every day we had the same conversation. I'd say, "You want to go look for work?"

Theshei would lift his head off the backpack he was using for a pillow and say, "There is no work."

I'd say, "That was yesterday."

And Theshei would say, "Why don't we go to college instead." He was being sarcastic. There weren't many colleges left, and the only people going to them were the sons and daughters of the rich. The Government had no money left for loans for ordinary people to go to college, and it certainly wasn't giving any money away. It was having enough trouble feeding everybody and trying to create work.

Sometimes I'd ignore him, and sometimes I'd play along. I'd say, "Which one?"

He'd say, "You already got a bachelor's degree in economics from Screw U. Why don't we go to Princeton and get doctorates? Then we could get jobs on some estate somewhere, raking leaves or babysitting." He wasn't kidding. There were people with Ph.D.'s in English a couple boxes down from us, and they'd have killed for a job like that.

Usually, I'd let it go though and then wait a minute and say, "You want to go get something to eat?"

That would usually get Theshei to prop his head up on his hand and say, "Walk an hour, wait six hours in line, and get some stuff without enough calories to make up for what you spent walking down there and standing around?" If he was particularly stiff and cranky from sleeping on the macadam, he'd add, "Assuming nobody tries to shoot you, stab you, or beat you up while you're waiting just because they're bored." That was certainly possible.

Then he might add, "Or if there isn't a riot." He knew there was hardly ever a disturbance, let alone a riot, but he liked to tell me this long theory he had about how lowering people's calories below a certain level took away their will to resist, and after a few months on a starvation diet, nobody had the energy to do much of anything, and that led to greater dependence on the Government, which strained the Government's resources even more and led to less calories, more depression, and a general apathy, which made things worse. I forget where it went after that, but it was depressing. It didn't depress Theshei though. He loved to think about how things worked, whether it was people, or galaxies, or the end of civilization.

It certainly looked like he was right, but I usually didn't want to hear it again, so I'd say, "Maybe we'll hear about some work."

Theshei would give a long sigh and say, "There was no work yesterday. There's no work today. There won't be any work tomorrow." And he was right.

But even so, I'd say, "Maybe things will change."

If he was awake enough by then, he'd go into a long explanation about how you lose the ability to cooperate when it's everybody for themself too long and how the downward spiral of expectations becomes a self-fulfilling prophecy leading to despair, despair leads to a reduction in the immune system, and reduced immunity leads to the eventual outbreak of worldwide epidemics, which in turn leads to an eventual restoration of civilization at a lower level of functioning, a resurgence of the environment, and a decreased reliance on technology. More often, he'd just say, "Wait ten years, enough people will be dead by then. There'll be plenty of jobs."

Sometimes I'd get mad at that and say so, and Theshei would say, "Yeah, well, everybody's got to have a dream to cheer them up."

It was a sort of a joke because that was what the Smiling Zombies always said if you asked them why they took Dylastic Sugar. It wasn't really that hard to understand; everything seemed to be disintegrating, and people needed something to hold onto. For a lot of people, it was Dylastic Sugar. Dylastic Sugar was supposed to be the Last Great Euphoric, the long-awaited, safe, and reversible psychedelic. It was just what the Great Party needed. It was cheap: A high school dropout could make it out of ordinary granulated sugar. It made you blissfully happy with whatever you were doing without wrecking your concentration or your dexterity, and you could reverse its effects just by drinking a couple glasses of ice water. It wasn't even illegal.

Faced with a scary reality, a lot of people just joined the Great Party and left. As long as they stayed away from ice water, everything felt fine and they had no worries. People who had jobs went and did them with big smiles on their faces, and went home with big smiles on their faces, and slept with big smiles on their faces. And people who didn't have jobs did the same. People who didn't take the Sugar One-Shot called them Smiling Zombies. The Smiling Zombies didn't care.

But not everybody went happily crazy on Dylastic Sugar. A lot more people turned to the cults. Of course, they weren't called cults then; they were called Nontraditional Theological Alternatives, and even Traditional Theological Alternatives started sprouting Nontraditional Alternatives like the Saltspeakers. Smiling Zombies called the Nontraditional Theological Alternatives, the NUTS. We were NUTS. We joined the Saltspeakers.

It was a spur-of-the-moment thing for me, but I think Theshei had been weighing the alternatives a long time before he brought it up. It was raining real hard one day and even though we'd waxed the box real good, the rain was dribbling in and practically rushing in under it, and Theshei asked me if I wanted to join the Saltspeakers with him, and I said, "Anything to get in out of the rain."

He said, "All right. Tomorrow we're going to college."

CHAPTER 2

US going to college didn't seem to make much sense to me until we got there. It was a real long walk, way out in the country. We started early, but it was late afternoon the next day before we got off the highway onto an old country road lined with woods and walked along that until we got to the big iron gate of the Saltspeaker Compound. Theshei was right. The compound used to be a small private college before it went bankrupt and the Saltspeakers bought it up, probably for next to nothing. It still felt like a college though, and it certainly looked like one. On one of the big stone pillars the gate was attached to, there was a metal plaque with a date from the 1800s on it. The big gate was closed, and there was a heavy chain keeping it that way, but you could still look in, and we did.

I never would have had much hope of going to a place like that even when middle-class people had a chance to go to college, but I felt at home the minute I looked in. There was a wide drive just inside the gate running straight down between two lines of big old oaks for about a hundred and fifty yards. At the end of the drive, there was a white building like an old mansion that they probably used for an administration building to impress the high school kids coming there to look the place over. You could see parts of more buildings beyond it, much taller ones that were probably dormitories once. They

11

were made out of the same gray stone as the gate pillars, but you could only see the top few floors of them because there were trees in the way. There were trees everywhere. Big trees. Old trees. Old like the stone. Everything was just saturated with tradition. It looked like heaven to me.

Theshei wasn't nearly as impressed. He looked in, but he was more interested in finding somebody to talk to. There didn't seem to be anybody around. There was an archway made of stone next to the right pillar with a smaller gate in it, and he turned away toward it, but he didn't get closer than five feet before we were surrounded.

One minute there was nobody there, and the next minute we were in the middle of a crowd of very big guys in camouflage suits. I figured they must have come from the trees on the far side of the road behind us or maybe from the trees and bushes that ran down the road in both directions from the gate, but wherever they came from, they certainly got there quickly. It was hard to tell whether they were there to keep people out or to keep people in. From what we knew of the Saltspeakers, it could have been both.

They looked like they thought we were spies and couldn't decide whether to kill us, or interrogate us and then kill us. They didn't point any guns at us, but it felt like they did, and I had the feeling somebody had us in their sights even if these guys didn't. It seemed to me that if we really were dangerous, their snipers would have to shoot a lot of their own before they got to us, and the guys around us looked like they knew that but didn't care. That was probably the scariest thing about them.

Finally one of them stopped looking us over and said, "What do you want?"

Theshei looked up at him and said, "We want to Sow the Salt."

The Saltspeakers were dedicated to Sowing Salt. Salt was the Saltspeaker theology. It tried to say everything as simply as possible. I think Theshei liked the Salt because of the way it answered his question about the nature of the universe. The Salt says, "Goodguy made stuff, all the stuff there is. Some of the stuff went bad and made Badguy. Badguy caught a bad case of Death. Goodguy made Niceplace. Goodguy made Whatzisname and Whatzername and gave them Niceplace. Whatzisname and Whatzername didn't understand their Anatomical Differences. Then Badguy showed up, screwed Whatzername, and gave her a case of Death. She screwed Whatzisname and gave him a case of Death. Ever since, everybody's got a bad case of Death. Stop screwing around and it'll go away."

It seemed reasonable at the time.

Except for the Great Party, people had been equating sex with death for years, ever since FastAIDS came out and people started dying before they could get up off one another. I wasn't all that attractive anyway, so it wasn't like celibacy was such a big sacrifice for me, but I don't think Theshei took his vow of chastity all that seriously. Even from the beginning, he seemed to think the Salt was negotiable; so it wasn't much of a surprise when he went Renegade. Just like it wasn't much of a surprise when I was the one who went to kill him. Except to Theshei.

But then I don't think Theshei understood anything the way the rest of us did. Of course, that sounds pretty obvious now that we understand Everything, but back before the Change things weren't so obvious, even to Theshei. And they were a lot less obvious to everybody else.

Not that the rest of us Saltspeakers knew it. We were like people in a foggy field. Everything seemed clear around *us;* it was everybody else that was lost in the fog. Of course, we thought that was because the Salt was so clear. It was so simple you couldn't misunderstand it. We just accepted it. Theshei was the only one who

thought there was more to it, and he kept going after
Deeper Meaning no matter how much it disturbed
everybody else.

He did that right from the beginning. In fact, I thought
he was going to get us both killed right there at the gate.
And even if he didn't, there was a fair chance we'd get
killed anyway, because the Saltspeakers did sometimes
Pound Salt into particularly dense converts until they
pounded them to death.

We knew from the beginning we'd either become
Saltspeakers or die in the attempt. They were dead
serious about Sowing the Salt; so even though it was easy
to join, once you joined, there was no way out alive. The
Saltspeakers were pretty secretive about a lot of the
things they did, and they weren't letting anybody take
those secrets out into the world. The guy in charge
looked at us like he thought there were only two groups
in the world: traitors and potential traitors. "So you
want to Sow the Salt," he said. But he didn't sound very
convinced. Theshei nodded, and the guy jerked his head
toward the little gate and said, "Through there."

I thought he'd go first, but he didn't. He gave a stern
nod to his men, and all but two of them faded back into
the leaves. The three of them fell in behind us and stayed
there all the way down the drive. I had the feeling they
were just waiting for us to bolt right or left so they could
run us down and cut our throats. But everything was
different when we got to the white building. The guy who
greeted us there was a middle-aged, soft, pink, chubby
guy with wispy red hair that stood out from his head like
flames. But if his head was on fire, it didn't seem to
bother him. He shook our hands and hovered around us,
smiling like a Zombie. It was probably his job, but he
couldn't have been more pleasant if he was getting a
commission on everybody who stayed. He said his name
was Uncle WillBe, and in all the time we were there after
that, I don't think I saw him outside that building more

than once or twice. I guess he was just too nice to waste on the people who were already inside and knew what it was like.

Uncle WillBe motioned for the guards to leave, and they looked disappointed that they weren't going to get to kill us after all, unless it was on the way out. But they left, and then he took us across campus. He went the long way, on these wide flagstone walks that snaked around the trees. He stopped and pointed out the Upper Dormitory where the senior staff had rooms. It had its back to us and blocked the view of the Great Hall. If I had known the Salt then, I would have said, "Everything is exactly what it is." And if Theshei had known the Salt, he would have said, "And what it isn't." And we'd have both been right.

But we didn't know anything then, and Uncle WillBe took us off to the right and there was the Quad, four big dormitories cut out of that gray stone and laid out in a square to form a wide courtyard with a big chestnut tree in one corner. Uncle WillBe walked us right out in the middle of it and swept his hand around at the buildings like he had built them personally and said, "I went to school here when this was a college." He pointed up to a window on the fifth floor, a little window high up under the eaves in the corner where two of the dormitories touched. "That was my room," he said. "It was a grand time." Then he stopped as if he thought somebody might be listening and said, "But not as good as now, of course." He said it very quickly, like he was correcting himself before somebody else did.

The main thing I noticed was that the windows were all shut, which meant they had air-conditioning. I couldn't get over that. Just having a roof over your head was a luxury for people like us, and here the Saltspeakers had an air-conditioned place to sleep at a time when about half the country was sleeping in abandoned cars. If Uncle WillBe was any example, they weren't starving either, and my guess was there wasn't any heavy lifting involved in Sowing the Salt, so even throwing celibacy and the possibility of conversion fatalities into the bargain, all in all, it didn't look like a bad deal. I just stood there looking up at the windows and thinking about real rooms with actual beds in them, and Uncle WillBe had to come back and take me by the arm to get me out of the Quad.

He took us down a sloping walkway along the backs of a couple other buildings, the dining hall, and what was probably a library at one time, and a little infirmary. There were some maintenance buildings, he said, but they were back off in the woods and weren't worth the walk, and there were some dormitories back the other way on the far side of the Welcome Building that he'd show us later.

Then he swung us around the last building, and you could tell the whole tour was arranged to come out right there. There was a huge rolling field that ran all the way back to the Upper Dormitory and out to the stretch of woods where the country road was and even a couple hundred yards off to our right. And about two-thirds of the way to the Upper Dormitory, there was the Great Hall.

It was a round building with walls about ten feet high and a huge dome rising out of it. It looked like a flying saucer ready to take off to another world. The ground sloped up toward it, and we walked across the grass without saying a word. All that empty space seemed to converge on it, as if the Great Hall wasn't in the field, the field was *around* the Great Hall. It seemed rooted there, and yet it seemed about to float away. I had the oddest feeling of connectedness, like I was imbedded in space, and there was no real distinction between where I ended and space began. I felt like a figure sculpted out of the world, like those faces of the presidents on Mount Rushmore, part of the living rock and yet not part of it. I felt solid as stone, and at the same time I felt like I wasn't really there at all. It was like I floated toward the Great Hall, like I was in a dream.

Everything felt like a dream for hours after that, places changed without transition, things happened that didn't seem related to the things that happened before them. Uncle WillBe must've introduced us to people, but all I remember is suddenly we were in these big wooden tubs filled with rose water, and then they were giving us those salt white robes with the hoods. I remember how soft the material felt. And how good we looked, standing there in that big stone room with granite pillars going up to that high mahogany roof, all of us in white, and the flames from the altar troughs dancing on the bone-colored walls all around the room, and the smell of spiceflower incense everywhere, and the lazy drone of some part of the Salt being mumbled over and over endlessly.

Then everything sort of congealed all at once, and I took one look around and knew I was Home.

Theshei just looked around like he knew he was on the right path but definitely wasn't at his destination. I always envied him that. He didn't always know where he was, and he didn't know where he was going, but he knew he was destined to go somewhere. So I guess he could be excused for what he did because all he was really doing was asking directions.

What he did was ask a question. Right in the middle of Sowing the Salt. We were sitting there on the floor right in the middle of all the other guys in white robes like we'd been there for months. We hadn't been there an hour, and I felt like we'd never been anywhere else. A huge bald guy named Orwoz was standing up on a platform with a dozen other Saltspeakers, Sowing, and he got to the part where the Salt says, "Badguy caught a bad case of Death," and Theshei said, "Who made Death?"

Orwoz was in the middle of this dramatic pause before

the next sentence, and everything else was so quiet the question bounced off the walls. I thought the incense was getting to me because the air seemed to rattle when he said it. I could see it rattle, like a big sheet of cellophane being shaken.

Then it struck me that suddenly I could see the air, literally see it. Instead of there just being empty space with people in it, we were suddenly in the middle of this thick transparent stuff, like water, only so clear you couldn't normally see it was there. I could feel it pressing on me, and when I looked down at my hands, I could see it pressing down on the sleeves of my robe. And I could see it cracking like ice between us when Orwoz shouted, *"What?"*

Everybody around him just stood there with their mouths making little pink O's, and all their eyebrows went up at once, like some sort of eyebrow drill team. Then all their eyebrows came down again so far they almost covered their eyes, and I figured they were going to Pound Salt into us until there was nothing left, especially when they started rolling up their sleeves.

But Theshei was oblivious to all that. He just looked at Orwoz and said, "Who made Death?"

Orwoz's head was turning bright red, and his hands were clenching and unclenching at his sides. He said, "*Who* made Death?"

Theshei nodded. "Who made Death?" he said.

I didn't know it then, but there was nothing Orwoz liked better than Pounding Salt. He personally had pounded a half-dozen rookies like us to death and at least twice that many unbelievers who refused to understand the Salt when he Sowed it on the street. But I had a pretty good idea that Theshei was on the brink of becoming bloody hamburger.

We also didn't know it, but Saltspeakers have a duty to answer whatever questions they can about the Salt. So Orwoz was obliged to try to answer Theshei's question before he began Pounding. The problem was, he didn't have an answer. He didn't even see how dangerous the wrong answer could be.

But I could see it. If Death was bad, Goodguy couldn't have made it because Goodguy is good. And if Goodguy didn't make it, then he didn't make everything. But the Salt says Goodguy made all the stuff there is. So he had to make it. But if he made it, and it's bad, how can he be completely good?

Orwoz scowled and opened his mouth to say something, but nothing came out. He looked around at the others, but all they could do was shrug and look at one another. I didn't know what the answer was, but it amazed me that *they* didn't have an answer ready. In fact, they looked like nobody'd ever thought to ask the question before. I should've expected that, but we were new, and I didn't know that the beauty of the Salt was that it didn't leave any room for questions.

Everybody else in the whole place seemed to be rolling up their sleeves, and I had the feeling if somebody didn't come up with some sort of answer soon, they were going to start Pounding us anyway.

But even though they all seemed to be edging toward us and the crowd was closing in all around us, they didn't do anything. Somebody said, "Ask the Wiseguy!" and everybody murmured something out of the Salt, which meant they agreed.

So Orwoz held up his hands and said, "Where's the Wiseguy?" and a path opened up through the crowd, and a scrawny old man with a scraggly white beard came through it. He had a black walking stick, and every time he brought it down, it struck the stone floor like a hammer.

But instead of walking all the way up to Orwoz, he stopped in front of me and Theshei. He leaned closer and looked at Theshei like his eyesight was bad and then he looked at me the same way, and then he looked back at Theshei. Then he smiled and nodded like he suddenly remembered who we were. The really weird thing was that he suddenly looked familiar to me too, even though I had no idea who he was. Finally, he looked up at Orwoz and said, "What?"

Orwoz looked like he wanted to get the formalities out of the way so he could start Pounding. "Who made Death?" he said.

The old guy smiled, and I expected him to give us the answer, but instead he turned around and touched me on the forehead with the top of his walking stick and said, "Tell him."

I looked around at the way the air was shimmering everywhere and thought it was a shame that just when I started seeing the air, I was going to be killed. But the old guy looked like he thought I knew the answer, so I took a wild guess. "Some of the stuff went bad?" I said.

Everybody kind of sucked in their breath like it was some kind of miracle, and the old guy looked at Theshei to see if he was satisfied. Some of the Saltspeakers were starting to roll down their sleeves, and I could tell that if Theshei just said, "Oh," everything would be all right and we'd be off the hook. But Theshei shook his head and said, "Goodguy made bad stuff?"

I had this tremendous urge to Pound Theshei myself. I thought it was because he couldn't keep his mouth shut even to keep us from getting killed, but I know now it was because I was already a Saltspeaker fanatic. I looked at the old guy, and he said, "Tell him."

So I said, "The stuff went bad after Goodguy made it."

Everybody made a low whistling sound like they were hearing something they never thought of before, and I knew if Theshei would only keep his mouth shut, we'd live at least until dinnertime. But he wouldn't. He screwed up his face like what I said was impossible and said, "Goodguy made defective stuff?"

The old guy smiled and said, "Tell him" for the third

time, like it was some sort of ritual, and I said, "He made good stuff. But stuff's not Goodguy. Only Goodguy's good."

Everybody let out a gasp like I'd just rewritten the Salt. Theshei considered it for a while, and I considered Pounding some sense into him if he asked one more question, but finally, finally, he nodded and said, "Oh."

Everybody but Orwoz let out a sigh of relief. He let out more of a growl like a dog somebody just snatched a bone away from, and I knew by the look on his face he wasn't going to rest until he got a chance to Pound the Salt into us.

The old guy had a big smile on his face, and he handed me the black walking stick. I thought it was some sort of ritual they hadn't explained to us yet, so I took it and held it out toward him just the way he gave it to me: straight up and down. I figured he needed his hands free to do some sort of symbolic gesture or something and then he'd take it back. But all he did was turn and start walking away.

I thought, "Well he's old, maybe he forgot he gave it to me." So I hissed at him to get his attention. He looked back over his shoulder, and I wiggled the stick at him to remind him it was his. He just smiled and started to turn away again. Everybody was quiet in that hushed way like a ceremony was going on, and I didn't think I was supposed to talk, but I didn't see anything else to do. So I said real quiet, so only he could hear, "You forgot your stick."

He laughed. A small private laugh just between the two of us. "*Your* stick," he said. "You're the new Wiseguy." Then he turned and walked away, and the crowd closed behind him.

I looked at Theshei for some suggestion, but all he did was shrug like he was asking me whether I would rather be Pounded, so I just stood there holding the stick out in front of me, still straight up and down like I thought he'd come back and take it off my hands. Nobody else moved, and they all seemed to be looking at me to see what I'd do next. I didn't know what to do, so I didn't do anything, but my arm started to get tired and the stick got heavier and heavier, and finally I let the stick down slowly until it touched the ground.

I let it down so slow the tip barely touched the ground, but it made a sound like rolling thunder. I didn't know what a Saltspeaker's Thunder was then, but even so, I knew I had found mine.

CHAPTER
3

FINDING your Thunder was a Saltspeaker religious experience where you discover whatever's destined to lead you to the cosmic adventure you've been created for. Defending the Salt was my Thunder. Seeing the air shimmering like water was just the outskirts of it; dead center was when the Old Wiseguy touched me on the forehead with his stick and I started answering Theshei. It felt to me like I had all the answers; I didn't know what the answers were, but I knew I had them. All I had to do was open my mouth and let them pop out.

That was the hard part: letting them pop out without thinking about them first. In fact, the more I *thought,* the more I was convinced the Old Wiseguy had made a terrible mistake and no answer would ever pop out of my mouth again. I wanted to go give him his stick back, but I didn't know where to go and I didn't think I was allowed. Actually, as the Wiseguy, I could go anywhere I wanted pretty much any time I wanted, but I didn't know it then, so I went with everybody else. Everybody else went back to the dorms.

When we got back there, everybody stood around in the courtyard of the Quad. At first I thought maybe it was some sort of tradition not to go right back to your room after a ceremony, but we didn't have a room, so I went up to the first guy I saw and said, "Where do we sleep?"

The guy went white. He was terrified. His eyes kept darting around, looking for a clue from somebody else, but nobody would meet his eyes. Everybody looked up or away or down, like they didn't want any part of what was going on. He kept trying to swallow, but his mouth must've been too dry because he couldn't do it. Sweat was beading out on his forehead, and he kept shifting his weight slightly from one foot to another like he was standing on coals that were getting hotter by the minute. I waited for him to calm down so I could at least find out what was wrong with him, but he just got more desperate looking the longer I waited.

Finally I realized what was wrong. He thought it was some kind of test, and if he didn't come up with an answer soon, I was going to do something to him with the Black Stick. He couldn't take his eyes off it, and the longer he looked at it, the wider they got. I was going to put it behind my back so he wouldn't have to look at it, but as soon as I started to move it, he leaned back like I was going to hit him with it and fainted dead away.

I didn't know what to do. I looked around for help, but everywhere I looked, the crowd just melted back away from me like they were afraid they were next. I turned to Theshei for help, but he was having all he could do not to burst out laughing. "I'm glad you're enjoying this," I said. He made an effort to keep a straight face, but he wasn't having much success. It annoyed me that he was having so much fun at my expense, and I said, "All right then, where *do* we sleep?" I must've said it too loud because everybody shrank back like they thought I was going to strike him down.

Theshei looked around at everybody and said, "Where does the Five-Hundred-Pound Dog sleep?"

It was an old joke, and I said the punchline right along with him. "Anywhere he wants."

That's when it dawned on me that they had all been standing around waiting to see where I was going to go. And they were still waiting. I didn't want to take

anybody else's room, but it was pretty clear that if I
didn't choose some room pretty soon, we were going to
end up standing around in the courtyard until morning.
I looked at Theshei for some direction, but he just
shrugged like *he* wasn't the Five-Hundred-Pound Dog,
so I looked around the Quad until it came to me: Uncle
WillBe's room.

I went in through the door to the dorm with Theshei
right behind me and the crowd right behind him. We
went up the wide central stairs, and they stayed a
respectful distance back, but it was like they were
waiting for something. By the time we got to the fifth
floor, they were lined up behind us down the stairs all
the way to the courtyard. They even packed the landings.
I had a general idea where the room should be, and I
turned right at the top landing, but things look different
inside a building than out, and the fact that all the doors
were closed as I went down the hall didn't help any
either.

I knew it had to be on the left side, and I figured it was
probably the last one, but the last room wasn't quite at
the end of the hall. Just as I went to open the door, I
noticed a little door at the very end of the hall almost
flush with the wall. All the other doors were light brown
and that one was dark mahogany. It was the only door
without a number, and it looked like the door to a broom
closet. I almost went into the one in front of me, but at
the last second, I looked at the broom closet door again
and all of a sudden I could see the air again. It shim-
mered and flowed like it was water cascading down over
the door.

I turned and went down to the very end of the hall and
opened the mahogany door. The minute I turned the
knob and opened it, I heard a commotion shoot down
the stairs like the fuse of a firecracker, and when it hit the
courtyard, there was a great shout.

All the guys I could see back at the top of the stairs
were laughing and smiling and nodding blissfully.

Theshei was still back at the landing too, and I knew they weren't going to tell *me* what it was all about because they assumed I already knew, but I thought they might explain it to Theshei, so I reached in and flicked on the light and went in to look around. As soon as the light went on, the sound of cheering came up from the courtyard.

It was a small room compared to the others, and the ceiling sloped down sharply from above the door so that the closer you got to the window the harder it was to stand, but it was huge compared to the cardboard box Theshei and I had shared. It was a little musty, like it hadn't been used since Uncle WillBe was a senior, and it looked like I'd picked the only room in the building that didn't have air-conditioning. I didn't think Theshei was going to be too happy about that, but compared to a leaky cardboard box, even without air-conditioning, it was a palace. I went over to see if I could get the window open, but when I bent down toward it, I could see everybody standing in the courtyard looking up at the window. I waved and they gave a loud cheer, and I stepped back before I did something else I didn't understand and set off a parade or something.

There were a couple of old beds in the room that looked like the ones Uncle WillBe and his roommate probably slept in, a pair of equally old and banged-up desks, and two small three-drawered bureaus on either side of the window. There was some cracked plaster partway up the slope of the ceiling, and the paint near it was stained light brown and was peeling away slowly. Right above it, there was a wire-mesh grate with a strip of metal hanging down from it. I had to go up on my toes to reach it, but when I pulled on it, louvers opened behind the mesh and a flood of cold air cascaded down on me. I had forgotten how good air-conditioning felt. I was still standing there letting it wash over me fifteen minutes later when Theshei came in.

He looked at me and shook his head. "You did it again," he said.

I thought he didn't like the room. "You want to go back to the box?" I said.

Theshei laughed. "No," he said. "This is perfect. You have no idea how perfect."

He walked over and looked out the window. It sounded like a lot of people having a good time down there. He turned back to me and said, "You know what this place is?"

"I've been in a room before," I said. "I wasn't born in a cardboard box."

Theshei shook his head. "This is the only room in the entire place that nobody is living in," he said.

"The whole building?" I said.

He said, "No. The whole place. Six dormitories. At least five hundred rooms. You picked the only vacancy."

I could see the air again. It was shimmering. I felt very strange, and it scared me a little. "That's a lot of rooms," I said.

"It should be," he said. "This isn't just an ordinary Saltspeaker Compound like the ones on the far side of the city. This is where everybody comes from all over the country for special training."

"You don't just walk in here then," I said.

Theshei nodded. "Apparently it's like walking up to the gate at Paris Island and telling them you want to be a Marine."

"No wonder those guards were all over us," I said.

Theshei shook his head. "There's something else going on here," he said. I thought he was going to give me one of his elaborate theories, but I could see he hadn't figured it out yet.

"Why'd they let us in then?" I said.

"Would you believe it?" he said. "This place should have been full. They had two last-minute dropouts, and they thought we were replacements."

That worried me. "You think they'll make us leave when they find out?" I said.

"Not now," he said. "You're a legend. The youngest Wiseguy ever." He could see it made me uncomfortable, and he laughed.

"That's some kind of mistake," I said. I knew things were too good to last. "As soon as they figure that out, they'll throw us out."

"Don't worry about it. If anybody says anything to you, just point that stick at them." I asked him why, and he said, "They think you can kill them if you touch them with it wrong."

"It didn't kill me," I said.

"Maybe it wasn't loaded," he said. He went over and laid down on the right-hand bed. It put a big smile on his face, and he stopped talking and just laid there enjoying it. I sat down on my bed and waited for him to tell me what else he'd found out. It took a while, but eventually he opened one eye and said, "Beats the box, doesn't it?"

"I don't know," I said. "I wouldn't get too used to it. This Wiseguy thing is a mistake. Sooner or later, they're going to throw us out." It made me feel sadder than I had in a long time. "Besides, I don't think that big guy likes you much."

Theshei laughed. "Orwoz?" he said. "He's supposed to be some sort of big shot in the national organization, but nobody knew exactly what. Everybody's terrified of him." You could see Theshei wasn't. "They think he's going to train us to death or something." He laughed. "One of them said if Goodguy wanted to punish Badguy, he'd send him here to Orwoz."

I hadn't seen anything that strenuous since we got there, but I thought it might be that things hadn't started yet. I laid back on the bed myself. "How hard can it be?" I said. It was one of those questions you come to regret. I looked up at the grate and felt the cool air all around me. "Besides, nothing comes for nothing."

Theshei nodded. "Air-conditioning doesn't come cheap," he said.

It didn't matter what it cost, I was ready to pay the price, but if they shut it off that instant, I'd still have wanted to stay more than anything else in my life. "They might throw us out," I said, "but they're not going to make me quit."

Theshei shook his head. "I don't think you *can* quit. You're in, you're in for life."

I didn't mind that. I was exactly where I wanted to be. "Not having second thoughts?" I said.

"No," he said, "but there's something going on here that hasn't got anything to do with Sowing the Salt. I can feel it."

All I felt was a kind of serenity I knew I didn't want to leave. It must have shown in my face because Theshei said, "Look, don't worry about Orwoz. He might run the place, but it's what the Wiseguy says that counts." He grinned. "And you're the Wiseguy."

"I'm not!" I said.

"You are unless the Old Wiseguy takes his stick back," he said.

"I'm not going to wait for him to take it back," I said. "I'm going to give it back to him as soon as I see him again."

Theshei just closed his eyes.

It was almost midnight before I got the chance. Theshei was asleep by then along with everybody else. I wasn't sleeping, I was just lying there feeling the serenity. I don't know what made me get up and go to the window, but when I looked down, there he was, sitting cross-legged under the tree in the far corner of the courtyard. The moon made him look like a silver statue. I picked up the Black Stick and went out of the room as quitely as I could.

Nobody said we couldn't be out of our rooms at night, but I had the feeling it was forbidden anyway. I went down the stairs as quietly as I could. I wanted to run down them before the Old Wiseguy disappeared again, but I didn't want to wake anybody up and have to answer a lot of questions. I went across the little lobby to the door, hoping he would still be there. Luckily, he was.

I closed the door softly behind me and tiptoed out to where he was, but I thought he was meditating or something and I didn't want to interrupt him. So I just stood in front of him, holding the stick out toward him, straight up and down, the way he gave it to me. He smiled without opening his eyes and said gently, "You don't have to hold it that way *all* of the time."

He was trying not to embarrass me, but I felt like an idiot anyway. "I don't want to hold it at all," I said. "Take it back."

He just laughed at me. It wasn't a loud laugh, but I felt like it would wake up the entire Quad. I was trying to keep my voice as low as possible, but I felt like shouting at him.

"Look," I said. "When you asked me that stuff, I didn't know what I was saying."

He nodded his head. "As it should be," he said.

I was trying to shout at him and whisper at the same time. "I don't know what I'm doing! I don't know what I'm doing!"

He just waited until I finished my tantrum, then he said, "How does a caterpillar dance?"

"I don't know," I told him.

Then he smiled that big dumb smile and said, "Neither does the caterpillar."

I was getting a little bit worried because he was starting to make sense to me.

Finally he stood up and took me over to one of the ground-floor windows and pointed to my reflection in the glass. "That's you," he said.

"I know my own reflection," I said.

He shook his head and tapped me on the chest with his finger. "Not you," he said. Then he pointed back to my reflection in the window and said, "That's *you*."

"That's just a trick of the light," I said.

He looked happy for a minute, as if I'd finally understood what Sowing was about. "Light's you," he said finally.

"Light's Goodguy," I said.

He looked astounded for a minute like he'd picked me on a whim and was amazed to discover that I really was something special. "Light's Goodguy," he said. He mulled it over for a few moments, and then he said, "Life's good."

And bad as things were almost everywhere, it *was* good.

CHAPTER 4

I think the Old Wiseguy knew even then how everything would turn out, even though he didn't know he knew it. So when the Change came, it was more like he was remembering it than like it was happening for the first time. I guess we all knew it all along, but we forgot. The truth used to be so hard to come by. It didn't even come easy to Theshei. Even his Thunder didn't come easy. I was there when Theshei found his Thunder. But it was quite a while later, and the delay caused him nothing but trouble.

They wanted you to find your Thunder pretty quick in the Saltspeakers, like I did mine. But Theshei never found his there, although the Saltspeakers were responsible for his finding it. Orwoz was always harassing him about it, like Theshei was some kind of Imposter because he didn't, even though there were Saltspeakers who'd been looking for years and years and hadn't found their Thunder.

Of course, Orwoz just wanted an excuse to Pound Salt into Theshei. I suppose he wanted to Pound me too, but he was too afraid of the Black Stick. As far as I could tell, it was only a black stick, but the Saltspeakers treated it as if it were Magic itself. They believed that if the Wiseguy touched them on the forehead with it, they'd die if they weren't true believers, and as devout as a lot of them were, they still weren't sure they believed enough. Of course, Theshei said anybody who was willing to become celibate ought to be given credit for believing enough whether they believed or not.

But then Theshei was always saying things that made the Saltspeakers mad, especially Orwoz. If I said the same thing, they thought it was a Profound Insight, but if Theshei said it, it was like a bulletin from Badguy. Not all the Saltspeakers thought that, but there was a group that revolved around Orwoz that never liked Theshei and never trusted him. As far as I was concerned, if Orwoz didn't like you, it was a letter of recommendation.

Still, he stood pretty high among the Saltspeakers because he Sowed Salt like nobody else in the congregation. He could work a crowd of unbelievers with just his tone of voice, and he didn't even have to use intimidation. If you saw him Sowing most of the time, you'd think he was the softest man on earth. But let someone heckle him, and he was ferocity itself.

In some ways I think he really believed the Salt and was committed to Sowing it, but he was too wrapped up in how well he did it and how many converts he got and how many Imposters he weeded out. Of course, to Theshei, Orwoz was just another bully.

We were there for about a week, and they acted like I already knew everything, but I went along with Theshei everywhere just like I was a rookie like him. There were long hours listening to Orwoz or somebody else Sow the Salt, and hours of silent contemplation every day, and hours memorizing the Salt, but they didn't come to more than three or four in any twenty-four, and the rest of the time didn't seem to have a lot to do with Sowing the Salt. The whole first week we never got more than three consecutive hours of sleep, and sometimes we were up for more than a day at a time.

Orwoz must have thought we were going to have to do a lot of Pounding because he trained us like we were preparing for a life of hand-to-hand combat with a race of giants. That beautiful ritual of first day was the Party on the Eve of Destruction; the rest was Destruction itself. We ran everywhere, especially up steps, and by the middle of the week I was beginning to regret not taking somebody's room on the first floor. It wasn't just that we ran everywhere, it was the way we ran. You can't run in those robes without hiking them up and, of course, nobody was allowed to do that. So we ran in a kind of flat-footed shuffle with our knees bent a little, like some sort of cartoon figures. By the end of the first week, it felt like I'd grown three new muscles in the back of my legs, and all three of them hurt worse than my normal muscles. And they didn't hurt half as bad as my lower back. If Orwoz had gone around every evening and given us ten good clouts with a baseball bat, working his way up from our heels to our shoulder blades, he couldn't have put us in more pain.

We went to bed knotted up like ropes, and as soon as sleep loosened our muscles enough for us to get comfortable, they'd have us up and scurrying somewhere. The shuffle run would have been bad enough in itself, but our rocks made it worse. The first day, after teaching us how to run in our robes without exposing our common humanity, Orwoz took us past the Great Hall to the far end of the field. There was still a ribbon of woods between us and the world outside the compound, and he told us to go into the woods, find a rock, and bring it back. Actually, he said, "Find your rock," like there was one in there with our name on it, and if we got the wrong one, he'd know it and make us wish we'd gotten the right one.

The problem was that there were no rocks, not above ground anyway. There were plenty buried in the ground with just a corner sticking up, but we had nothing to dig them up with. Somebody promptly pointed that out to Orwoz, and Orwoz Pounded him bloody for being a Slacker and a Troublemaker. He didn't say so, but it was pretty clear we were supposed to dig them up with our bare hands, and that was what we did. It took hours, but Orwoz didn't seem pressed for time. He walked around and stood over people as they dug, and sometimes he'd start yelling at somebody, usually when they had one halfway dug up, "That's not your rock! Get your own rock. Not somebody else's rock." Usually the rookie stood there looking bewildered with Orwoz screaming in his face, "Find it! Find it now!" until the recruit would start rushing everywhere at once like a desperate squirrel.

He even stopped me after I had mine partway uncovered and took me to another place near the edge of the treeline and pointed to the one he wanted me to dig up. After a while, he went back out into the field at the edge of the trees, and everybody had to carry their rock out to him for approval. When about half the people had their rocks, I began to notice that they were all about the size of a bowling ball, except mine. Some were a little bigger than others, but none of them was smaller than that, and mine was the size of a grapefruit. I had the feeling Orwoz had supervised their burial, probably by the last group that fell into his clutches, and he knew the size of every rock there. It didn't look good for Theshei.

I knew he wasn't going to accept Theshei's rock, and so did Theshei, but he dug it up and took it out to Orwoz anyway. Orwoz took it and turned it over in his hands a couple times and shook his head, and Theshei went back into the woods without saying a word.

It took him an hour to dig up the next one, and by then, most of the recruits were standing around holding their rocks in front of them in their cupped hands. Theshei took it out to Orwoz, and Orwoz hefted it in one hand and then another and finally shook his head. Theshei went back without saying a word. He did it twice more, and by then, Theshei's hands were caked with dirt and blood, but he didn't even frown. I thought he'd snap when Orwoz turned down the last one, but I should have known Theshei had dealt with enough bullies not to make his confrontation on their terms.

Even the stragglers had been standing in the field for an hour by the time Theshei brought him the last rock. The sun was going down. Everybody was hungry and tired and miserable. Our shoulders hurt, our necks hurt, our hands hurt. Theshei put the rock in Orwoz's hands, turned, and went back in the woods. Orwoz looked like he thought he'd won, but I could see Theshei was taking the offensive. It was up to Theshei after that how long we stayed out there. He could keep bringing rocks back and going back into the woods before Orwoz could reject them for as long as he wanted. After he came out with the next rock an hour later and did the same thing, even Orwoz figured it out.

It was dark by then, and when Theshei came up to him, Orwoz shook his head and said, "I'll show you your rock, or we'll be out here all night," and he walked past Theshei into the woods. Theshei gave me a smile and a wink and went in after him. About an hour and a half later, they came back out with Theshei carrying a rock the size of a basketball. My rock felt like it was the size of a stuffed chair by then, and I knew Theshei's must feel like his was the size of a couch. But he walked behind Orwoz like he wasn't carrying anything at all. Orwoz looked like he'd had the last laugh, but he was the only one who thought so.

He had a couple of assistants bring him two big bags that looked like they were stuffed with old laundry, and he reached in and pulled out a white sling. He looped the narrow end over his head and around his neck and picked up one of the rejected rocks and held it over his head. "I don't want to see anybody without their rock," he said. "I never want to see anybody with anybody else's rock." He looked at Theshei like he expected him to switch with somebody the minute his back was turned. "You carry it in your hands." He took it down and put it in the big loop of the sling. "If we have something for you to do with your hands, you don't put it down. You put it in this." He waited for it to sink in, and then he said, "But you never, never, never put it naked on the ground!"

Then he had us all line up and file past him, and he gave each one of us a sling. When we all had one, he said, "Just for practice, we're going to let you use your slings on the way back in." He acted like he was a teacher granting special recess. Then he looked at Theshei and said, "Except for you." And we all went trudging back to the Great Hall, then down the back way to the cafeteria and a hot meal. There was never much of it, certainly not more calories than we expended, but it was hot and a lot better than what Theshei and I were used to eating.

By the end of the next day, it was pretty clear that Orwoz hadn't done us much of a favor giving us the slings. The way we had to run in those robes made us lean forward a little, and all the slings did was use our bodies as a lever to shift the strain down into our lower backs. The only way to take the pressure off was to run with your back perfectly straight and your chin up, but if you did that, you couldn't see the ground right, and it sent rookie after rookie tumbling end over end around his rock, trying to keep it from popping out and touching the ground as he fell. Most of the time, before the fallen hit the ground Orwoz was on top of them, cursing them for their stupidity and clumsiness. Theshei never dropped his once. Even when we were running in line and somebody went down, Theshei never stumbled. There might be a pileup five men deep, but Theshei always managed to avoid it without even breaking stride.

It drove Orwoz crazy. Worse still, Theshei never even seemed to be carrying a rock. Big as it was, he carried it effortlessly whether he was running or standing or sitting down. Everybody else's rock seemed to gain weight during the night so that by the fourth day, it felt like they were carrying a small car around. Even my little rock felt like a cannonball, but Theshei's seemed to get lighter. Orwoz ran us more than ever, and he took to running us in line everywhere we went and putting Theshei in the middle behind the clumsiest rookies he could find. It didn't work. There was pileup after pileup, but Theshei never went down once. Everybody else was covered with cuts and bruises from taking hard falls to protect their rock. There were separated shoulders and dislocated elbows and a couple broken bones, but Theshei didn't even seem to get sore. By the end of the week, those who weren't in the infirmary looked like a band of casualties retreating from a battle. Except for Theshei.

Two days into the next week, Orwoz had us take one last in-line run across the field and bury our rocks again in the woods. I would have bet anything we were the first group who didn't carry their rocks to the very last day.

CHAPTER
5

ALWAYS after a particularly grueling day, they would wake us up in the middle of the night to go stand in the courtyard and chant the Salt. And Orwoz or somebody else would walk around between the lines listening, and if you said anything the wrong way, they were on you like they'd uncovered an Imposter.

They were fanatical about Imposters, but they were absolutely paranoid about Intruders. Imposters were guys just trying to stay off the street and faking their interest in the Salt. Most of them either developed a genuine feeling for the Salt or had one Pounded into them. The others just vanished. We assumed they died under the stress of being Pounded and some of them did, but I think they let us think that to keep us in line. In the first week or so, we really didn't learn anything about the Saltspeakers that wasn't already common knowledge, so none of the Imposters they got rid of then was any kind of real threat to them. I believe they threatened to assassinate them for revealing Saltspeaker secrets, and when they were good and terrified, they let them escape, knowing they'd keep their mouths shut. Either that or the Defenders shot them and buried them in the woods.

But the ones they were really looking for were the Intruders—spies sent to infiltrate the Saltspeakers—even though nobody would say who was sending the spies or what they would do with the information even if they got any. As I understood it, everything we knew about the Salt was supposed to be used to Sow it, which meant it was to be public knowledge so the whole idea of secrecy didn't make any sense.

Orwoz thought from the first that we were Imposters, which wasn't too far from right, but the longer we stayed, the more convinced he was that Theshei was an Intruder. I don't know if he thought I was one or not, but he kept away from me as much as he could, either because he couldn't stand being close to me knowing he could never Pound me or because he was afraid I'd Stick him. I could put the Black Stick on the forehead of anybody I suspected was an Imposter, and I think Orwoz believed enough for it to kill him.

He couldn't Pound me, of course, because I was the Wiseguy, and I knew more than he did about the Salt, even if I didn't even know how I knew it. When it came to matters of interpretation, I was right no matter what I said. I don't know if the Old Wiseguy could have challenged me, but Orwoz couldn't without proclaiming himself the new Wiseguy and you can't proclaim yourself. I could have made Orwoz the new Wiseguy, but he couldn't do it himself.

So he left me alone, but he was always on Theshei, towering over him, screaming at him, threatening to Pound the Salt into him if he didn't get it all right soon. Actually, I was surprised that Theshei took as much of it as he did. Everybody thinks Theshei was some kind of pacifist saint, but he wasn't like that all his life. I'd seen him snap a couple times back in school, and Orwoz didn't know how much danger he was in.

Still, he kept on Theshei, but Theshei usually acted like he was locked in some back ward of a mental hospital and Orwoz was just another lunatic inmate who made a lot of noise but didn't have enough contact with reality to do any damage. Theshei never did care what anybody thought of him, and it drove Orwoz crazy. He'd come running up to Theshei and demand to know what

Goodguy had to say about marriage or something, and Theshei would look at him like he was an escaped psychopath. Then Orwoz would go off on a five-minute tirade about everything from the reptilian nature of Theshei's ancestry to the nine and forty ways Orwoz was going to break all the bones in Theshei's body. That was supposed to be the Saltspeaker calling card. If they caught a real Intruder, they broke all the bones in his body at least twice and sent the body back to whoever sent him neatly folded in a package about the size of couch cushion.

When Orwoz was sputtering with rage so bad he couldn't form any coherent words or when he couldn't think of what to say next, Theshei would rattle off every appropriate phrase from the Salt in chronological order. It took Theshei about three days to memorize the entire six hundred and sixty-six pages of the Salt, five hundred of which were Commentaries by the most important Wiseguys since Saltspeech was founded. He knew it better than Orwoz, which made Orwoz even crazier. Then he'd add a couple quotes about losing your temper, and Orwoz would usually stalk away or turn on some other poor unfortunate rookie.

By the sixth week, Orwoz was frothing at the mouth every time he saw Theshei, and things finally came to a head. We were on our knees scrubbing the marble floor in the Great Hall. Scrubbing the floor was supposed to show your humility and your love for the Great Hall. It was also supposed to put you into a blissful state, which for me, at least, it did.

When your body does something over and over, you lose track of it, and the same thing for your mind. We were supposed to repeat the same phrase from the Salt with every stroke. After a few hundred strokes, I would sort of disappear. It was like the kind of dreaming where you're aware of the dream while it's going on, but you can't remember any of it when you wake up.

Maybe because that's where it first happened, I was

able to see the air again more often there than anywhere else. We would be scrubbing away, and suddenly I'd see it flowing between me and the floor, between me and the brush. I'd watch it eddy up off the hot water, and I'd watch it wave and wrinkle as it flowed past under me like currents in a river. I never saw the air without feeling a kind of delight, and even now, when the world is like that all the time, it's still always new to me.

The Saltspeakers had a ritual for everything, and there was even a right and wrong way to scrub the floor. The right way was to make short strokes back and forth about a foot long and covering a circle. The circle was like a clockface, and the first stroke was supposed to start at twelve and end at six, the second beginning at one and ending at seven, the third between two and eight and so on. You had to stop and rotate the brush slightly under your palm after each stroke. It made things a lot slower, but that was the point.

We'd been scrubbing for about half an hour when Orwoz came shrieking across the floor straight for Theshei. The floor was wet and soapy, and he was barefoot; I expected him to go flying up in the air like somebody stepping on a banana peel with every running step. But even though he lost his balance a little and listed to one side and then the other a couple of times, the wet marble didn't even slow him down, and he came to a sliding stop that carried him into Theshei's little bucket and spilled it. The water ran over the floor in front of him, and he stood there towering over Theshei and screaming at the top of his lungs. "You motherless scum! I knew it! I knew it!" He kept jabbing his finger down at Theshei with every word. "I was just waiting for the proof, and now you gave yourself away, you pig-on Happy Dancer!"

The Happy Dancers were another Nontraditional Theological Alternative. They believed primarily in na-ked dancing, moonlight sex, and the intelligent awareness of trees, especially birch trees. Orwoz probably meant *pagan* by *pig-on,* but the Saltspeakers had a way of mispronouncing everything to fit their opinion of it.

In any case, they were the mortal enemies of the Saltspeakers, at least as far as Orwoz was concerned. Actually, we had considered joining the Happy Dancers before we decided on the Saltspeakers, but they weren't much better off than we were then, except they tried to set up their cardboard boxes out in the woods or the parks, so we didn't see much point in it. Theshei was really a lot more like the Happy Dancers than he was like the Saltspeakers, and he wasn't as desperate as I was for a steady place to stay, so I don't know what made him want to join the Saltspeakers instead except an intuitive knowledge that they were along the path to his destiny.

So Theshei wasn't really insulted at being called a Happy Dancer the way most of the Saltspeakers would have been. I expected him to keep scrubbing away like Orwoz was a hallucination he couldn't even see. But he didn't. He finished making the complete circle, and then he stood up. Orwoz was right on top of him so it wasn't easy. The top of his head even brushed Orwoz's chin and made him take a step backward.

He and Orwoz were nose to nose, or actually nose to chest since Orwoz was so much taller. Theshei looked up at him and said, "What are you talking about?"

"Counterclockwise!" Orwoz screamed. "Counter-clockwise!"

Theshei said, "What?"

Orwoz pointed to the floor as if Theshei was still down there scrubbing. "Counterclockwise, you Happy Dancing scum. You were scrubbing counterclockwise!"

I knew what he meant right away. The Happy Dancers did everything counterclockwise and left-handed. They did everything in circles in their rituals, and when they danced, they always danced around in a circle counter-clockwise. I think what decided me against joining the

Happy Dancers was that I didn't want to become left-handed. But Theshei didn't seem to remember anything about them. "What do you mean scrubbing counter-clockwise?"

Orwoz was livid. "Don't play dumb with me!" he said.

"If dumb's being played," Theshei said, "you're playing with yourself."

I'm sure he said *with* instead of *by* on purpose. Masturbation was a taboo subject among the Salt-speakers, and accusing somebody of indulging in it was a mortal insult. It was the last straw, and Theshei knew it.

Orwoz sputtered, looking for a comeback, but he was so outraged all he could do was throw a punch at Theshei. I didn't think he would hit him, and he didn't. Theshei used to stand still and let people punch at him when we were at school, and most of them couldn't hit him one time in a hundred. So I thought he'd stand there ducking and leaning and bobbing until Orwoz got arm weary or slipped on the water underfoot from the spilled bucket and went down. But I was wrong.

Theshei was moving around while Orwoz was shouting at him, and he was shifted to Orwoz's right, off to the side, facing him. His right shoulder was even with Orwoz's right shoulder, and all he had to do was lean to his left and the punch would have gone right by him. Instead, he took a short step to his left, and when the punch went whistling by his head, he reached inside it and leaned forward. His hand went up over Orwoz's shoulder and down his back until Theshei's fingers hooked under the shoulder blade. Then he stepped on Orwoz's right foot and snapped the shoulder forward and down.

The foot stopped where it was, and the rest of Orwoz's body went over it and down. His forehead hit the marble like the tip of a ballpeen hammer, and if there hadn't been a thin layer of water on the floor to make it slide as it hit, I think it would have killed him. As it was, it looked like he was dead. His head hit and skidded forward, his body followed it, and Theshei stepped off the foot and let it slid out at full length. There was a thin splash as the body flattened out along the floor. Then it just lay there, twitched a couple times, and got real still.

Nothing in the Great Hall moved. The sound of Orwoz's head hitting the marble floor was still echoing around the room. Everybody thought he was dead for sure. Just like everybody thought it was an accident. Theshei moved so fast only he, Orwoz, and I knew otherwise. To everybody else, it looked like Orwoz threw a punch, slipped in the water, and hit his head. I only saw it because I knew what to expect. And even I thought Orwoz was dead.

He wasn't though. It took eight rookies to carry him out of the Great Hall, and they kept him in the infirmary for over a week before they were sure there wasn't any permanent brain damage. Theshei wanted to know how they'd tell.

But when Orwoz came back, he seemed exactly the same as before except for a fist-sized egg right in the middle of his upper forehead. He didn't even let up on Theshei. The impact gave him what's called *event amnesia*. The moments immediately before the impact and the hours afterward were knocked completely out of his head. All he knew about the fall was what other people told him, and what they told him was that he threw a punch at Theshei, slipped on the wet floor, and fell. In the short run at least, it would've been better for everybody if he'd remembered.

CHAPTER 6

THINGS got easier after a couple weeks and the physical side slowed down although the mental harassment stayed pretty constant. There was more time spent in contemplation and Sowing the Salt, and we even began to have a little free time of our own, although you were expected to spend it in private meditation on the Salt.

Things went back to normal between Theshei and Orwoz after a little while. I guess at first, Orwoz was still a little rocky from the concussion, and he wanted to wait until he got his strength back before he took on Theshei again. He may not have consciously remembered how he ended up in the infirmary, but deep down he knew, and he didn't want to end up there again.

If all he was was just another musclehead trying to show he was nastier than Nasty it would have been all right, but Orwoz wasn't as dumb as he looked. Of course, the lump in the middle of his forehead didn't make him look any smarter. For some reason, it was calcifying into a permanent little knob.

Orwoz could have had it removed overnight, but he didn't think the Salt could spare him for that long. He implied we'd be overrun with Intruders while he was gone, and he couldn't take the chance. Even though it would have just been a matter of slitting the skin and scraping out the calcified tissue, it couldn't be done in the infirmary and he would have to go to a hospital, and he was afraid a hospital would kill him. He was probably right.

Unless you were in the five percent of the country with the right medical insurance, the only time they found out what was wrong with you was at the autopsy. As often as not, the hospital was the reason you needed one. People used to say the Government only investigates a hospital if you get better. A lot of people even thought it was Government policy for the hospitals to get rid of as many of the Indigent as possible, but the real reason so many died was probably that it just wasn't profitable to treat them properly.

The big insurance companies had most of their money tied up in investments so they went belly-up like everybody else when the economy crashed. The few that didn't found there was nobody to insure but the rich. It's hard to make a profit off people who have nothing, and when the Government stopped paying the medical bills for the poor because there were just too many of them, doctors naturally turned their attention to those who could pay. To keep their profit margin up, the hospitals replaced nurses with "paraprofessionals," mostly ex-kitchen staff who took a two-week course, and before long, hospitals were mostly warehouses where the desperate went to die, usually sooner than they would have otherwise.

In any case, most people chose to die at home, even if home was a parked car or a cardboard box; it was more convenient and usually less painful. Of course, the Saltspeakers had the right insurance, and back then, money talked. But Orwoz thought it was a hostile world made up of Saltspeakers and non-Saltspeakers, and hospitals definitely weren't Saltspeakers.

He also thought the Government was after the Salt-speakers, but the truth was there were hundreds of

Nontraditional Theological Alternatives and the Salt-speakers were neither the largest nor the most obnoxious.

Besides, the Government had its hands full just keeping the Smiling Zombies from getting run over in traffic. It just didn't have the manpower to infiltrate every group that could have been a threat. It had real terrorists to look for and not enough people to do the looking. The Government was less than a tenth as big as it was before the collapse of the world economy, so it had its hands full just keeping the water running.

So to keep the Government and unnamed conspirators from taking over the Saltspeakers while he was gone, Orwoz let his bump solidify into a permanent knob. Theshei, of course, insisted it was a horn and started referring to Orwoz as the Rhino. Orwoz was still riding him, but dumping Orwoz on his head seemed to have satisfied Theshei for a while, although it may have been that Theshei himself was afraid he'd killed Orwoz and was relieved that he hadn't. For whatever reason, Theshei had gone back to treating Orwoz as an escaped lunatic, and Orwoz was still treating Theshei as Badguy's chief representative on earth.

Most of the rookies were rooting for Theshei except for a few fanatics who wanted to grow up to become Orwoz. Theshei called them the Rhinettes, backup group for the Rhino, and said the only good thing about them was that celibacy was at least going to keep them from reproducing. There were about ten of them who seemed to be leftovers from previous training sessions who had permanently attached themselves to Orwoz and lived in the Upper Dormitory along with the staff who ran the infirmary and the cafeteria and the parts of the campus where rookies were discouraged from going. The rest of the Rhinettes, about twice as many, were rookies who just naturally sucked up to whoever was in power. Most of them seemed to think the greatest reward possible on earth was to live in the Upper Dormitory and serve Orwoz. In better times they would have been the kind of young men who sniped and fawned and politicked their way up through corporate hierarchy or the government bureaucracy.

All the rookies lived in the Quad, and one of the other dormitories beyond the Welcome Building housed a lot of older Saltspeakers, like Uncle WillBe, whose sole purpose seemed to be to talk about the Salt among themselves and provide a full house for Orwoz when he Sowed the Salt. They didn't mix with the rookies very much outside of the rituals. Theshei's guess was that they were no good at Sowing the Salt and had been prematurely retired to a life of contemplation because the Saltspeakers didn't know what else to do with them.

Theshei was a lot more interested in the other dorm, which was completely off limits. It housed the Defenders of the Faith, those camouflaged paranoids who'd surrounded us at the gate. They didn't mix with us at all and tried to be as invisible as possible. And there was a smaller group who dressed like the rest of the Saltspeakers but still seemed to be a part of the Defenders. Some of them lived on the floor above Orwoz in the Upper Dormitory, and Theshei noticed that even though Orwoz was supposed to be in charge of things, he showed a lot of deference to most of them. They were a puzzle to Theshei for about three weeks, and then one night I heard him coming into the room well after midnight when I hadn't even known he went out.

I asked him where he'd been, even though I had a pretty good idea it was wherever Orwoz didn't want him to be.

"The Ghost Dorm," he said. Everybody who dared to talk about it called it that because the Saltspeakers in it might as well have been ghosts for all we saw of them. "I told you something is going on here besides the Salt."

I didn't ask him exactly what was going on partly because I knew he was going to tell me anyway and partly because I wasn't sure I wanted to know. Theshei told me anyway. "The top four floors are filled with a lot of sophisticated monitoring equipment, and there's a couple long-range transmission towers on the roof. This is some sort of Intelligence center." That made him laugh. "Who in their right mind would put Orwoz in charge of a place dealing with Intelligence?" he said. The idea made him laugh even harder. He went over and laid down on his bed, shaking his head. "Orwoz," he said, "head of the SIA." He was still chuckling when he fell asleep.

He pretty much lost interest in the Ghost Dorm after that. He seemed convinced that whoever they were monitoring were probably the safest people on the planet if Orwoz had anything to do with it, and it wasn't worth any more of his sleep time to find out who it was. They were keeping us pretty busy anyway, and Theshei's battle against Orwoz was dividing the rookies into two sharply divided camps.

About the only rookie who was neutral about Theshei was a guy renamed Morzon, the guy who fainted when I asked him where our room was.

Morzon was one of those short, scrawny ugly ducklings who desperately want to please. He didn't need actual praise; all he wanted was an occasional confirmation that he wasn't entirely hopeless. It seems people like that always picked somebody like Orwoz to try to please, like people used to always be falling in love with somebody who couldn't stand the sight of them.

Morzon certainly wasn't in love with Orwoz; in fact, he was terrified of him, but he still wanted to please him. He just couldn't get out of his own way. The first time Orwoz stood in front of him and commanded him to recite the opening of the Salt, Morzon threw up all over him. It was all down hill for him after that.

Theshei and I tried to reassure him that Orwoz despised all of us, but it didn't do much good. It was hard to encourage Morzon about anything else because he never did anything right, and the harder he tried, the worse he did. Nobody was particularly fond of him, but most of the rookies pitied him. If Orwoz hadn't been so preoccupied with Theshei, he probably would've taken a personal interest in making Morzon's life a misery.

The Rhinettes were another story. They followed Orwoz around like a flock of ducklings. They always buzzed and whispered whenever Theshei went by, and at least one of them was always following him around. I doubt there was anything they saw him do that wasn't reported back to Orwoz. They even coerced Morzon into shadowing Theshei, but he only went through the motions, and no matter how easy Theshei made it for Morzon to follow him, Morzon almost immediately lost track of him and reported back to the Rhinettes, who had no trouble believing it was just ineptitude.

The Rhinettes didn't mean very much to Theshei except as a source of amusement. When they were really obvious about following him around, he would go to the Great Hall and sit in the middle of the great open room. The only place they could keep an eye on him was from behind one of the pillars, but that meant they'd have to keep peeking around the pillar to see him and still stay hidden. At first they'd peek around the curve of the pillar every few seconds, but after a few minutes, they'd take longer and longer between peeks.

Once he got their rhythm down, he'd wait until they ducked back and then he'd sprint for the pillar. Theshei could run quieter than most people could tiptoe, so they never heard him coming. The next time they peeked around the corner, Theshei would be peeking back at them from the other side of the pillar.

Sometimes he just stayed on the other side of the pillar, and when they peeked around again, they'd think he was gone. They didn't know what to do then. They knew he must've gone out one of the other doors, but the only way to catch up with him was to pick the right door and make a dash for it. The problem, of course, was that they were supposed to have too much respect for the

Great Hall to run in it. If they gave up and went back to
Orwoz and told him they'd lost Theshei, Theshei'd let
them alone and not play any more tricks on them.

If not, he could do Orwoz's voice pretty well, and
when the Rhinette ran across the Hall to one of the
doors, Theshei did his Orwoz impression. He always let
them get up to top speed before he stepped out and
shouted, "Stop running!" in Orwoz's voice. One of them
fainted in midstride when he did it, and the rest pulled a
variety of muscles trying to go from full speed to full
stop in one step.

If he really wanted to drive them crazy, he'd go all the
way around the pillar and come up behind them. When
they stepped out to see where he went, he'd step right
into their footprints. He had such a good sense of
people's rhythms, he could fit himself right in behind
them, almost touching them, and mimic every gesture as
they made it. Most people's movements are habitual and
they don't vary much, so once he got into their rhythm
of walking across the Hall, it was easy for him to move
an arm or a leg just as they did but a half inch under
theirs. If they turned around, he swung right around
with them still behind them, and if they looked over
their shoulder, he just dropped his head down their back
so they couldn't see him. The first time I saw him
shadow one of them across the Hall, I almost wet myself
laughing.

He didn't just do it to them in the Hall either. If one of
them was walking across the grounds, Theshei would fall
in step behind him and then close the gap between them
until he was almost touching the Rhinette's back, and
then Theshei'd shadow every move he made. Everywhere the poor Rhinette went, rookies fell down laughing at him, and he could never figure out why until some
other Rhinette came along and told him Theshei was
stuck to his back. As often as not, it would take five
minutes to convince him, as he swung in circles with

Theshei swinging right with him. Inevitably, when the second Rhinette walked away, Theshei fell in behind him and did the same thing.

It made the Rhinettes a laughingstock everywhere they went, and sometimes the other rookies would drive them crazy by laughing as if Theshei was shadowing them even when he wasn't. You would think they would have realized after a while that they were backing the wrong horse, but they never did, and nobody gloated more when the death sentence came down on Theshei than the Rhinettes.

That was still a long way off, but everything Theshei did to them brought it a step nearer. He never did take them seriously enough. There's a tendency in everybody to think that because you can make somebody *look* ridiculous, they *are* ridiculous. But a lot of the time, even ridiculous people are dangerous. The Rhinettes were a lot more dangerous than Theshei ever gave them credit for.

So was Orwoz, but Theshei couldn't see it. Or didn't want to. I suppose if he admitted to himself that Orwoz was dangerous, he would've had to do something fatal about it, and he didn't want to. Not that that kept him from making Orwoz's life as miserable as possible. He didn't have to try very hard. To Orwoz, the fact that Theshei was alive and inside the Saltspeakers was more than enough reason to be miserable. Theshei was an obsession for him, and he schemed constantly to destroy Theshei one way or another. It took him a long time, but eventually he was successful.

I can see now that it was all part of Theshei's destiny, but it looked like just a dangerous diversion then, and Theshei never took it seriously. There was nowhere Orwoz or the Rhinettes were safe from him. The training was rough for rookies, and Theshei made them laugh whenever he could, as often as not by doing his Rhino impression, which consisted of putting the back of his hand against the middle of his forehead and extending his middle finger like a horn. Then he'd charge over to whoever Orwoz had just chewed out and say exactly the same thing Orwoz said in Orwoz's voice. It helped a lot of them get through.

The Saltspeakers were easy to get into, hard to stay in, and impossible to get out of. But they didn't have to worry about many rookies going back into the world with their secrets because their training worked almost universally. The techniques were as old as organized religion itself. Keep us without sleep, lower our calories below a thousand a day, isolate us from "outsiders" who might point out the inconsistencies between what the Salt said and what some Saltspeakers did, work us nearly to death doing repetitious jobs, threaten and intimidate us, beat the slow learners and anybody else who shows signs of individuality, and indoctrinate us with the Salt every waking minute.

It was irresistible, or at least it would have been if not for Theshei. Theshei was the outside world, the non-Saltspeaker view of the Saltspeakers. He had a knack for showing everything the way it was instead of the way it imagined itself. Orwoz probably had a near perfect success rate before Theshei came along, but he didn't have one while Theshei was there. Most of the rookies did develop an attachment to the Salt, but they weren't the mindless believers Orwoz wanted. So Orwoz hated Theshei for that as well.

Of course, he had so many things to hate Theshei for, and Theshei was always adding to the list. But Theshei didn't go completely over the line until we were at our lowest point. They never let us get more than three hours sleep in a row, and when they couldn't think of any work for us to do, they woke us up in the middle of the night to discuss the Salt.

We weren't supposed to discuss it in the sense of trying to understand it or argue about it; we were supposed to trade quotes from it. When Saltspeakers talked, they always quoted from the Salt about what they were going to say before they said it. In fact, some of them never said anything unless it was directly quoted from the Salt. Saltspeakers like Orwoz just referred to the page and line. They sounded like mathematicians arguing. One would say, "150/35," and the other would say, "Yes, but 430/16." The numbers under 100 carried more weight because the Salt itself only had 100 pages. Pages 101 to 666 were all commentaries, and the Commentaries were debatable.

Anyway, near the end of the training, we had a really bad day. Orwoz was driving us without let up, we were in the third day of a total fast, and nobody'd slept for forty-eight hours. When Orwoz humiliated Morzon in front of everybody because he couldn't clear his mind enough to recite the first two pages of the Salt, nobody thought that much of it except to be glad it wasn't them. But Morzon took the Salt more seriously than most, and he was harder on himself than even Orwoz. When Orwoz told him to get out of his sight, he did. Permanently. He went and hanged himself from a showerhead.

When Morzon didn't show up at the dining hall with the rookies to sit and watch the rest of the Saltspeakers eat, Orwoz sent the Rhinettes looking for him. When they found him, he might have been still alive, but they were too dumb or too afraid to cut him down, and he hung there until they sent for Orwoz. Orwoz cursed at the body for about ten minutes, but he didn't take it down. Instead, he gave us a tirade about what sorry excuses for Saltspeakers we were and what a despicable and ungrateful pig-on pig the dead man was. Then he had us line up and file past the body.

After that, he put us on Holy Silence and sent us to bed. We went without even a murmur of resistance. We were so weary, all we cared about was sleep. We couldn't even remember Morzon's name, and we were just too tired to care. It made us ashamed, but it didn't keep us awake. We were numb and on the point of breaking, and

Orwoz could see it. It was what he'd been waiting for all along, and if he'd known Morzon's suicide would have gotten us there sooner, he'd have hung the rookie himself.

In the middle of the night, the official Rhinettes came through the dorms blowing bugles and banging on doors and rousting us out of our beds. Sometimes a little sleep is worse than none at all, and we staggered to our feet and stumbled into our clothes. Everybody had a bad taste in their mouth, and things looked fuzzy and out of focus. The lights were pure glare, and our bodies ached for more sleep. When they told us to run to the Great Hall to Sow Salt, all we could do was shuffle.

Once we got there, the battle was just starting. Everybody knew Orwoz would be watching for one of us to fall asleep, and we tried everything to stay awake. Even sitting on the cold marble floor didn't help much. We sat there trying to clear our heads before Orwoz asked us a question.

Theoretically, rookies could ask questions about the Salt during these sessions, but nobody ever did because the Salt needs no explanation. Nobody except Theshei. Orwoz was up on the platform testing us on how much we knew of the Salt, and Theshei said, "Doesn't Badguy have a horn?"

The Salt says nothing about what Badguy looks like, but the Commentaries do, so Orwoz said, "320/34," thinking Theshei's ignorance would shame him into shutting up.

But, of course, Theshei knew the Salt and the Commentaries as well as Orwoz, and he said, "Badguy came to me in a dream. His horn was stiff and proud. We struggled, and I woke with Badguy's horn sticking out of me."

Before we got used to being celibate, we all woke with Badguy's horn sticking out of us. It was a rookie joke, and as soon as Theshei quoted the passage, everybody woke up. There were rookies everywhere biting their lips to keep from laughing. The idea of joking about the Salt was completely beyond Orwoz, and he didn't know what was going on, but he was wary whenever Theshei asked a question, and he waited for Theshei to say the unthinkable. Theshei didn't disappoint him. Theshei said, "Now exactly where was this horn located?"

About half the rookies were turning red trying to stifle their laughter, and the other half had tears in their eyes from biting their lips so hard. To Orwoz, all the question showed was Theshei's ignorance. "470/21," he said.

And Theshei said, "Right, right. In his forehead." Orwoz nodded, and Theshei said, "In the middle of his forehead?" and when Orwoz nodded again, Theshei put the back of his hand to his forehead and stuck out his finger. "Like this?" he said.

And as soon as he made his Rhino gesture, the rookies just disintegrated. The laughter just burst out of them. It was like all the laughter they'd been holding in came out at once, and once out, there was no controlling it. Every time they managed to force themselves to stop laughing, it would last about two seconds, and then they'd lose it again. Once or twice, all of them got quiet at the same time, but every time they did, some muffled snigger would start them off again.

Orwoz looked like he wanted to kill each of them individually, but there was no precedent for Pounding an entire group of rookies to death, so he didn't know what to do. He didn't know what was going on, so he bellowed, "Shut up! The Salt is not for laughing at!" The rookies tried to stop laughing, but the harder they tried, the more it made them laugh. Orwoz didn't know why they were laughing, but he knew Theshei was behind it, and he said, "You Happy Dancing pig-on pig, how dare you laugh at the Salt!"

Of course, Theshei was the only one of us not laughing. I was laughing. The Old Wiseguy was laughing. Even

Saltspeakers who didn't know why they were laughing were laughing. Rookies were stuffing their robes into their mouths to keep from laughing.

When it got quiet enough for everybody to hear him, Theshei said, "100/17."

Everybody knew that one because it was what every Saltspeaker was supposed to say when things went bad. It said, "Badguy does his worst. Goodguy laughs." It made everybody laugh harder than the Rhino impression.

Orwoz didn't know what to say. He could see we were all out of his control, but there was no blaming Theshei. Everything Theshei did was within the rules, and Orwoz had no justification for Pounding any of us. When he tried to start grilling us again, Theshei cut him off. "I have another question," he said, but he didn't wait for Orwoz to ask him what it was. "If Goodguy doesn't have a sense of humor, why would he give the most prominent Saltspeaker in the congregation a horn just like Badguy's?"

There was no doubt he meant Orwoz, and the rookies were delighted with its outrageousness. It was all they could do to keep from cheering Theshei. But Orwoz didn't find it funny. He fingered his lump unconsciously, and when the laughter stopped, he was frowning at Theshei with one of those scowls that lead to murder. "You'll trifle with me once too often," he said, "before I Pound the Salt into you." But he didn't make any gesture toward coming down and doing it. But I knew even then he was planning some way to make Theshei's being a hero to the rookies work against him. It was the Sandscripti, those luminous ghosts from outer space, who finally gave him his chance.

The Sandscripti pretty much kept to themselves, and most people didn't think about them. But Orwoz did, and that made all the difference.

CHAPTER 7

I don't think the hypocrisy of the Saltspeakers bothered Theshei all that much, but it bothered me, at least at first, because without my realizing it, I'd become very serious about the Salt. But after a while I saw hypocrisy as the normal failings of people who just didn't understand what it was all about. The more I read the Salt, the more certain I became that, although what people did might be wrong, there was really nothing wrong with the people themselves.

That wasn't any brilliant insight on my part; the Salt said it perfectly. "I didn't hurt you. You didn't hurt me. Badguy did it. Badguy does his worst. Goodguy laughs!"

What I understood that to mean is that we're all momentary expressions of one force or the other, and in the end, just as the last line of the Salt says, "Goodguy wins! You win! Next game." Of course, I had to learn from Theshei and the Sandscripti what that last line really meant.

Now, of course, everybody understands it, and they feel like they always understood it, even before the Change. But if they did, they certainly didn't act like it. Then, just about everybody misunderstood just about everything. Especially people like Orwoz.

Orwoz acted like "Badguy did it" was an excuse for anything he did. Not that he thought anything he did was wrong, but if it was, it was just the temporary influence of Badguy.

And it was.

But that didn't make it all right. The minute you think "Badguy's doing it," it stops being Badguy and starts being you. So you have to stop. You don't have to apologize for what Badguy did while he was you, but you have to set to work right away making things right again. You have to undo the work of Badguy. You have to put everything back to good. Orwoz never did that. Or Badguy never stopped being Orwoz long enough for him to do it.

Still, I didn't hold it against Orwoz. He just had no clue as to what was going on. After a while, even when I hated what he did, I didn't hate Orwoz. Theshei could never understand that then. We both had a lot to learn. I think the only time I ever fought with Theshei was over Orwoz, and it was right after Morzon killed himself.

We were alone in the Great Hall; everybody'd gone back to bed after the Sowing except us. Theshei was there because Orwoz told him not to be. I was there because Theshei was there. I was there whenever Theshei had a bad case of the Whys. I never had any answers for him the whole time we were in school, but I thought I'd finally found them.

Theshei said, "Why is that harmless little idiot Morzon dead and he's still alive?" It sounded like he was dangerously close to correcting the mistake of Orwoz's continuing existence.

I quoted him what he'd quoted Orwoz. "Badguy does his worst. Goodguy laughs!"

Theshei looked at me like he was annoyed. "You're going to tell me Badguy drove that little idiot to hang himself?" he said.

I nodded. Theshei shook his head in disbelief. "What's the matter with you?" he said. "Did you forget why we came in here?"

I knew what he meant, and I said it. "To get out of the rain."

"Right!" he said. "To get out of the rain." He looked like he thought I didn't really remember. "You were tired sleeping in a cardboard box," he said.

I knew that had happened, but it seemed like a story about something that happened to somebody else. "*You* picked the Saltspeakers," I reminded him.

He had to think about that one, because whatever was wrong with the Saltspeakers, they were still a stop on the road of his destiny, and he knew it. However unbearable the Saltspeakers might be, joining them was still the right decision. He couldn't get around that. I knew what was bothering him. There was something right about the Salt, even though it wasn't right enough, but he just couldn't tell what it was. Something about it attracted him, and that wasn't really part of his plan, although his plan was really the same as always: "Do what it comes to you to do." He didn't like the fact that he couldn't stand outside the Salt and be untouched by it. He had the Salt and Orwoz mixed up and couldn't get them apart.

I told him the obvious. "Orwoz isn't the Salt."

"I know that," he said. But I felt like he needed reminding, so I said it again. All it did was annoy him. I knew he was annoyed because he was having trouble separating them. He knew I knew it. That annoyed him more. "You're letting that stick go to your head," he said.

I just shrugged like it wasn't my fault that the truth was the truth. "Is, is," I said. That came out of the Salt too. I might as well have quoted Orwoz.

"Don't quote Salt at me!" he shouted. "Can't you think any more? Does the Rhino have your brain along with everybody else's?" He didn't let me answer. "Badguy didn't kill that kid; Orwoz did!"

"Badguy did it," I said.

"Yeah," he said. "Badguy with a horn in the middle of his forehead." He put his hand to his head and made his

Rhino. He was right, of course. For the moment, maybe for most moments, Orwoz was Badguy, and Badguy was Orwoz. That was literally and absolutely true. So I nodded in agreement. But he knew I meant it differently than he did, and that just made him madder. He grabbed the Black Stick out of my hand and shook it in my face. "This is just a stick!" he shouted. "And you didn't become a prophet just because some idiot gave it to you."

He threw it back at me, and I caught it at arm's length. It was like it jumped into my hands. I felt like no matter how close he was or how hard he threw it, I'd catch it just the same. As I caught it, I saw someone scurry away from behind one of the pillars. I knew he was on his way to tell Orwoz we were arguing. What I didn't know was that that was going to make all the difference. I told Theshei the truth about what was bothering him. "Hurts to stay, hurts to go," I said.

"What do you know about what hurts?" he said, but he knew I was right. Whatever he was searching for had to go through the Saltspeakers, however much he wanted to leave them, and he knew it. He could feel he was where he was supposed to be for the moment, however uncomfortable. That annoyed him too. "You pompous asshole, you're getting just like the Rhino!"

"We are what we are," I said.

That infuriated him. "You say one more word to me that isn't yours, I'm going to punch your face in!" he said.

I wasn't mad at Theshei when he said that. I really wanted to shut up and let it go, even if I was only trying to help him. But most of the time, we're not ourselves. "Badguy does his worst," I said.

He didn't let me finish. He just drew back his fist and threw a hard overhand right at my head. Normally, Theshei was way too fast for me, and it would have hit me right between the eyes. But this time I rolled out of the way to the right and flicked it aside with the Black

Stick. Theshei went sailing past me. I didn't even intend to put a foot out. But I did. And Theshei tripped over it and went sprawling on the floor.

I could hear the Rhinettes whispering behind me and scurrying from pillar to pillar. I had no doubt Orwoz was going to get a blow by blow, but it never occurred to me that he would think Theshei and I were enemies. I wasn't even mad at Theshei, and he wasn't really mad at me. He was just a little crazy at the moment, and I knew he'd get over it. But he wasn't quite over it yet, and he pushed himself up and came at me again.

I would have reasoned with him, but he didn't give me a chance. He just tried to tackle me. It amazed me even as I did it, but I sort of swung my body away from him like a door being pushed open. This time I stuck the Black Stick between his ankles as he went by, and he went sprawling again. I didn't plan it; I didn't even think about it; it just happened. It took absolutely no effort. It was like it wasn't even me, it was so graceful and smooth.

Even Theshei couldn't believe it. I don't think Theshei and I ever fought because we assumed he would win, no contest. And before we joined the Saltspeakers, that would have been true. But now something else was moving me, and it felt too good to be Badguy.

I really wished Theshei would stay down, but there was too much grief and frustration in him for that. Ordinarily I would have run away and given Theshei a chance to cool down, but it didn't occur to me to run. When Theshei stood up, he gave a strangled cry and started to come at me again. I had let the Stick slide down so I had it by the knob at the top, and as he started to take a step toward me, I put the tip of it under the hem of his robe and flicked the robe up over his head.

He had his hands out around it, and he staggered forward groping for me. I spun away and around him and hit him across the back of both knees with the Black Stick. His knees caved in and dropped him to the floor.

Then I stuck the point of the stick between his shoulder blades and shoved him forward. When he hit, I left the stick in the middle of his back and leaned on it a little, pinning him to the floor like a bug on a pin. I was surprised at how little force I needed to hold him there. He kept trying to push himself up, but it was like the entire weight of the Great Hall was on top of him. I think I could have held him there with one finger if I had to. It astonished me that I could do that. It astonished Theshei too.

"If you get up again," I said, "I'm going to have to fake a seizure." It made Theshei chuckle in spite of himself. It made him seem to realize for the first time what he'd been doing and how ridiculous a position he was in. That made him laugh. I let him up, and he laughed until tears rolled out of his eyes. I knew that was as close as he was going to come to grieving. After a while, he looked at me and shook his head. "It's still a stick," he said.

I said, "Yeah, but it's a *black* stick."

That made him start laughing all over again, and I realized that he was always making somebody else laugh to take the pressure off them, but nobody was taking the pressure off him. I wanted to say something to him to let him know I understood, but everything that came to mind came out of the Salt, and I didn't want to start things all over again.

"I'm sorry," he said.

I shrugged. "Badguy did it," I said. Theshei laughed.

CHAPTER
8

THE next day Orwoz took me by the sleeve while everybody else was on their knees trimming the lawn with scissors. We'd been doing it since just before sunrise, and it was almost noon. Orwoz had been running around sticking a long metal ruler in the ground and screaming at everybody whose grass was taller than an inch or shorter than a half. There would have been a bald spot wherever Morzon went, but Morzon wasn't there anymore.

Everybody else seemed to be making up for it and the lawn in front of the Great Hall looked like sheep had grazed it. Orwoz was livid. He alternated between cursing us all for idiots and warning us that the conspiracy wasn't going to work. But even when he started making some of the rookies eat the overcut grass, everybody still kept trimming it down to the dirt. And Theshei stopped him from doing that by eating a handful of grass every time Orwoz made some rookie eat one. By the third handful, everybody ate grass if anybody was forced to eat it.

Orwoz gave us a tirade on arrogance and the path to destruction and stalked away, warning us that he'd be back and everything better look right. It was a retreat, but he made it look as much as possible like a strategic withdrawal. I was a little surprised that nobody stopped cutting when he left, even Theshei, but then Theshei needed to stay in the Saltspeakers, and he conformed even to Orwoz's craziness as often as he could.

When Orwoz came back, he led me over behind a big tree. It was unusual because he never talked to any of the rookies privately, except for the Rhinettes, who reported everything they knew about Theshei to him in private. He never really accepted the idea that I was the new Wiseguy; as far as he was concerned, it was just another of the Old Wiseguy's little jokes. Still, even while he talked to me, he tried to keep on the other side of me from the Black Stick.

"We have an Intruder," he said.

"Nobody's who they seem," I said. "Not even Badguy." It was out of the Salt, and I thought I understood exactly what that meant. Events proved me wrong. After the Change, I understood it differently. So did the Saltspeakers.

Orwoz nodded toward the tree as if Theshei were on the other side of it, which I thought might be the case. "That guy," he said.

"That guy what?" I said.

Orwoz looked at me with withering contempt. "That guy's an Intruder."

I said, "Be serious."

He looked insulted, but he let it pass. "And I know who sent him."

"I sent him," I said. It was at least partly true. "I've known Theshei all my life. If he's an Intruder, I'm an Intruder."

He looked like I was only confirming what he thought already, and I couldn't understand why he would want to tell one Intruder that another Intruder has been discovered. It worried me a little because Orwoz was a master at manipulating people, and I had a feeling he was involved in a deeper scheme than I could recognize and I was its target as much as Theshei. It meant he thought he had me figured out.

"*They* sent him," he said. Considering the number of agencies Orwoz believed were conspiring against the Saltspeakers, it was impossible to guess who "They" were.

"Which They?" I said.

"The Ghosts!" he said. It was what a lot of people called the Sandscripti. Some even called them the Holy Ghosts but not Orwoz. He wasn't even convinced that they were from off planet.

"Theshei never even saw a Ghost," I said. But I'd seen one. It looked like a sail to me, a great boatless sail puffed out by the wind, with a moving humanoid picture on it in luminous paint. It floated by, about three times as big as a man, very graceful and beautiful and serene. You could see through it, but everything you saw on the far side of it was distorted somehow. It glowed with a foggy kind of light, sort of like fuzzy sunlight but not as bright.

After it was past, it sort of floated to a stop and turned and looked at me like it thought it recognized me. Then it made some swirls and flashes with its light wand and looked at me a little closer. Finally, it decided it didn't know me after all, and it turned and glided away. I just stood there and stared at it until it faded away in the distance, the way I did the first time I ever saw a rainbow. They were about as rare as rainbows.

Nobody knew what the Sandscripti were really up to, but I doubted that it had anything at all to do with the Saltspeakers. Orwoz looked like he was expecting more cooperation from me and couldn't figure out why he wasn't getting it. I probably looked at him like I thought he'd finally snapped.

"We've seen them," he said. "Beyond the trees. At night. Going back and forth."

Beyond the trees was the road. "Headlights," I said.

He ignored it and rightly so. The Sandscripti have a

very special kind of light and you really couldn't confuse it with any other kind of light. "They're waiting for some kind of message from him," he said.

"Don't be ridiculous," I said. "You can only talk to them with a light wand, and you know what happens if you try to use one of those."

Orwoz looked like he hoped we'd both try it. "We're watching them all the time," he said. Suddenly I understood who all that monitoring equipment in the Ghost Dorm was directed at. Theshei was right, there was something going on there beside Sowing the Salt. "We see," he said. "We're not fooled. And we know who's who."

"Nothing you know is true," I said. It was right out of the Salt.

Orwoz scowled. He never liked to hear me quote the Salt, and he hated to hear Theshei say anything from it. "In the end, you only betray yourself," he said. I was surprised at what he said; he usually took his quotes from the Commentaries instead of the Salt itself.

"Why are you telling me all this?" I said.

Orwoz smiled. "So you'll know!" he said.

I didn't like the sound of that. I knew he thought he had some irresistible plan set up, and there wasn't going to be time when the hammer fell to let me know where it was coming from. Half the fun of revenge is letting the victim know where it came from. He was telling me in advance so that if I had a half second before the end, I'd know he set it all up long before.

CHAPTER 9

WHEN I came back, I knelt down beside Theshei and started clipping the grass. He kept cutting away and then changing direction. And the others were doing the same thing, so I knew something was going on. Theshei said, "What'd the Rhino want?"

I was surprised he didn't already know. Even while I was listening to Orwoz, I half expected to look up into the tree and see Theshei smiling down at me. "Weren't you listening?" I said.

Theshei looked like I accused him of opening my mail.

"It's all right with me if you were," I told him. "I have nothing to say to Orwoz you couldn't hear." He nodded, but he still looked skeptical. "You're getting as paranoid as he is," I said. "You can't hate anything without becoming it, you know." The Salt was right about so many things, and it always said it better than I could, even if it did annoy Theshei.

"I sound like the Rhino?" he said. "I'm not the one quoting him every five minutes."

"Just because they come out his mouth, doesn't mean they're his words," I said. "Orwoz is not the Salt."

"And you are?" he said. I thought we'd put that argument behind us, and I couldn't figure out why he wanted to start it up again.

"Who knows anything?" I said. It was the Salt again.

"You sound like one of the Rhinettes," he said.

"There's a big difference between the Rhinettes and Saltspeakers, and a bigger difference between Saltspeakers and the Salt," I told him.

I don't know whether he couldn't understand how I felt about the Salt or wouldn't. But I knew something was bothering him. He shook his head at me. "You're getting to be just like the rest of them," he said.

"You're one of them too," I said.

"No," he said, "I'm beginning to think I don't belong here anymore." I hated to hear him say that. If he felt like moving on, then whatever had driven him here was calling him somewhere else, and I'd have to choose between him and the Salt. Even though the Saltspeakers were not the Salt, I couldn't imagine the Salt without them. I couldn't imagine leaving.

"You're going to go?" I said.

"You're going to stay?" he said.

I told him I didn't know, I hadn't thought about it. And I really didn't know. But Theshei knew. He wasn't hurt or angry about it. "Look," he said. "Maybe this is where you're supposed to be."

"I thought it was where you were supposed to be too," I told him. I wanted it to be. I didn't want to have to choose, and I didn't want to have to go.

"I'm not sure anymore," he said.

"It's almost over," I said. I sounded to myself like I did when we were kids and I was pleading with him to do something. "In another couple weeks, we'll be Saltspeakers, and Orwoz'll be just another guy in a white robe."

"It's not the Rhino," he said. I knew what it was, but I didn't really want him to tell me. It was his destiny again, that sense of being on his way somewhere and knowing whether he was on the right road or not, even if he didn't know where the road was going. "Something's happened here," he said. "This place just doesn't feel right anymore."

I didn't know what to do. "Give it another month," I

said. "Then if you still want to go, I'll go with you." I hoped by then he'd want to stay, and I didn't want to think about what I'd do if he didn't. I really believed I'd go. I didn't even think about whether the Saltspeakers would let us go. I should have. Theshei did.

"You better think about that," he said. "You know the pledge: No way out but death."

I knew the pledge; in two weeks we'd be making it in earnest, but we already knew too much for Orwoz's paranoia to let us go alive.

"Goodguy lives forever. So do you," I said. I wanted to say things my own way when I talked to Theshei, but the Salt always came out instead.

Theshei shook his head like I was hopeless. "Simple sayings don't make you bulletproof," he said. "I don't think you understand what we're in here."

I didn't think *he* understood. To me, it had nothing to do with organizations. "Two people in the same different place," I said. Even now it's funny how much of the Salt still holds up, even if the meaning is totally different than it was then. Then, I thought it meant, any two people experience the same thing differently. Now, I know it means much more.

"These people are everywhere," he said. "There's going to be no place to hide." I could see he was trying to talk me out of it, and that made me feel real bad because I knew that it meant deep down he'd already made up his mind. "You think the Rhino is going to let us walk away?"

"He'll never expect us to go," I said.

"He'll never expect you to go," he said.

I said, "No, no, he thinks you're an Intruder. He'd never expect you to leave, especially after we take the pledge." I knew Orwoz would think even the inscrutable Sandscripti wouldn't waste their time getting a spy that deep in the Saltspeakers and then pull him out.

Theshei was amused. "I'm an Intruder?" he said. "Who does he think I'm spying for?"

It was so preposterous, I almost didn't want to tell him. "The Sandscripti," I said. "That's who they're monitoring from the Ghost Dorm."

Theshei started to laugh. "That man's crazier than I thought," he said. "Why would the Ghosts care about the Saltspeakers?"

"It's worse than that," I said. "He thinks they're going back and forth beyond the trees waiting for a message from you."

Theshei stopped clipping for a minute. "Where does he get these ideas?" he said. "I think that horn's growing inward and squeezing his brain." He shook his head at the sheer looniness of it. "I never even saw one."

"I did," I said. Theshei looked surprised. "A little while before we started looking for some place to get in out of the rain."

"I almost saw one then," he said. "In Municipal Park, down by the lake. I could see the glow just over the hill, but when I got there, it was gone." He sounded disappointed. He looked puzzled. "Maybe I saw it and don't remember it," he said. People believed the Sandscripti could do that, cloud your mind if you saw something they didn't want you to see, but then people believed the Sandscripti could do a lot of things they couldn't.

"You'd remember if you ever saw one," I said.

"What'd it look like?" he said. Everybody'd seen pictures of them; there was even one on the front page of one of the newspapers I'd lined the cardboard box with. But the pictures were always blurry and grainy, the way newspaper pictures always are but worse.

"I thought it was a sailboat coming down the road," I said. "A big glowing sail. Or maybe a balloon out of the Thanksgiving parade, only smaller and glowing." I couldn't help thinking about it without some of that uniqueness coming back. "But it wasn't the way it looked; it was something else."

Even while I was trying to explain it to him, I knew it was one of those things all you can say about is "You hadda be there." But I tried. "It made me feel . . . like the Salt." I knew that was hopeless because Theshei didn't feel the Salt the way I did, but it was as close as I could come. I wondered for a minute why we didn't join the Sandscripti, but then I remembered what a suicidal thing it would have been.

"You don't think we could be Sandscripti spies and not know it, do you?" Theshei said.

"What? Sleeper agents?" I said. "You're getting to be as crazy as Orwoz." Theshei just shrugged. The whole idea gave me the creeps. "What made you say a crazy thing like that?" I said.

"I don't know," he said. "I just feel like I know more about them than I do." He looked like he wasn't sure exactly what he meant; it was like he was with his destiny—he didn't know what it was but he knew when he was on the right track. "You know what I mean?" he said.

I knew what he meant, but for me, it was that way with the Salt. It wasn't like I learned the Salt, I just remembered it. But the Sandscripti were something different. Little chills of apprehension went shooting up my back when I thought about them and Theshei. I could see the plan forming in his head. Not a plan for the moment but a backup plan. A bolt-hole we could disappear down as a last resort.

I think it was one of those things you get whole; you don't figure out the details, they come complete with the idea the first time you get it. He said, "If something happens to me or if we ever get separated . . ." I knew right then he was planning to leave me behind. I didn't know whether it was because he knew he couldn't get both of us out or he knew I was where I belonged. "Just remember this conversation if you ever want to find me again."

I said, "You're not planning to leave me here, are you?" I shouldn't have had to remind him. "We go back a long way."

"Only Goodguy plans," Theshei said. He didn't quote the Salt much, so it was ominous when he did. But he put his finger horn up to his forehead and made me laugh.

I was starting to trim away from him, and he put his hand out to stop me. He drew a little curvy line where he wanted it cut. "Like that," he said. When I was done, he looked around and nodded his head like he was satisfied. Then he looked across the lawn. Orwoz was storming across it toward us. Theshei smiled. "Right on time," he said.

You couldn't see it from the ground, but from Orwoz's room in the Upper Dormitory, we'd cut a perfect portrait of Morzon too close to the ground for even lawnmowers to erase.

CHAPTER
10

I thought it was the showdown even though I didn't know why. From the top steps of the Upper Dormitory, you could see it was a face, but you had to get up a couple stories to see it was Morzon. Kneeling in the grass, it didn't look like anything.

But I could tell from the way Orwoz was walking that he'd reached the breaking point; his head was so red he looked like somebody had heated a bowling ball in a fire. He was slapping his metal ruler against his palm with every step, and it looked like it should have stung, but he didn't look like he was feeling it. I doubted he was coming to measure the grass.

He was coming straight for Theshei, and Theshei stood up before he got to us. The ruler had a straightedge on it that could cut like a knife, but I wasn't afraid for Theshei. I was afraid he'd take it off Orwoz and cut his throat with it. He came striding up to us, and I expected him to raise the ruler over his head and bringing it slashing down like a sword. But he stopped short of arm's reach, like he didn't trust himself to get any closer.

He pointed his ruler right and left at the ground. "What this?" he shouted.

Theshei gave him an innocent look, but he looked more like he was trying not to laugh. "What's what?" he said.

"This . . . this picture!" Orwoz said. I didn't know

what he was talking about, but when I stood up beside Theshei, I could see we weren't just cutting random patterns.

Theshei looked at him like he was surprised Orwoz wasn't delighted. "A Saltspeaker memorial," he said.

"That pig-on wasn't a Saltspeaker!" Orwoz shouted.

"He was trying to be," Theshei said.

"He killed himself!" Orwoz was actually shaking with rage.

I expected Theshei to say, "You killed him." But instead he said, "Badguy did it."

Orwoz was so outraged all he could do was sputter. He couldn't deny it without denying the Salt. And if Badguy killed Morzon, there was no reason not to have a memorial. He knew the rest of the Saltspeakers wouldn't support him if he had it removed, and he knew Theshei and the rookies weren't going to obliterate it if he told them to. He couldn't afford to lose any more confrontations with Theshei, so he had no choice but to say what he did when he finally got himself under control. "Leave it," he said. Then he turned on his heel and stalked away.

About ten feet away, he turned on us again and pointed his ruler at Theshei. "You remember this," he said. "Your time is coming." Then he walked away without looking back.

It was all the rookies could do to keep from cheering, but nobody wanted to be a scapegoat for the Rhino's rage. I didn't feel like cheering. If Orwoz could keep himself under control, it meant he had some better way to get Theshei, and I didn't like it. And the longer we went without Orwoz springing his trap, the less I liked it.

Orwoz was a lot less dangerous when he was raging out of control. It was when he was quiet and patient that I really worried. But it wasn't fear of assassination that bothered me. It wasn't even that I knew he wanted to kill Theshei, because Orwoz was really no match for him. It was leaving the Salt. One way or another, I knew that was going to happen.

But it didn't happen right away. The two weeks between us and being full Saltspeakers went by like two days. Even Orwoz seemed to ease up on everybody as the ceremony got closer. He was almost pleasant, and some of the rookies even began to wonder if maybe he hadn't just been tough on us to keep out all but the most devout. Theshei said it was the Stockholm syndrome: you torture people long enough, they want to be on your side. Prisoners want to love their captors. The Salt said, "I didn't hurt you. You didn't hurt me." Theshei didn't think that was what it was.

I thought Orwoz was setting us up, and at first I thought he'd spring his trap before the ceremony, but then I realized that he was waiting until we were Saltspeakers and had whatever secrets they were going to tell us at the ceremony before he denounced us. But after a while, even I began to think it was all over. Orwoz had no evidence Theshei was an Intruder; maybe he was just testing both of us. I was kidding myself and I knew it. Orwoz had some long-range plan and the patience to wait.

The night of the ceremony, all the rookies were gathered out near the trees, waiting to begin the long procession across the field to the Great Hall. We were the last ones to get there, and the other rookies looked like giant fireflies flying slowly between the trees. Everything seemed special, and I could see the air rolling in big slow waves across the lawn. Everybody had a candle they were supposed to keep lit, and they concentrated on that, they concentrated hard. Orwoz told them theirs might go out from time to time, but an Imposter's candle would never stay lit, especially in the Great Hall, where the true Saltspeaker's flame burned without letup.

We were on Holy Silence, so if your candle went out, you just lit it off somebody else's without asking. Theshei said he would keep as silent as they wanted after he was dead, and the candles were just something to keep us distracted—worrying over our candles made us frightened and afraid and easy to manipulate. But I didn't see it that way.

I thought it was what the Salt was all about: lighting one candle from another. "What belongs to one belongs to all," the Salt says. The candles were just a way of helping us see that for ourselves. I think we were supposed to see that we were candles also and would go out but could be relit by the Salt. It made me feel like I was a part of something bigger than myself, and I think more of the rookies felt like I did than like Theshei.

There was only a little breeze, and everybody's candle guttered, but cupping your hand around it kept it lit until the gust would die down. Theshei's went out early, and he left it out. Occasionally one of the rookies would pass by and light it without saying anything, like they thought Theshei didn't notice it was out. Everybody but him could feel the magic of it. In a way I felt sorry for him. I knew this wasn't his Thunder, but I wished it was more to him than it was. We'd both come in to get out of the rain, but it was still raining on him.

I lit his candle for the last time just before Orwoz came and started shaping us up in one long line. It twisted and curved back on itself, but there wasn't enough room and those of us at the end were back in the trees so far we could see the road. I was surprised that there was no traffic on it. And then I saw a light coming down it, like headlights at the very outer edge of their beams. It wasn't until it got brighter that I knew what it was. Everybody else was looking forward, waiting for the signal to start the procession across the field. I tapped Theshei on the shoulder and pointed back toward the road just as the Sandscripti came into view.

The whole woods started to glow, and I don't know how it was that the rest of the rookies didn't notice it. You could see the glow on the trees across the road and on the trees around us like yellowish silver. It floated, large and luminous and beautiful. Even the air flowed right through it. It was even more beautiful than the one I'd seen before. It looked like a woman made out of light. And I knew the minute I looked at Theshei that he had found his Thunder.

She was so stately, so serene. I never saw anything before or since so stunning. The Sandscripti moved pretty much like we did, but because nothing affected them on our world, they didn't need to move much as they floated along, so they looked mostly like incandescent pictures. Theshei was mesmerized.

When she got opposite us, she turned toward us and looked directly at us, first at me and then at Theshei. Then she moved a little closer to see us better. I can see now that we were all shadows dancing at the edge of the dark to the Sandscripti, and they couldn't see us very well even in the best of circumstances. She came almost to the edge of the road before she paused. Then she looked at me as if she recognized me, and when she looked at Theshei, she smiled.

The Sandscripti were gorgeous at their worst, but when this one smiled, she gave beauty a whole new meaning. It was impossible to be in the presence of that smile and not feel significant. To be the center of it, like Theshei, was more than our world could offer and all we needed as proof that there was a world beyond. "If the Salt was alive," I thought, "this is what it would look like."

She smiled at Theshei for a long time, and then she raised her light wand and wrote something in the air. I had no idea what it meant, but the way the swirls of light lingered and sparkled was beautiful enough in itself to be as much meaning as I needed. I could have watched her write like that forever. Then she turned again and drifted away. We watched her go until the last glow of her having been there died away. And when she was gone, we stood there still. I looked at Theshei's candle; it was burning like a torch.

By the time we turned back to the procession, the tail

end of it was already leaving the woods. We ran to catch up, but neither my candle nor Theshei's even guttered as we ran. Theshei kept looking back over his shoulder like he wanted to go back, but we both knew it was suicide. Orwoz would have somebody there waiting for us, and they'd gun us down as soon as we hit the road.

So we caught up with the rest and took our places at the end of the line. Other candles flickered, and a few went out, only to be relit by others of the Salt. Even Theshei smiled when he saw that. But then he'd been smiling ever since we saw the Sandscripti.

I was glad for Theshei that he had found his Thunder, but I was also sorry. It meant that before long, if I knew Theshei, he would be gone. And I knew exactly where he'd be going.

"There is only the moment," the Salt says, and I concentrated on that. It was a spectacular moment, and even Theshei seemed suddenly in the spirit of it. Orwoz was at the door as we filed up the steps, and as we went in, Theshei leaned over and lit Orwoz's candle. But it went out again as Orwoz followed us in.

The Great Hall was blazing; hundreds and hundreds of Saltspeakers packed it almost to the walls, all in white robes, each holding a candle. It gave the room a golden glow, like Sandscripti light. The line that had stretched in front of us had coiled into a tight spiral around the huge golden bowl at the center. The faces were beaming, even in their solemnity. The floor rose from the center outward, and Saltspeakers from all over the country and all over the world packed the slope. I could see from their faces, they were not all like Orwoz. "Look for the Glow," the Salt says, and the Glow was everywhere.

When the last coil of the spiral closed into place, the doors of the Great Hall all slammed shut at once. The bang from each rolled down to the center, canceled each other out, and dissolved into silence. The voice that came from the platform was rich and deep. "Goodguy sowed Salt," the Speaker said. As one, the thick circle of Saltspeakers shouted, "From the Salt grew men." The sound rattled the stone pillars, and the candles flickered and danced. It was one voice.

The voice from the platform said, "From the Salt grew men."

And the Saltspeakers answered as one, "To Sow the Salt."

Then the Speaker said, "Are you willing to Sow the Salt?"

And the rookies answered, "Yes."

Then the Speaker said, "By what will you pledge?"

And the rookies answered, "Our life's blood."

Then we filed up to the great bowl and held out our right arm. Orwoz took a gold knife in his right hand and held a gold cup under our arm with his left. With the tip of the knife, he opened the vein and our blood poured out into the cup. When the cup was filled, he turned and poured it into the great bowl, which was already filled with blood. Then he took a handful of salt from a vessel and rubbed it into the wound.

When Theshei stepped before him, Orwoz smiled, and I was afraid for an instant he was going to plunge the knife into Theshei's heart. But the cut he made on Theshei was only a little wider and a little deeper than on anyone else. Even standing next in line as I was, the difference wouldn't have been noticeable to anyone who wasn't looking for it. When he filled the cup and poured it, it was only slightly closer to the brim than any other. When he rubbed the salt into the wound, I could see his thumb working it in. But Theshei didn't flinch. Orwoz rubbed as long and hard as he could without breaking the rhythm of the ceremony, but at the end Theshei was still smiling.

He had the same smile for me, but my cut was no deeper than anyone else's, and he massaged salt into the cut almost gently. It stung and then burned, a deep, searing fire, but no one in the entire line cried out, and I did not break the chain. I knew the symbolism. We accepted the pain Sowing the Salt would bring. Our silence was our pledge never to complain.

When it was done, Orwoz smiled at me, and I knew we were doing exactly what he wanted. Once we had made our pledge, nothing could excuse us from it. If we ran, everyone there would hunt us for as long as breath was in them. The hand of every Saltspeaker would be turned against us. None of them would rest while we lived.

We filed back into our places and the Speaker spoke again. "This is the blood of the Saltspeakers." And he meant that literally. Every Saltspeaker from every country had contributed to it. "Yours mingles with it. You are one with us now. Will you take the pledge?"

We said, "Yes!" in one voice, and again the line filed toward the great bowl. This time Orwoz stood beside a golden step, where we kneeled. He dipped a gold ladle into the blood and offered it to us. We took it and said, "No way out but death." Then we drank, and handed the dipper back. Orwoz lifted it, and we leaned our heads over the great bowl. Then he poured the blood down over us, and it was done.

Theshei drank and leaned forward, and Orwoz poured the blood of the Saltspeakers over him. There was no going back. He watched the blood spill down over Theshei's head, and he looked to me as if he poured a curse instead of a welcome. He looked at the blood on Theshei as if it was Theshei's blood, as if the whole bowl was Theshei's blood, and now he had the power to make it happen.

When he handed the dipper to me, I raised it and said the words, "No way out but death." I knew I was giving Orwoz my death warrant, but even if they killed me the moment I stepped away form the great bowl, I wouldn't have turned that dipper away. I drank.

The blood had been heating for hours. It was warm and coppery. I thought it would be transformed, but it was only blood. Not until I swallowed it did I feel anything different. And then it was as if the candles were sliding in procession down my throat and pooling in a lake of fire in my stomach. For an instant, I was afraid Orwoz had somehow poisoned it. But the feeling passed, and I felt filled with a warm glow that made everything change.

When I bent my head over the great bowl, the blood gleamed and glistened. And when the first drops cascaded off my head, they sent out ripples that made it shimmer. Everything seemed to be saturated with golden light. I knew I was where I should be.

When I got up to walk back to my place, Orwoz leaned close and whispered, "No way out but death."

When we stood ringed around the great bowl again, the Speaker said, "Do you swear to keep faith with the brotherhood even in death?"

And we said, "Yes."

"Do you swear to hunt those who do not while breath is in you?" he said.

And we said, "Yes."

Then everyone at once said, "No way out but death."

Simultaneously, all candles were snuffed out, leaving us in total darkness. For a moment everything was as silent as death itself and as dark. The moment lengthened. The dark and the silence deepened. Then with a great clang, the hoods of the fire troughs were thrown back, and the flames leaped up. We were all reborn, and we were reborn Saltspeakers.

CHAPTER
11

THE next day, things had changed. The fasting and the interrupted sleep, the meaningless labor, even the harassment, became things of the past. When Orwoz met us on the paths or outside the Great Hall, he would smile and nod or greet us with some words from the Salt. It seemed like a nightmare was over, and nothing of it remained in the light of day. Everything seemed changed except Theshei.

I went to the room, but his cot was unmade and I thought he was gone. I felt a great emptiness. His friendship was the only consistent thing in my life. I told myself he would be back before long, but I was afraid he was gone for good. Still, I couldn't believe he'd go without me, and after an hour, I decided to go and look for him. I thought I knew where to find him, but when I got to the Great Hall, he wasn't there. The rest of the rookies were. They were on their hands and knees in the grass, trimming away Morzon's picture.

Nobody told them to do it. Not even Orwoz. None of them seemed to know whose idea it was. They said they came by and others were doing it, and they just joined in. I asked one of them if it was the Rhinettes who were cutting first, and he said to me, "We're all Saltspeakers now."

There was nothing I could say to that. That was the way it was supposed to be. But I realized every one of them would have cut my throat if they thought I had any intention of leaving. And they'd cut Theshei's just as quick. "Nothing comes before the Salt," I said. It had always been just a greeting until that moment, but I realized it was true. There was nothing any of them would not sacrifice for the Salt, including themselves. They were going to be merciless pursuers.

I stood on the steps watching them obliterate everything Theshei had taught them. There wasn't a question left in them. They believed, and the Salt requires no explanation. None of them could explain it. They could repeat it flawlessly, they would be able to exhort others to follow it with genuine fervor, they would Sow it among the educated and the ignorant alike, they would accept being beaten and reviled and even killed for its sake, but not one of them could explain the least part of it.

They knew what the rest of the Saltspeakers knew. If one of them knew it was good to eradicate the last trace of Morzon, they all knew it. And when they didn't know, they had me and my Black Stick to tell them. Or they had Orwoz to tell them. They had the whole brotherhood to tell them. And they were willing, even anxious, to be told. Their faith was as beautifully trusting as it was frightening.

I left them shaving the grass down to the nub. Most of Morzon was already gone. By the time I reached the trees, it would all be gone. I wondered if Theshei knew. I wondered if he had seen them. I knew if he was still around at all, I would find him in the woods where we saw the Sandscripti, and I was right.

He was sitting at the base of a tree looking out at the road. Cars whizzed by occasionally, but I doubted that he saw them. I believe he could still see the Sandscripti, floating there, radiant with her unearthly light. I can still see her, even though the Change makes me see her differently. I looked across at the trees that had reflected her glow, and at first I thought the glint back in the underbrush was a fragment of that light, left like some piece of cloth snagged on a twig. Only gradually did I realize it was a gun barrel.

I realized that for Theshei and I nothing had changed. Orwoz was waiting for us to make our break. All around the perimeter there were Saltspeakers with the patience to wait until we broke cover, Saltspeakers who would be relieved by other Saltspeakers when their shift was up. Night and day, rotation after rotation, they would lie in wait meditating on our deaths, waiting for us or anyone else to transgress the perimeter.

"Sit down before they blow your head off," Theshei said.

I sat down opposite him, with my back to the road, between him and the gunsight. Theshei smiled and shook his head. "Who do you think you're fooling?" he said.

"I don't want them to get the wrong idea," I said.

Theshei laughed. "You don't want them to get the right idea."

He was right, but I ignored it. "We're not supposed to be out here," I said. I sounded like one of the Rhinettes, and I knew it.

Theshei corrected me. "Rookies aren't supposed to be out here. We're Saltspeakers now. We can go anywhere as long as we don't cross the road." His voice was sharp with bitterness and disappointment. I didn't know what to say to him; even the Salt couldn't help me. "Don't worry," he said. "They don't shoot unless you cross the road."

"How do you know?" I said.

He said, "I asked them." I must've looked surprised. "I went over and asked that one."

"When?" I said.

"When the barrel drooped," he said. "Even Saltspeakers doze and daydream."

I understood how he did it. He was definitely quick enough. And patient. The shooter's eyelids drooped, the gun lowered slightly, and Theshei was gone behind the nearest tree. When they sagged again, to another. One more to cross the road and roll into the ditch. In twenty minutes, he could have been on the other side of the shooter and gone. What I didn't understand was why he came back. "Why would he tell you that?" I said.

Theshei smiled. "Orwoz chewed him out for taking his eyes off me and told him to keep his eyes on the road instead of turning around." I knew he meant he told him using Orwoz's voice. "It's amazing," he said. "As long as you stay on this side of the road, you can go all the way around the compound, and nobody'll shoot you." I knew he'd done just that. "But if you cross the road . . ." He left the rest unfinished.

"Simple rules are best," I said. It was from the Salt, but I meant it as a joke.

"And simple minds," he said.

"Simplicity is the friend of faith," I said.

Theshei laughed. "That's not from the Salt," he said.

"It's from the New Commentaries," I told him. "I just haven't had a chance to write it down yet."

"It doesn't matter," he said. "They won't understand it anyway."

"They're not supposed to understand," I said. "They're supposed to know." It was true. Reason only corrupts faith for most people. The things I knew best were things I didn't even know I knew until somebody asked me.

Theshei shook his head at their gullibility. And mine. "A little spicy tomato soup laced with Dylastic Sugar, and everybody's a believer," he said.

"It was blood to me," I said. It didn't matter if what he said was true. Belief doesn't change your understanding of the world; it changes the world. For him it was soup and Dylastic Sugar. For me, it was blood and enlightenment.

"Before you drank it or after?" he said.

I knew he knew the answer, but I gave it to him anyway. "Before."

"The miracle of faith," he said. There was a touch of envy in it, as if he wanted to believe something that much, he just didn't know what yet. "The Salt is made of Dylastic Sugar," he said. He seemed just a bit disappointed.

"How'd you know it was Dylastic Sugar?" I said.

"Misspent youth," he said. "You were there." I remembered. School was a drugstore. A Sugar One-Shot was the least of what was available. Euphoria and suggestibility on demand. You could get it from the school nurse, and if you didn't stay in line, you got it from the school principal in megadoses. It was amazing that Theshei wasn't a Smiling Zombie. I guess it just doesn't take on some people. I never got as far out of line as Theshei, so nobody tried to put a Smile on my face, and I didn't want to try it on my own. I had enough problems.

"Flashback," I said. But we both knew he was probably right. What we disagreed on was what it meant. To Theshei, it was just one more trick played in the name of truth and justice. To me, it was no trick at all. "Besides, it's where you get, not how you get there."

Theshei raised an eyebrow. "You're telling me the end justifies the means?"

"I'm telling you the end *makes* the means," I said. "That's the difference between a Sugar One-Shot and a miracle."

"A Smiling Zombie by any other name . . ." he said.

I knew they weren't the same; even if Orwoz was turning the rookies into an army of Rhinettes, sooner or later, they would break through into True Knowing. "One sugar dream doesn't make a Smiling Zombie," I said.

"Then why are they back there snipping Morzon into oblivion?" His voice was full of anger and disappointment.

"You think they betrayed you," I said.

Theshei snorted. "I think they betrayed themselves. The Rhino can have them."

"The Rhino may have them for the moment," I said, "but they're still the Salt's. You can't come in contact with the Salt without knowing enlightenment sooner or later."

Theshei laughed, but he wasn't amused. "I did," he said.

It was my turn to smile. "How do you know?" I said. "Maybe it's already transformed you in spite of your self."

"It's not the Salt," he said. Then he said a very strange thing. He said, "Have you ever been in love?"

I said, "What?"

"In love," he said. "Have you ever been in love?"

"I was in heat a lot," I said. "It never did me much good. It never did me any good at all in fact."

"I'm serious," he said.

I told him I hadn't, but it wasn't true. The moment I said it, I realized that I was in love with the Salt.

"You know the woman we saw," he said.

"The Sandscripti?" I said. Theshei nodded. I said, "That's not going to work out. You can reach right through her."

"That doesn't matter," he said. He said it just like I would have said it if he said I couldn't be in love with the Salt, and I realized it was the same thing. Reason had nothing to do with it. Theshei was in love with his Thunder. There was no precedent for it, but then Theshei was always finding new alternatives. Either finding love or finding your Thunder could change your life; finding them both together was more powerful than destiny.

"Then why'd you come back?" I said. "You were past them. You could've kept right on going."

"Time wasn't right," he said. "There's still things to do."

"What things?" I said.

He looked at me for a long time. "We go back a long way," he said. It wasn't really all that long, but it was most of our lives. "Listen to me, no matter what happens, don't take it personally."

"You're not going to tell me what you're going to do?" I said. It seemed to me that I deserved to know. "What do you think, I'm going to tell Orwoz?" It was a spiteful thing to say, but I was hurt that he suddenly didn't trust me.

"It's better that you don't know," he said. "Trust me."

"Trust's a two-way street," I told him. But I knew he wasn't going to tell me anything else.

"You know what the weakness of the rhinoceros is?" he said. He didn't give me a chance to tell him. "It's nearsighted, so it can only attack one target at a time."

"Look," I said. "I don't care what your plan is as long as you don't go without me."

He looked like I was making it real hard for him. "Would you kill me if I asked you to?" he said. He knew the answer. "Then don't ask me to kill you," he said.

Logic was on his side. I was dead weight. I didn't have half his skills. It would take him twice as long to get us both across the road. Two people can't disappear as easily as one. I didn't really want to go, and sooner or later, that alone would get one or both of us killed. I knew he couldn't stay either. Not just because Orwoz wanted him dead, but because that unerring sense of destiny was pulling him elsewhere. It left me without an argument.

Theshei stood up and started back toward the Great Hall. I always worried when Theshei quoted the Salt. "Nothing lost. Nothing gained. Everything that goes remains. No good-byes." It was what Saltspeakers said over the dead.

CHAPTER
12

THAT was the last Theshei said to me about escape. For a few weeks, things moved along but without direction. There was no routine except for mealtimes, and even they weren't mandatory. In between, we did whatever it came to us to do. Small groups were always forming to "discuss" the Salt, even though discussion amounted to exchanging quotations, but they weren't organized or moderated. They were more like games, where whoever had the quotation with the lowest number won the point. More and more, everybody spoke in numbers from the Salt.

Or one or another would stand up and begin Sowing the Salt as if everyone else was an outsider who needed conversion. It was practice for what we had all pledged ourselves to, and spontaneously, the group would take on the role of the unconverted and heckle or question or scoff, and whoever was Sowing would have to feel his way to what the best response was. Whenever he was finished, the others would critique his technique.

It amazed me that nobody organized those groups. The rookies just congregated and began, and just as spontaneously, they dispersed, only to form up again in new combinations somewhere else. Somebody was always sitting in the Great Hall meditating or just sitting blissfully in the residual glow of the initiation ceremony except when somebody would get up on the platform and begin to Sow. And even then, many of them would sit, still oblivious to the fact that somebody was speaking.

Theshei and I wandered around the grounds, watching what was going on or making up part of a mob for someone to Sow to. I was surprised that Theshei didn't automatically take on the role of sceptic and demolish whoever was Sowing, but he never did. But sometimes just his being there intimidated one or another of them into silence. It was as if they wanted to forget all about Theshei, as if he had come to represent rebellion and doubt, and they had repudiated all that. He made them nervous.

After a while, he became invisible. No one would acknowledge he was there unless they couldn't help it. If they talked to him, their conversation was short and full of awkward pauses. When we went past, they looked the other way or talked to one another as if they were too deep in conversation to see us. It was like he was somebody out of a shady past they wanted to forget.

Alone, they'd greet me with some line from the Salt, but with Theshei, I was equally invisible. It was just as well; it allowed us to spend time in the woods, scouting the perimeter, without anybody being suspicious. People were always glad to see us go, and nobody ever encouraged us to Sow. It seemed assumed that I wouldn't have to, that the Black Stick singled me out for interpretation and not exhortation. And I believe they were afraid that Theshei would make them see things about themselves they didn't want to see or remind them of things they didn't want to remember.

We put a damper on the air of expectation that seemed to get stronger by the day, as if they expected Orwoz to throw open the gate when he thought they were ready and let them all stream forth into the world to Sow the Salt. We were a reminder, or at least Theshei was, of all the misery of being rookies, of all the doubts and fears. I don't believe Orwoz even encouraged any of it, though it probably didn't displease him. It was the unpremeditated shrinking back from an unpleasant truth. The natural tendency to deny unpleasant memories. But it wasn't just that Theshei reminded them of a time when Orwoz was a living nightmare to them. Theshei was a man lightning was going to strike, and nobody wanted to be close to him. It was a contradiction they didn't want to think about. Benevolent Orwoz, who had become their kindly though distant mentor, who was not at all the monster they had thought as rookies, was going to get Theshei, and they all knew it. They didn't want to face that that vindictiveness might lie in wait for them as well.

More and more, Theshei and I retired to the cupola on top of the Great Hall, where we'd stand and look out over the compound and the marksmen beyond. We didn't talk as much as we used to. Not that the silences were uncomfortable, it was just that they made it seem like Theshei was leaving a little bit at a time. We were like the rookies; we didn't want to acknowledge that he was living on borrowed time, and unless he escaped soon, Orwoz would put an end to him. I didn't want to think about being left behind or probably never seeing him again, and maybe he didn't want to think about it either. So at first we said nothing about it, until finally we said almost nothing at all.

I began to stay down in the Great Hall when Theshei went up into the cupola. I felt comfortable there, as if I belonged. Danger and destiny seemed remote from me, and I would disappear out of myself for hours on end. All there was of me was peacefulness, a great quiet void.

Up in the cupola, Theshei watched the changing of the guard all around the perimeter. He watched the rhythms of the day rise and fall and the attentiveness of the marksmen with it. He watched the countryside beyond and the distant city, marking out landmarks he could use, estimating what lay in the folds of the earth he couldn't see between the hills, figuring out obstacles, routes, and destinations. But whenever I went up, he was always looking out toward the road in the direction the Sandscripti woman disappeared.

He had that look of deep and unquenchable longing, and I didn't know what he was waiting for; he could have gone anytime he wanted, day or night. I tried to pretend he was figuring out a way for both of us to get away, but I knew that whatever his plan was, it was already made when we walked out of the woods and he was just waiting for his opportunity. As he probably expected, Orwoz gave it to him.

A month to the day after the initiation ceremony, one of the Rhinettes came up to me and told me we were all to meet in the Great Hall an hour after full dark for our Destinations. It never occurred to me that we would go anywhere else. I thought we would go out to the city in the morning and Sow the Salt and come back again at night. Even though a lot of the rookies came from as far away as California, it never occurred to me that they would go anywhere. I knew the compound was only a training center; I just never thought about it.

Theshei didn't seem the least surprised. He just looked out over the compound toward the road. I asked him if he wasn't shocked that they were going to send us somewhere different all along. He said, "If I step off the edge of the roof, should I be shocked when I hit the ground?"

I couldn't believe it. I said, "If you knew how this was going to turn out, why'd you get us into it?"

"When you step off the roof," he said, "you can only control *how* you fall, not where."

I said, "I don't want to hear all that destiny business!" I didn't want to hear it because I knew it was true. I had to come to find the Salt, and Theshei had to come so he could be standing in the woods at the edge of the road when the Sandscripti woman passed.

It always annoyed Theshei when I wouldn't listen to him. "What do you want to hear?" he said. "The Salt?"

I didn't want to hear anything that had to do with separation or being sent away somewhere. I didn't want to hear I was talking to him for the last time, but I was afraid I was.

"Everything changes," he said. "Everything stays the same."

I knew that line from the Salt as well as he did, and I finished it for him. "Nothing lost. Nothing gained. Everything that goes remains. No good-byes."

Theshei smiled, and we went down to get ready. When we got to the Great Hall, a lot of the Saltspeakers from the ceremony were there, but the hall wasn't as full. There were no candles, and the light of the flame troughs reflected off the walls. It was bright and businesslike, and the Hall did not seem itself. I knew the Saltspeakers from elsewhere were there to take some of the rookies with them. When Orwoz welcomed us, he said as much. Up on the platform, he looked like an auctioneer auctioning off slaves.

He called each of the rookies by their chosen names and gave them a Destination. Then he introduced them to the Saltspeaker from there and wished them luck in their journey. He made everything an opportunity, but I knew some of the places he named and I'd heard about others, and all we'd gotten for our troubles was a chance to die for the Salt in some place nobody'd want to live in anyway.

But the rookies welcomed their Destinations as if they'd picked them themselves. The tougher the place, the more anti-Saltspeaker it was, the happier they were. "No better place to Sow the Salt," they said, "than barren ground." Official toleration didn't mean any of the Nontraditional Theological Alternatives condoned the existence of any of the others, and some of them made the murder of their competitors a virtue. And even the Traditional Theological Alternatives weren't averse to cracking a few heads to keep their followers from being seduced away by false orthodoxies.

It's hard to tell an American old enough to remember the Days of Affluence that the deterioration of their life is Goodguy's doing. It tends to make them look for the nearest representative of Goodguy to take it out on. The rookies looked on their suicide missions as gifts. They were, universally, grateful for the opportunity to bring the Salt to those who were most resistant to it.

Theshei and I were last as usual, and Orwoz called Theshei's name with a big smile, as if he had been Orwoz's favorite rookie. "We are in grave danger," he said. "The Salt is in grave danger. Plots have been uncovered, and some may remain hidden still." He paused until the murmurs died down. I thought he was going to denounce Theshei with or without evidence, but it was worse.

"What is needed is a brave man. An ingenious man. A man willing to risk his life to infiltrate the very heart of our enemy and uncover these plots at their source." I think he expected applause, but there was only stunned silence. "There is only one man with these qualities new enough to the Saltspeakers to be unrecognized by our enemies. Of all your Destinations, his is the most deadly and the most terrifying. To go among our most dangerous enemies and bring them down."

Two Saltspeakers stepped forward on the platform. They looked like they had been police at one time, big burly men who could do whatever was necessary without a qualm of conscience. I knew if Theshei went with them, he'd never be heard of again except for a memorial service in a few months to honor a Saltspeaker who gave his life for the Salt. Orwoz would get up at it and tell us how Theshei, on the verge of uncovering a monstrous plot by the pig-on Happy Dancers, had been discovered and martyred. Knowing Orwoz, I didn't doubt he would tell us that unfortunately there was no body left because the Happy Dancers killed Theshei and ate him.

I was as certain of that as I was that everybody would believe it, whether they believed it or not. I had no doubt they believed it already.

"Theshei," Orwoz said, "your time for service has come!" He looked like it was taking all of his willpower to keep from laughing.

I looked for Theshei, but the next instant a pair of hands came over my shoulders, the Black Stick slammed against my throat, and I was being dragged backward toward the door. I couldn't decide whether it was harder to breathe or keep my balance. I grabbed at the Stick with both hands, but all I could do was loosen it enough to catch a short breath before it slammed back under my chin. I thought it was one of Orwoz's goons, and I tried to catch sight of whoever had Theshei the same way, but I couldn't see Theshei. And then I heard his voice. It was right next to my ear. "If anybody moves, I'll kill him!" it said.

I was surprised that anybody listened. I'm not sure if they were just afraid he would turn the Black Stick on them or if they were just afraid of him period or whether they thought a Wiseguy was too important to be sacrificed or if they just didn't have any orders and they didn't know what to do on their own. Or if it's like the Salt says, "There's no courage in a lie." But for whatever reason, a path parted all the way to the door.

I knew Theshei wouldn't kill me, and he kept kicking my feet out from under me to make it look like I was struggling. When we got to the door, he slid his hands in over my thumbs and made it look like I'd pulled free and twisted the Stick almost out of his hands. He twisted and shook the Stick and made me dance like a puppet, but it looked to everyone else like we were locked in mortal combat, and I was about to wrench the Stick free at any moment.

Orwoz and his assassins had jumped down off the platform and were running up the aisle between the stunned Saltspeakers toward us. Theshei made our battle last until they were almost to us, and then he shoved me away. As I staggered back, he held the Black Stick out parallel to the ground in front of him and snapped it like a twig.

It was an unthinkable thing to do. Even Orwoz was stunned, and the two giants with him stumbled and lost a half step as if Theshei had hit them with it. The sound of it snapping was sickening, like a bone breaking. I felt like he had broken a part of me.

He stood there for an instant, holding the two halves. It had split down the long axis, leaving two sharp tapering points, and he held the knobbed end like a spear and the other like a sword. I stumbled toward him as if I could put it back together. As I took a step with my right, he took a step to his. It made it look like I was moving in front of Orwoz to protect him. I couldn't believe it when Theshei threw the spear end right at my head.

He was too close for me to duck, and the point sliced open my forehead as it went past. It would have stuck Orwoz in the throat if the knobbed end hadn't hit me in the right forehead like a hammer. I felt it hit, I even heard it hit. It sounded like he'd smacked the Stick against one of the marble columns, and it snapped my head back. But I didn't feel the pain. I didn't feel anything. Then I couldn't see anything, and I couldn't think. It was like I vanished. Or the world did.

CHAPTER
13

I didn't so much wake up as come back to life. It was slow, and intermittent, and I wasn't really part of it. I was aware of people around me and fussing over me, but I just had no interest in what was going on. It was like there was a sheet of thick glass between me and everything else. And I kept falling back to sleep. I'm not sure I wanted to wake up. I didn't remember much of the details, but I knew Theshei'd tried to kill me. But I couldn't remember why. So I stayed asleep so I wouldn't have to think about it.

And there was the problem of the pain. It felt like there was a dent above my right eye, a wedge of numbness I could have stuck my thumb in. The skin around it was stretched, like something had driven it inward and it hadn't come back out. I didn't feel any pain from it, just tightness and a sense of damage. The pain was inside, an inch or two deeper than the point of the wedge. It spread out from there like the shadow of the wedge, back and up through my whole head, darkening parts of my brain.

My head felt fragile, like an egg somebody'd dropped and then tried to salvage. I felt like it was cracked, with a dozen fissures spreading all over it, and if I moved in the slightest, the pieces would all come apart and my head would disintegrate. If I just kept still, I thought it would be all right. But no matter how still I kept, my head kept vibrating, the way a struck bell keeps quivering long after it stops making a sound. And the vibrations came in waves, going outward into my head from just beyond the point of the wedge and then bouncing back off the inside of my skull and making crosscurrents and eddies.

During the ebb of it I could see if I concentrated on focusing my eyes, but during the surge, my whole body rattled, and I couldn't even think about seeing. I was indifferent to everything else. I had no questions, no answers, no expectations. If I slept, the pain would come rattling through like a freight train, waking me up and shaking the walls of my skull. I'd have to wait until even the echo of it died away before I could doze again.

I don't know how long it went on like that, but it seemed to me that they should have taken me to a hospital, and I kept thinking about telling them about that, but I kept dozing off before I could get the words out. The one time I did manage to say something, one of the Rhinettes who was hovering over me looked at me like I was speaking Sandscripti. It didn't seem to matter enough to try again.

I had no track of anything, night or day, sitting or lying, awake or asleep. Whatever happened to me happened to somebody else, and I followed the events with lukewarm interest. But gradually things seemed less remote, and the pain and the echoes of the pain finally died away to a dull ache. They never dwindled beyond that, but after a while it seemed so second nature that I didn't pay any attention to it.

I believe I was hiding in that pain so I didn't have to face a worse pain: what Theshei had done and what had been done to him. I remembered him telling me not to take it personally, but the fact remained that he'd tried to kill me and almost succeeded. After all we'd been through together, I just couldn't believe that he'd sacrifice me to save himself. My guess was that he didn't expect Orwoz to make his move that way, and in the heat of the moment, self-preservation kicked in.

But long trains of thought just made my head start hurting again, so I let it go. Until Orwoz came in. He sat down beside the bed and looked at me for a long while like he wasn't sure what to say. Finally, he said, "I never thought the Wiseguy made the right choice with you." He paused, but I wasn't sure whether it was for me to say something or because he was still picking his words. I wasn't saying anything until I knew where I stood. They were taking care of me pretty good, but I wasn't sure I wasn't just a prisoner Orwoz wanted to interrogate.

"I'm not used to being wrong," he said. "That was a courageous thing you did."

I wasn't really sure what he was talking about. There were gaps in what happened, and a lot of what I did remember was blurry at best. I must've looked at him blankly because he said, "That stick was meant for me."

"He broke the Stick!" I said. It was like he'd just broken it. I could still hear the crack. I felt a lot of things when I thought about Theshei trying to kill me, but all I felt when I thought about the Stick was rage and grief. It was such an irreparable loss, not just to me but to all the Saltspeakers.

"Yes," Orwoz said, "and tried to kill me with half of it." The thought still outraged him. "You threw yourself between us and shielded me." It seemed to surprise him as much as it did me.

I put a hand gingerly to my head. There was still a big lump, and I wondered if I was going to have a horn like Orwoz. I was surprised that there was a long cut along the side of my head. I knew he'd hit me with something, but I kept remembering it as a spear. I didn't even remember Orwoz being behind me until he mentioned it. I had trouble believing I'd sacrificed myself for him.

"The point cut your head," he said, "and then the knob hit you." He shook his head like it was a wonder I was still alive. "We thought you had a fractured skull for a while."

I wanted to ask him why he didn't take me to a

hospital then, but he didn't give me a chance, and I knew it probably had something to do with imaginary pig-on spies or Sandscripti assassins. "You're going to be all right now, though," he said.

I couldn't imagine what would have made me do a thing like that. I thought maybe it was the Stick. Or maybe it was just that I had to choose between the Salt and Theshei, and I took the Salt. Or maybe I just got in the way by accident. I could hardly remember doing it, and trying to figure out the reasons was one of those things that made my head start to rattle again.

I still had enough of my mind to know that if Orwoz thought I'd saved his life, I was a lot better off than if he thought I was part of Theshei's escape, so I kept my mouth shut. I wanted to know what happened to Theshei, but I didn't want to seem too anxious about it and make them suspicious again. So I asked the usual question. "How long?"

"Till you're completely better?" he said.

I shook my head. It was a big mistake. It made me dizzy and everything started to throb. I had to lay my head back in the pillows with both my hands and not move for a while before it tapered off. I didn't want to talk anymore, but there were things I had to know.

"I'll come back later," Orwoz said.

But I motioned for him to stay. "How long since it happened?" I said.

"Oh," Orwoz said. He laughed at the misunderstanding. "Almost a week. You were out completely for more than a day and in and out of consciousness ever since." He seemed like he was genuinely concerned. He seemed like a different person with Theshei gone. I wondered if Theshei *was* gone.

There was no easy way to ask directly. I tried the indirect approach. "The Stick," I said. "Where is it?" If Theshei threw half, he must have kept half. I hoped he didn't take it with him.

"We recovered the other half in the woods across the road," he said. I was glad. It meant Theshei was free. Even if he tried to kill me, I didn't want him dead. Besides, I wanted to know why.

"We're going to need it," he said, "and you. We think he had a confederate in the woods. One of the Defenders named Maljik."

I wanted to ask him why the "Defenders" had their guns pointed inward, but it was something Theshei would have said and I knew I'd only get myself in trouble. If Theshei had any confederates, I should have been at the top of the list of suspects. "Nobody stopped him?" I said. I tried to make it sound like I wished they had.

Orwoz looked embarrassed. "No," he said, "I'm afraid they were all too stunned to move. By the time anybody could react, he was out the door and gone." He shook his head as if it was a bad miscalculation. "We didn't think he'd get off the grounds."

That didn't surprise me. I was sure Orwoz must've had the outside covered just in case Theshei didn't go along quietly, but they probably didn't expect him to be armed, and Orwoz had probably told them to take him alive so he could kill Theshei himself later.

"Two of the brotherhood from New Jersey did try to stop him just outside the door, but he slashed one and stabbed the other with the bottom half of the Black Stick." I felt bad about that, not because some thugs had gotten cut up but because the Black Stick had been used to draw blood. It just seemed wrong. But then the Black Stick didn't mean anything to Theshei. He was always telling me it was just a stick.

But it was a lot more than that to me. It represented the Salt and my connection with the Salt, and I hated to see it misused. I supposed Theshei didn't have any choice, but I still held it against him, and I was going to have a lot to say to him about abusing it the next time I saw him. That made me wonder if I ever was going to see him again. In a way I hoped I wouldn't, because if I did, it would probably be if Orwoz caught him.

"Well," Orwoz said, "I'll let you get some rest. We're going to need you as soon as possible."

I didn't really want to know what they'd need me for, and I was surprised at how tired I was just from talking that much. But the surprise must've showed in my face, and Orwoz thought I wanted to know what they needed me for. "Only the Wiseguy can use the Black Stick," he said, "and we have to know about this confederate."

I knew what he meant. They needed me to touch the Black Stick to Maljik's forehead to test his faith. I knew he was innocent, but I knew also that if he thought he was guilty, the touch would kill him. I wasn't looking forward to that, and besides the Stick was broken. But it was such an effort to say that. I just let my eyes close and drifted off to sleep again.

When I opened them again, it was hours later. The sun was setting, and the wall opposite the window was pink. I was feeling a little better. Out of every sleep I seemed to wake stronger, and my appetite was coming back. One of the Rhinettes brought me a tray in a little later, and I was surprised at how hungry I was. I wolfed it down and asked for more. The Rhinette looked pleased and went to get me some. I tried to wait for him, but I dozed off again.

It was a full day when I woke up again. I was still hungry, and it seemed like as soon as I opened my eyes one of the Rhinettes popped up in front of me asking if they could get me anything. They seemed as anxious to please me as they did to please Orwoz, but it didn't endear them to me. I don't think they cared who they sucked up to as long as they got to suck up to somebody.

Still, I figured he might know something. The Rhinettes were a pack of little weasels who lived on what they could snoop out. The spy's main vice is always gossip. "You're looking better," he said.

I said, "Thanks, uh . . ." I'd thought of them as a group for so long that I'd forgotten his name.

"Malmun," he said.

I repeated it for all the good it was going to do me. They all looked alike to me. We all had to have new names nobody'd ever had before, but I didn't think much of his. I figured I probably wouldn't have liked his old name much either. "What's been going on while I've been gone?" I said.

He looked like he was honored to talk to me. The Rhinettes were easily honored. "Oh, a lot," he said. "Most of the people we were rookies with are gone to new Destinations, and people are coming in all the time, trying to pick up the Intruder's trail." He knew Theshei's name, so I assumed it wasn't something Salt-speakers were permitted to utter. Or maybe being so close to Orwoz, they wanted to spare his feelings. Or keep from annoying him.

"No luck though," I said.

"No," he said, "but that'll change as soon as you're up and around."

I wasn't sure I wanted it to change. I certainly didn't want to be part of killing anybody. "You think this Maljik guy knows something?"

He looked delighted to be able to tell me something nobody else could. "He's tough. They've tried every-thing, but he still says the same thing."

"What's that?" I said.

"He says Orwoz came in the afternoon and told him not to shoot if somebody came running out of the woods after dark," he said. "No matter what they do to him, he swears it."

"He swears it was Orwoz," I said, "but he never actually saw him."

He looked astounded. "How did . . . ?" He stopped himself. I was the Wiseguy after all. I was supposed to do things like that. I had no doubt it would be a legend by the time the Rhinette rumor mill got finished embellishing on the story. The problem with faith is it makes you gullible. I didn't correct him. One of the things I always wanted to add to the Commentaries is "It's a hard life for an idiot." It didn't seem my place to make his life any easier.

As far as the Rhinettes were concerned, I was a hero. I figured it wouldn't hurt if they thought I was a holy man as well. They were going to believe it anyway. When we were all old and gray, they wanted to be able to go around saying to the rookies, "Back when me and the Old Wiseguy were rookies together . . ." As long as *I* didn't start believing it, I figured I'd be all right. There's nothing like being looked up to by idiots to remind you what fame is worth.

"Orwoz'll be here in less than a minute," I told him. Forty-two seconds later, Orwoz walked in. Malmun's mouth dropped open. It seemed to me that all the scurrying in the hall was so obvious a sign of Orwoz's arrival, nobody could miss it. But Malmun did. People like the Rhinettes went flying around like startled quail half a block ahead of wherever Orwoz went. As soon as I saw one Saltspeaker go skidding past the door and then two others, I knew Orwoz had to be at the far end of the hall.

It was such a simple trick it shouldn't have fooled a child. But Malmun wanted to believe that the Wiseguy had special powers, so almost anything was evidence to him. If I'd told him the sun was going to set and eventually it did, he'd have taken it as proof of second sight. They all wanted to be witnesses to miracles. They never expected to perform miracles themselves, but reflected glory was good enough. Very special people had supernatural powers; special people got to see them used. They wanted to be special, so they saw miracles whenever they looked at me. Being their idol was like being elected king of the sheep. It kept me humble.

There was no way I could take myself seriously as long as *they* took me seriously. It made me understand the Old Wiseguy a little better.

When Orwoz came in, he looked at Malmun standing there stupefied with awe and shook his head. I almost felt sorry for him, having to battle Theshei with the likes of the Rhinettes. "You're looking better," he said.

I didn't want to risk nodding my head, so I said, "I'm getting there."

He said, "Good." Then he kind of shuffled around what he wanted to say. Finally, he said, "Look, I don't want to force you into a relapse, but we need you to test the confederate's faith, and we can't wait. The trail's cold already, and we have to find out where the Intruder went."

"He doesn't know," I said. It seemed to me that I didn't owe Theshei anything, and whatever I had to tell them about him would save some poor Saltspeaker from his worst nightmare.

Orwoz scowled. He had his mind made up that Maljik was lying, and he didn't want to be confused with the facts. "Then why's he still lying?" he said.

"He's not," I said.

Orwoz looked insulted. "I was never in the woods, and I never gave him an order not to shoot anybody."

"Theshei did," I said. Malmun winced when I said Theshei's name and rolled his eyes up into his head. "Theshei's a natural mimic. He could do your voice better than you can."

Orwoz mulled it over for a moment. Finally, he said, "Well, we have to test this guy anyway to see if his faith is still strong." He was just unwilling to give up on the idea of Sticking the poor guy. Once he got his mind set on a thing, he would do it no matter how stupid you showed him it was. It seemed to me that a week of being tortured by Saltspeakers from New Jersey would do serious damage to your faith, but I didn't want to think what would happen to the poor guy if they'd broken him of everything except his belief in the Black Stick.

But I didn't see any way out of it without becoming a prime suspect myself, and I didn't want Orwoz interrogating me until I was a lot stronger, because I knew where Theshei was. Besides, I thought maybe when I got close to Maljik I'd be able to calm him down and tell him it was OK. So I said I'd do it.

Orwoz looked like he wanted it done now, and I saw my chance. I threw my legs over the bed and stood up as fast as I could. It worked perfectly. Except for the pain. It was like somebody hit me in the face with a long-handled shovel, and it wasn't until I was back in bed that I realized I was the handle and the floor was what hit me flat in the face.

My nose was bleeding, and the blood was pouring down into my mouth and for a minute I thought maybe Theshei was right and the Blood of the Saltspeakers didn't really taste like blood. But then I realized there was nothing to transform this blood and it *should* taste different. Then I thought what a strange thing it was to be thinking about, and then I stopped thinking at all.

CHAPTER
14

THEY went slow with me after that, and I didn't push myself. Orwoz came by again and apologized for not realizing I wasn't up to it, and after that, he dropped in every day but he didn't say any more about the test and I began to worry that they'd tortured Maljik, the poor Defender, to death and didn't need me anymore. I wanted to stretch it out to a month before Orwoz started asking me questions in earnest, but worrying about Maljik made me put some effort into getting better. The pain went away completely for periods, and the periods got longer and longer until the pain was the exception rather than the rule. I was standing by the twelfth day and walking fairly well by the thirteenth, except that I got dizzy occasionally.

On the fourteenth day, Orwoz asked if I was ready, and I said I was. "Time for you to go and see the old Wiseguy," he said. It was my thought exactly. I had a lot to figure out, and without Theshei to talk to, it was hard. I needed some other outlook besides my own. Sometimes it isn't what other people tell *you* but what you tell *them* that gets it all straight in your head.

Orwoz nodded to Malmun and said, "He'll take you." At the doorway he said, "We'll test this Maljik tonight." He didn't say it with any relish, and the more I got to see Orwoz, the surer I was that he really believed he had no personal vendetta against Theshei. He really believed Theshei was an Intruder; he really believed the Sand-scripti were plotting against the Saltspeakers; he really believed what he was doing was right.

The problem was that Orwoz was as dedicated to the Saltspeakers as I was to the Salt, and he didn't under-stand that they weren't the same thing. He wasn't evil, only ruthless, which comes to the same thing especially if you're ruthless in the name of some higher cause. I don't think he wanted to destroy Maljik particularly; he just wanted to protect the Saltspeakers from Theshei, and he wasn't taking any chances. He was one of those people who gets an idea in his head and then can't get it out. The idea controlled him, and no matter what form it took, the idea was always the same: The Saltspeakers were in danger, and he was the only one who could save them. I suppose that was his Thunder.

He had this simple narrow view of the world, and he never let anything interfere with it. I almost envied him that. Much as I loved the Salt, I had no idea what I was supposed to do about it, and most of the time I wasn't even sure what it was about. I thought maybe the Old Wiseguy would help me find out.

I was surprised that I didn't get to talk to him after the night in the courtyard. I thought he'd be around to give me advice and tell me what I was supposed to do, but he wasn't. I rarely saw him in the crowd at the Great Hall; I never saw him at meals or walking around the com-pound. It was like he'd given me the Stick and vanished. Of course, I had Theshei to talk to then, and I didn't need any more help than that to figure things out.

At first I thought we were going to the Great Hall, but Malmun took me down the back way past the cafeteria and the infirmary and back toward the out buildings that Uncle WillBe said weren't worth the walk. Out beyond them, we went into the woods beyond. Theshei and I had gone the same way a couple times when we were checking out the perimeter, but Malmun turned off the main path after a little while and the trees got thicker. About ten minutes further on, we crossed a small stream and came to the edge of a little clearing with a huge pile of leaves and branches backed against two trees.

There was a little wisp of smoke curling out of the top of the pile, and I thought at first that it was smoldering and about to burst into flames. It seemed like we were in the middle of nowhere, but I knew from scouting the perimeter with Theshei that there were roads not too far away. I could hear a car horn and the sound of a truck laboring up a hill from beyond the rest of the trees and the sound of a jet going by overhead. Malmun said he would wait for me back over the stream and left. He looked like he was in awe of the place, but then the Rhinettes were in awe of just about everything.

Still, it did seem like a special place, and it got very quiet the second he was out of sight. I stood in the clearing for a while, looking around. I couldn't hear any of the traffic anymore. There was some bird noise and that hum of indistinguishable sounds that you always hear deep in the woods, but otherwise it was amazingly still. I might as well have been a hundred miles from civilization. There was a serenity to it that seemed unnatural considering where it was.

Eventually, a patch of leaves in the pile opened out to make a door, and the Old Wiseguy came out. He had a walking stick about as tall as he was, but it was light brown instead of black. He shaded his eyes against the sun like he wasn't used to the light, and it looked for a minute like he was going to go back inside and leave me there. But when he got to the door, he waved me in after him and I went.

The mound was dark except for a shaft of light that poured in through the hole where the smoke went out, and it reminded me of the Great Hall somehow. He had a small fire going made of twigs and a little charcoal. It was dry and cool but not really cool enough for a fire. He saw me looking at it and said, "I like the way the smoke looks in the light."

I could see why. The curls of smoke broke and twisted as they went up, and the light shone through them and seemed to be bent by them as well. "It never looks the same twice," he said. "A thing like that will tell you a lot."

"About what?" I said. I didn't doubt him, I just wanted to learn.

"Everything," he said. "Now and Then. Here and There. You'll see." He sat down on the dirt floor on one side of the fire and motioned me to do the same on the other.

"Why did they put you out here?" I said.

He laughed. "Put me?" he said. He laughed again. I don't know whether it amused him more to think he could be put somewhere or that the Saltspeakers could do it. "I always wanted to be out here right from the beginning," he said. "Or some place like this."

"Why?" I said. Compared to living out on the street, he had pretty good accommodations, but after a year in a cardboard box it wasn't something I would have picked.

"It's quiet," he said. "And I don't have to see any-body." He smiled. "Not that I mind seeing you. It's good to talk to somebody with some sense now and again. You learn things."

I didn't know why he thought I had any sense. "You'll learn more from the smoke than you will from me," I said.

He laughed again. I think it pleased him to laugh, and I had no doubt he laughed even when nobody was around. He seemed very happy, very contented. I suppose it was because he was in his place. It made me wonder if I would ever find mine. Your Thunder is supposed to lead you to your place eventually, but I felt like I was a long way from mine, so far from it that I was lost. He sensed that. "I'll learn a lot from you when you find your place," he said. "The whole world will." I started to tell him I was lost, but he anticipated me. "You *will* find your place," he said. "Even though it won't be in this world."

I didn't like the sound of that. "Where will it be?" I said.

He just smiled and turned his palms up. "Only you know that," he said. "And even you won't know until you get there."

"Will I get there soon?" I said.

He laughed again. "What do you think I am, a fortune-teller? How would I know?"

I felt foolish, but I said it anyway. "You're the Wiseguy."

He shook his head. "No," he said firmly, "you're the Wiseguy."

It wasn't much consolation. "But I don't know anything!" I told him.

"You don't *remember* anything," he said. "You *know* everything." He looked up at the smoke and smiled. "You're still a man trying to escape from a mirror."

If he'd told me that the first time he showed me my reflection, it would have puzzled me, but I understood it the minute he said it. I not only understood it, it was as if he'd just reminded me of something I always knew. "He isn't in the mirror," I said.

He smiled and nodded. "It's nice to talk to somebody with common sense," he said. Then he got up and went over by where he had a pile of quilts that must have been his bed and took something out of the shadows. When he came back, he held it out into the shaft of light that streamed down, swirling through the smoke. It was the Black Stick. Whole!

I was so excited I jumped up. I couldn't believe it. "It's whole!" I said. "How did you do it?"

The Old Wiseguy smiled, "White glue," he said. "Always did work best on wood."

"But it's the Black Stick!" I said.

He looked at me like I was one of the Rhinettes. "It's only a stick," he said.

"That's what Theshei always said," I said.

He nodded. "But it is a *black* stick," he said.

It made me laugh. It was what I always said back to Theshei. I wondered how he knew. I told him that. He said, "It's what anybody with any sense would say."

I knew what he meant. That even if it stood for the Salt and my connection with it, it was still only a stick. It was an ordinary stick and a Black Stick at the same time. It never stopped being ordinary; it never stopped being holy. Two worlds occur at the same time in the same place. You live in one or you live in the other. That was why his clearing was so quiet. It wasn't entirely in the world of ordinary things when people like Malmun weren't around. The traffic didn't go away; it just stopped having an effect.

"It's very quiet here," I said.

"And very noisy," he said. "Sometimes you can barely hear the smoke."

I didn't hear the smoke until he said that, but I could suddenly hear it, a sifting sound like falling snow, only lighter, softer. When I looked at it, I could hear it change as it curled and twisted. And then I couldn't hear it at all. I looked at the Old Wiseguy. He shrugged. "It's just smoke," he said.

I laughed. "Is is," I said, "and Is isn't." I wondered if there was anything worth knowing that wasn't already in the Salt.

"It's just the Salt," he said. "There's nothing in it you don't already know. You mustn't forget that."

I knew what he meant. If I started treating it like something *only* sacred, something outside myself, I'd end up like Orwoz, a prisoner of a deformed idea. It was truth, but it was also only words. "You have to live in both worlds?" I said.

He held up a cautionary finger. "Simultaneously," he said.

I could hear another truck grinding up the hill beyond the woods, and then in midnoise it was gone. He smiled again. "Not an easy thing," he said. "That's why it's so much easier here, so much nicer away from all of them." He shook his head sadly. "They're in so much pain," he said, "and they make most of it themselves. It gets hard to watch after a while."

"And harder to listen to," I said.

He nodded. "They wouldn't believe that stick is a curse," he said. "You have no idea how many of them envy you."

"Why don't I just give it to one of them?" I said. But I knew why as well as he did: for the same reason you don't give a gun to a child.

He sighed. "No," he said, "when you go, you'll have to give it back to me." He shook his head sadly. "And I'll have to take it." He looked at the light and the smoke, at the shadows and the little fire. "I hate to leave all this," he said.

I said, "When I go?" I'd forgotten they didn't get around to me when they were giving out Destinations. "Where am I going to go?"

"How should I know?" he said.

"Well, you know I'm going," I said.

"I know the smoke is going too," he said. "I don't know where."

I watched the smoke rise up through the light. I knew it wasn't coming back. I knew the same was true for me. But I wanted to hear him say it. "Do you know if I'm coming back?" I said. I couldn't keep the fear out of my voice.

He laughed as if he knew the punch line to some cosmic joke. "There'll be nothing to come back to," he said. "Everything we know now will be gone."

Those old turn-of-the-century fears about the end of

the world came flooding back to me. "The Saltspeakers are going to be destroyed?" I said. I couldn't imagine them all gone, and if they weren't gone, I couldn't imagine not coming back.

He winced like my pain was giving him pain. "Changed," he said. "Nothing gets destroyed."

"If this place is still here," I said, "I *will* be back."

He shook his head as if I had forgotten everything I'd remembered. "Here?" he said. "Here is disappearing as we speak." He waved an arm around the room. "The hut you entered has already vanished."

I felt like the world was dissolving around me. It made me dizzy and frightened. The Salt says, "There is only Change; nothing changes," but somehow it didn't comfort me.

"But you will come back," he said. "More or less." It seemed to amuse him that I didn't, couldn't, know what he meant. I don't believe *he* even knew, not in any concrete way. And how could he know? The Change was beyond our comprehension then. We couldn't even have imagined it. Now it becomes more impossible every day to imagine what life was like before the Change.

"You won't be here when I come back, will you?" I said.

He said, "As I am? No. But as I will be . . ." He shrugged. "Who knows?"

I wanted somebody to know. And I wanted them to tell me. It would have been better not to know at all than to know some terrible change was coming that would wipe out everything. "Why did you tell me that if I can't do anything about it?!" I wasn't really mad at him; I was just afraid, but I sounded mad. "What was the point in telling me about it if I can't stop it?"

I heard the blare of an air horn as if a huge truck was about to come crashing through the clearing, but it was gone in midnote.

"Stop it?" he said. "You *cause* it. You and Theshei."

It made me feel so weak I could hardly stand. I pressed the Black Stick into the ground so I could lean on it, but it didn't seem to be there. It was like the whole world was made out of smoky light and something was blowing it away. I said, "Theshei and I are going to cause the end of the world?" I didn't want it to be true.

"As we know it," he said.

"But how?" I shouted at him. "How?"

"How do I know?" he said. "I don't know everything." Then he paused like somebody trying to recall the details of a dream. "In a flash," he said, "a bright flash of light."

All I could think of was the world incinerating in one giant nuclear flash. Everything burned beyond recognition. "Why?" I cried. "Why?"

He shrugged. "You just do, that's all." He frowned as if more details were coming back to him from a dream he could hardly even remember having. "At least Theshei does."

For a moment, I could remember everything that would happen, but as soon as I remembered it, I forgot it again. I knew what I had to do, but I didn't want to do it. The Old Wiseguy looked like my pain was tormenting him. "Sit down," he said, "and watch the smoke for a while. It will soothe you."

But I didn't sit. I turned and stumbled out of the hut, knocking the door open and tripping over the Black Stick. I fell to the ground, and when I hit, my head felt like it was broken open. I lay there feeling the ground with my hands, thankful that it was still solid, waiting for it to be turned to radioactive ash at any moment. Somewhere Theshei was doing something that would bring about the end of the world; it could happen at any second.

I forced myself up and ran, my head throbbing. I stumbled and fell again, got up, and ran until I collapsed. I lay there gasping for breath. I tried to calm myself, tried to tell myself nobody had the power to annihilate the world in a single flash. And then I realized who did, and Theshei was with them.

The thought of it made me get up and run again, even though I didn't know where I was running. I ran in circles around the clearing until finally I came to the stream and splashed across it, but the terrible idea was still with me. Theshei and the end of the world. Theshei and the end of the world. Theshei and the end of the world.

CHAPTER
15

MALMUN looked like he was seeing a ghost when I came stumbling out of the stream. I was covered with mud and leaves, the branches and falls had torn my robe and scratched my face. I was wild-eyed and half crazy with fear. I kept trying to say something to him, but I couldn't catch my breath, and he just stood there looking like he wanted to run away but was afraid I'd drag him down from behind. When I finally got my breath, I said, "It's just me."

I don't know whether it was the way he looked, or the fact that it really *was* just me and not the savior of the world, but I started to laugh. That only scared Malmun more. And that just made me laugh harder. I understood how the Old Wiseguy felt. I knew something Malmun didn't know, but there were huge gaps in what I knew, so many that what I knew probably wasn't true at all, at least in the way I understood it. I could see why the Old Wiseguy laughed; it was the only thing anybody with any sense could do.

I knew the Old Wiseguy was right: I should have sat and looked at the smoke. I needed soothing. I knew where I needed to go. My heart was slowing down, and my breathing was getting back to normal. I was coming back into the ordinary world more with each breath. In a few minutes, I was almost ready to go. And then

Malmun said for probably the fiftieth time but the first I actually heard him, "What's wrong?"

That made me start to laugh again. What could I say to him? "Nothing much. My best friend is about to destroy the world, that's all. Other than that everything's fine." No wonder Goodguy laughs.

My laughing only made Malmun more frightened, and I felt sorry for him. There was no point in telling him anything. He couldn't do anything about it. I wasn't even sure I could. And in ten minutes, every other Saltspeaker in the compound would know the world was coming to an end. There'd be panic and a stampede. They'd probably all go running off in all directions just like I did, trying to run away from the truth. I could see why the Old Wiseguy hurt so bad. There was nothing either of us could do to help them much.

"I got lost," I said.

Malmun looked skeptical. The clearing wasn't more than fifty yards on the other side of the stream, and a blind man could have found the path. "Did you ever visit the Old Wiseguy?" I said.

He shook his head. "No," he said, "he won't let any of us even cross the stream. We have to leave his food over here."

"But you've been in the clearing," I said.

"Just this once," he said.

"Did that seem like an ordinary clearing to you?" I said. I knew it didn't, and that would be enough of an explanation for Malmun. Miracles occurred there. He'd been nearby when one occurred; he didn't have to know what it was. Two Wiseguys in the same place was too much for Malmun to think about anyway. Anything on the other side of the stream was already miracle country. I'd just confirmed it for him.

He didn't even ask me any more questions on the way back. He wanted to believe that whatever had driven me into such a state was safely on the other side of the stream, and he didn't want to hear anything to the contrary. Besides, whatever happened was Wiseguy business in any case and nothing he should concern himself about.

When we got to the Great Hall, I told him I had to go inside and meditate for a little while alone. He said he'd wait outside for me. There was no use telling him he didn't have to; Orwoz had made me his responsibility and he was already afraid he was in deep water because of whatever had happened to me.

The second I got inside the Great Hall I felt better. My head was starting to hurt in earnest, but I felt at home. It made me sad to think I'd never get to sit there in the middle of that tranquility again. In a few hours I'd be gone, and I'd never see it again. Unless I stopped Theshei from ending the world.

I wasn't certain that he *could* be stopped. I tried to put it into a series of scenarios. In the worst case, if it looked like Theshei was about to do whatever he would do to end the world, I would have to kill him. I could look at that thought coldly and objectively in the Great Hall. Out in the woods, it seemed the only option, and I couldn't accept that I would have to do it. Now it seemed like I had alternatives.

The only way he could destroy the world would be through the Sandscripti. If I could get him away from them in time, the end of the world wouldn't happen. I could take him away by force, or maybe I could convince him that he had to leave or everything would be destroyed. If he was doing it on purpose, maybe I could convince him not to.

I put how to deal with Theshei aside for a moment. I was going to have to leave right away, and I didn't even know where to go. I was going to have to get help from Orwoz for that, and I was going to have to convince him that he should let me go after Theshei. I was going to have to give the Old Wiseguy the Black Stick back. Every time I thought of something that had to be done, it made me calmer because I knew there was one more thing I could do.

I had no time for grief, but I savored my last moments in the Great Hall. I couldn't believe there was any place where I would feel that good again. I told myself that I was leaving the Saltspeakers, not the Salt. I told myself if I stopped Theshei, I'd be back; if I didn't, it wouldn't matter. I thought of the test I was supposed to perform there. It wasn't necessary now, but if I didn't do it, Maljik would never be able to clear himself. I could tell them he wasn't guilty, but unless he passed the test, nobody would fully accept it.

When I was completely calm, I sent Malmun to tell Orwoz I had to see him in my room. Then I went back to my room and cleaned up. I rolled up a couple robes and tied them together, but then I thought Theshei had gone with nothing and I ought to do the same. There wasn't anything else I needed. Orwoz arrived just as I finished unrolling them again. I told him I needed to talk to him alone, and he scowled Malmun out of the room.

I told him he was right, the Sandscripti were planning to destroy the Saltspeakers, but they were planning to destroy the world as well. I said Theshei was going to be their tool and he had to be stopped.

He was surprised to hear me say that, but he said Theshei would be stopped as soon as they found him.

I said, "No, *I* have to do it. I'm the only one who can."

Orwoz said, "We have people who handle things like that. You've risked yourself enough."

I said, "You don't understand. He's with the Sandscripti. I'm the only one who can get close to him."

I thought it would shock him, but it didn't, and the old suspicion was back in his voice. "How do you know he's with the Sandscripti?" he said.

"I saw one of them flash him a signal with her light wand," I said.

"With the Sandscripti where?" he said. At first I thought he just wasn't convinced I was the one to go after Theshei, but I could feel there was something more.

"You tell *me,*" I said. "The Sandscripti woman was on the road traveling north to south. Are there any Sandscripti sanctuaries on that road in either direction?"

He nodded that there were, but he didn't say where. He had a plan already for dealing with Theshei, and it was going to be next to impossible to swerve him from it no matter how stupid the plan. "We have people with the Ghosts," he said.

"You had people outside the Great Hall too," I said. There was no time to be subtle, and I was tired pretending I didn't know what was going on. "You had marksmen outside the perimeter. What good did they do you?"

Orwoz was ruffled. He didn't want to admit he had set Theshei up, but he knew I was right. He tried a lame excuse. "He took them by surprise," he said.

"And you think he's run out of surprises?" I said. He didn't answer.

"What's the matter?" I said. "You're afraid I won't come back? What secrets do I know that Theshei doesn't?"

"No," he said, "that's not it. I didn't trust you in the beginning, but I don't think you'd betray the Salt."

I said, "Well, what is it then? We don't have a lot of time. He could be triggering the end of the world at any minute."

He hesitated, struggling to tell me something without telling me too much. "We have a plan in place,' he said. "It'll look like an accident. There's no need for you to go."

All of a sudden it dawned on me. "You knew he's there!" I said. Orwoz looked sheepish and wouldn't meet my eyes. "You've known for days," I said. It explained why he'd been so patient about my recovering. "How long have you known?" I demanded.

Orwoz looked at me like I was still a rookie. "It's not yours to question," he said.

"No?" I said. "I'm going to lay this black knob against your forehead, and we'll see whether all this resistance is faith or stubbornness!"

I don't know how long it had been since somebody threatened him, probably so long he'd forgotten what it was like, but it made him turn pale. He got himself back under control with outrage. "You can't threaten me!" he said.

I said, "No, but I can test you, and I will."

We both knew he was opposing me out of sheer pigheadedness. All I had to do was put that stick against his head and ask him why he was letting the Saltspeakers be put in danger of annihilation, and he'd either have to tell the truth or die for it. It was just a black stick, but Orwoz believed its touch could kill him for lying, or for betraying the Saltspeakers, or for not having enough faith. For all his bluster, he had enough doubts about his own faith to worry him, and he looked at the Black Stick like it was a poisonous snake poised to strike.

"I'm not going to see the Saltspeakers destroyed because you're too stubborn to change your plan," I said. "You're going to have a hard time explaining why you won't let me kill somebody we've all sworn an oath to kill already." He knew it was true. There was no way he could win. I could see why he resisted giving in; he probably thought with Theshei gone he'd never lose another confrontation, and here he was faced with another one he couldn't win.

He didn't like being treated like he treated everybody else, but he respected it. If our places were reversed, he'd have said exactly the same thing. It was just a question of how long it was going to take him to swallow his pride and do the right thing. It took about another thirty seconds. When I saw him starting to crack, I asked him again, "How long have you known Theshei was there?"

He didn't want to answer, but he looked like he thought I might put the stick on his head right then and it was more than he wanted to risk. "Only a few days," he said. He waited to see if it was enough. "Four," he said. I moved the stick an inch. "All right, six. Four days since it was confirmed."

I didn't think Orwoz would wait six days even to make it look like an accident. "How?" I said.

He was still being evasive, even with the stick looming in front of him. "I told you, we have people with the Ghosts. We monitor them constantly."

"You have half a dorm full of monitoring equipment, and it took you a week to find out he was there?" I said.

He looked as if he thought the Ghost Dorm was an impenetrable secret. "How did you know about the equipment?" he said.

I ignored him. "Why did it take you a week?" I said. "You said you monitor them constantly."

"We do," he said. "There's a lot of interference around the Ghosts. Our people have to get far enough away from them to transmit. It's not easy. And even when they do, the light pens damage the equipment." I suspected that if Orwoz's spies were as inept as the Rhinettes, the Sandscripti probably burned out their equipment on purpose and steered them away from anything they didn't want them to know. Orwoz assumed anybody he trained would be undetectable, and he couldn't imagine the Sandscripti not eliminating a spy in their midst. But he should have known it's better to manipulate a spy you know than to kill him and have your enemies send another you might not detect. Whatever Orwoz's plan was, the Sandscripti were probably a dozen steps ahead of him.

"When did he get there?" I said.

"The night he left," Orwoz said. "He went straight there, the little pig-on traitor."

"So your people knew he was there for six days and

couldn't get you a message out?" There was no way they could have missed Theshei in his white robe, and they must have known he wasn't somebody Orwoz sent.

"There were technical problems," he said. I could see he was holding something back, and I tried to fire questions at him too quick for him to hedge.

"What technical problems?"

"I told you. Interference. Defective equipment. Security was too tight," he said.

"And all that cleared up after a week?" I said.

He looked embarrassed, as if for all his efforts his plan was being thwarted at every turn and he couldn't figure out why. "One of them finally had to come out," he said.

"And the Defenders were there waiting for him," I said. It wasn't as dumb as I made it sound. You could leave the Sandscripti sanctuary anytime you wanted; most people didn't because somebody was waiting for them. The Saltspeakers were as likely a group as any to pick up a dropout.

"We roughed him up," he said indignantly. "They never suspected. They—"

I cut him off. "Why didn't he come out right away?" I said.

"He couldn't," Orwoz said.

"Why not?"

"He just couldn't," he said. I could see there was a line I was going to have to force him across, and I closed the space between us. I could reach out and touch him with the Black Stick and he wouldn't even see it coming. Orwoz was starting to sweat. "You don't need to know," he said.

"I *do* need to know. I'm going in there, and I need to know what's going on," I said.

"You're not going in," he said. I didn't need to say I was, and he didn't need to hear it to back down. "And even if you did, the less you know, the less they can torture out of you."

It was a reasonable argument; there was nothing to do

but ignore it. "Why couldn't he leave?" I said.

He held it back as long as he could, and then he blurted it out. His voice was filled with rage and frustration. "Because we're too far from critical number as it is."

Critical number is what you need for a nuclear reaction, but I couldn't imagine even Orwoz smuggling nuclear material in there or the Sandscripti not noticing. "Critical number for what?"

"The accident," he said. He was still trying to tell me as little as he could, and I was starting to lose patience.

"Wait a minute," I said. "You had to be putting these people in there for months. How could you be arranging an accident for Theshei if you only knew he was there a week ago?"

"It's not for him," he said. "It's for all of them. Every one of those damn shiny Ghosts and all the scum that are in there with them."

It sent a chill up my back. An "accident" big enough to destroy a whole Sandscripti sanctuary would have to be enormous. And if it involved Theshei, it might be the trigger to the end of the world. It made it even more important that I get in there and stop Theshei.

"How?" I said. I had to lift the stick off the ground to get him to answer.

"A gigantic flare-out," he said. "Saltspeaker martyrs all pushing their light pens to the limit at the same time!" It was a lunatic idea. If you didn't work the light pen right, you vanished in a flash of light, but nobody had any idea what kind of force would be unleashed with dozens of light pens flaring out all at once. But there was no use telling Orwoz that, and it was Theshei who was the problem. The Old Wiseguy didn't tell me the Saltspeakers caused the end of the world; he said Theshei did. There was no time to wait. It was clear Orwoz had been going for his critical number for a long time and still hadn't gotten it.

"How many more do you need for critical number?" I said.

Orwoz said nothing. I looked at that Black Stick. "We don't know," he said.

"Why not?" I said.

He looked humiliated. "We don't know how many people we have left," he said finally.

"But you monitor them constantly," I said.

"We try. We try." It was clear the monitoring didn't really work. They probably only kept at it because they couldn't admit the failure to themselves. I almost felt sorry for him. "But there's always this interference," he said, "it's like looking for fish in murky water."

"You know how many you sent in, don't you?" I said.

He nodded. "But we keep losing them. The pens are hard to control. They keep flaring out one at a time." I didn't want to think how many deaths were on his hands. It wasn't hard to get people into the Sandscripti; they took anybody who expressed an interest. As long as you worked diligently with the light pen the Sandscripti didn't ask any questions about where you were from or why you were there, but it was hard to stay in. It was hard to stay alive.

"We don't have time for this fiasco." I said. "Theshei could end the world at any minute! How are you going to stop that while you wait for your grand scheme to get into place?"

"Our people will stop him," he said. He just couldn't give up the power.

"Look," I said. "You're only going to get one shot at him, because if you miss, and maybe even if you don't, the Sandscripti are going to retaliate, and there will never be a second chance, even if some of the Saltspeakers survive."

Nobody had any idea what Sandscripti retaliation would be like because nobody dared tempt it. Anybody who accepted sanctuary from the Sandscripti was left alone by everybody: organized crime, the government, even fanatic groups like us. The annihilation of the Saltspeakers was clearly within possibility.

"What'll make it any different if *you* do it?" he said.

"I'm his friend," I said. "If I do it, they'll think it was personal. If some stranger does it, they'll trace him to the Saltspeakers and that will be the end of all of us. If you don't believe me, just ask the Old Wiseguy."

I knew he wouldn't take me up on that. Even Orwoz was a little daunted by that clearing. He scowled.

"There's no time," I said. "I have to go in after him and I have to go now."

He knew I was right and he did what people who don't have an answer always do: He changed the subject. "What about his confederate?" he said.

I said, "Who? That poor Saltspeaker you've been torturing all week? He's not the confederate. Think about it! How did Theshei get across the road? How did he get behind Maljik to use your voice in the first place?" I knew he had no answers to those questions; it was why he clung to his confederate-in-the-ranks theory. "Who can influence your thinking? Who could distract him long enough for Theshei to cross unnoticed?"

He knew who I meant, but he didn't want to give up on his theory. He'd rather be wrong than rethink anything. But I wasn't going to let him get away with it. "Did you ever see one of the Sandscripti?" I said.

"I've seen Ghosts," he said.

"And you couldn't take your eyes off them, could you?" I said. I could see by the look on his face he couldn't. The first time anybody sees the Sandscripti, they can't take their eyes off them. He wouldn't meet my eyes. "Just think what that poor Saltspeaker sitting in the trees did when that Sandscripti glided by. Theshei could have stood in the middle of the road for ten minutes without being noticed."

I knew Theshei didn't need a Sandscripti for distraction, but Orwoz would never have believed that he could have slipped across otherwise, and I had to play on his paranoia about the Sandscripti if I was going to go after Theshei with his help. It was like getting an ocean liner to make a U-turn. He mulled over everything I said, and he could see I was right, but he just couldn't let go of his intentions. I could see even if he gave in, he'd only change his mind after I'd gone and that would be it for poor Maljik.

"All right," I said. "I'll test him. And then I'm leaving. All you have to do now is tell me where to go."

I didn't even have to tip the stick toward him. "North on the road for two miles then turn left and go down a mile," he said. "I'll have somebody take you."

"And do what?" I said. "Tell the Sandscripti it's OK to let me in because I'm not really a spy, I'm an assassin?" It was no wonder the Old Wiseguy couldn't stand dealing with the Saltspeakers. Most of them were block-heads. "I'll go myself. The same way Theshei went: across the road and straight cross-country. Let them think I've escaped too."

He liked that idea. He probably would've thought it was a great idea if I told him I wanted to go in disguise too. I had the feeling when I got inside the Sandscripti temple, I'd be able to tell the undercover Saltspeakers without even trying. "And tell your idiots inside the Sandscripti to stay away from me. This is too important for them to screw everything up playing spy." I could've been more tactful, but I knew if I didn't put Orwoz in his place right away, he'd do something stupid. I knew he'd probably have his men do something stupid anyway.

"They won't bother you," he said.

I said, "Good. Don't even tell them I'm there." Orwoz nodded reluctantly. "In fact, don't tell anybody I'm gone. Tell them I've gone to the Old Wiseguy's clearing to recuperate. Leave the food on this side of the stream. The Old Wiseguy will get rid of it."

He liked that idea too. I figured the more time he had to spend tricking the Rhinettes and the rest of the Saltspeakers, the less time he'd have to get in my way. I don't think Orwoz cared who he was conspiring against as long as he got to conspire. "You'll need safe conduct across the road," he said. "I'll arrange it."

I could probably have gotten across the same way as Theshei, but it would have taken too long. "Good," I said. "I'll leave while everybody is still in the Great Hall. Is everything ready?"

He said, "Everybody will be there in fifteen minutes."

I said, "Good. You go on ahead of me. I have some things to do." I didn't have anything else to do. I just wanted him to think there were things even he didn't know about.

At the door he turned back. He nodded toward the Black Stick. "You were the right choice," he said, "however it turns out."

I figured that was the least he could say to somebody who was going to kill his best friend and probably get killed in the process, but I answered him with the Salt. "All choices are the right choice."

CHAPTER 16

WHEN he was gone, I went out into the field and sat down. It amazed me how much I'd gotten attached to the place in such a short time. I would've lived there the rest of my life, Orwoz and all, if I had a choice. But I was just the intersection of opposing forces. A shadow of brighter light created by the overlap of Badguy and Goodguy. As soon as I accepted that, everything got easier. I knew what I had to do, and I knew I could do it. The air was moving in huge curtains across the lawn. When it was time, I got up and walked back to the Great Hall.

The rest of the Saltspeakers were already there. There weren't as many as there were before the rookies dispersed, and they didn't fill the Hall out to the walls, but there were enough. Orwoz and a few others were up on the platform with Maljik next to him. He was younger than I expected, or maybe being frightened just made him look helpless and looking helpless made him look younger. His eyes were very wide, and he kept running his tongue over his lip and looking around like I was going to pop up out of nowhere and press his death against his forehead. When he saw me, he started to sweat.

I walked through the crowd, and it opened in front of me like fog melting away as you walk through it. It made me wonder if any of it was real. Even the faces I knew looked at me differently than before, like I wasn't me at all but the Wiseguy. I went up the steps and stood in front of Maljik.

Orwoz said, "Saltspeaker Maljik, you are accused of betraying your oath and the Saltspeakers. The Wiseguy will test you."

I took Maljik by the sleeve and led him to the corner of the platform as far away from Orwoz as I could. He looked like he was going to cry, and his knees almost buckled under him twice before we got there. I leaned close to him and said, "Do you know what this is?"

And he said, "It's the Black Stick."

I said, "No. It's *a* black stick."

He gave me a bewildered look, and then he looked around the Hall like somebody in the audience could give him a hint about what was going on. But nobody did. "I didn't do it," he said.

I said, "I know that. I know who did." He looked like he thought I *should* know who did, but he wasn't sure it would save his life. "The trouble is," I told him, "none of these other people know that. So I'm going to have to touch you with this stick to show them you're innocent." He looked at the Stick like it was a gun I proposed putting to his head and pulling the trigger. "It's just a stick," I said. "It won't hurt you."

He looked bewildered again. I could see what it was: He just couldn't imagine that it was only a stick. He could only see the symbolic side of it. I realized I could never make him see it was also ordinary. I was just making it more likely that he'd die when I touched him by confusing him. I took the only course open to me. "You know it won't hurt you if you're innocent," I said. He nodded, but he didn't take his eyes off the Stick. "You didn't help Theshei escape, did you?" I said. He shook his head. "Then you'll be all right. Just remember that."

I walked him back to the center of the platform. He knelt down, and I laid the knob of the stick against his forehead. The sweat was running down out of his hairline and out of the pores in his forehead. Little beads of water just seemed to materialize on the skin. I was fascinated by it. I watched them pop out, hang where they were for a moment, and then elongate and slide down his forehead. It seemed miraculous to me that they could appear like that, wave after wave of them. I had a hand on his shoulder and the side of the knob pressed against his forehead. "Did you let Theshei escape?" I said.

He shut his eyes tight. "No," he said. He squeezed his closed eyes together like he expected to be struck dead immediately.

"Did you hear what you thought was the voice of Orwoz telling you not to shoot whoever crossed the road?" I said.

He took a deep breath; it shuddered when he released it. "Yes," he said.

His hands were shaking. "Did you ever betray the Saltspeakers?" I said.

He shook his head. "Never," he said. He tensed up as if he expected to be incinerated on the spot. When nothing happened, he opened one eye and then the other. He seemed amazed that he was still alive.

I looked at Orwoz to see if he was satisfied. He nodded. I said to the rest of the Saltspeakers, "Saltspeaker Maljik is without blame and true to the Saltspeakers. Let whoever says otherwise come up here and take his place." I waited for somebody to raise an objection, but it was all formality. Nobody was getting any closer to the Black Stick than they had to.

When nobody objected, I left the platform and went out through the crowd. The Old Wiseguy was waiting for me outside the door. He looked older than he did in the clearing and tired. I said, "Orwoz will tell them I'm gone to recuperate in your clearing." He nodded as if he knew.

I handed him the Black Stick. "This is yours again," I said.

He took it and handed me his stick. The light brown wood seemed gray white with age. It was a beautiful staff, and I was grateful. "It's just a stick," he said.

"Is there anything else I should know?" I said.

He laughed. "A lot," he said, "but I don't know it."

"No advice?" I said. I knew as well as he did that I'd have to find everything out for myself by living it. Everybody does. But I was still looking for shortcuts. I was surprised that he had an answer.

"Yes," he said, "don't take the Salt too seriously."

It made me smile in spite of the sadness I felt to be leaving him there without much hope of coming back. "Which part," I said.

He smiled too and put a hand on my shoulder. "You'll know when you come to it," he said.

And I did. But by then it was too late.

CHAPTER
17

I ran across the lawn toward the trees. They seemed very far away, and I had that sense of urgency again. There were stars out—not the full Milky Way, just early stars—but they were enough. I wondered which of them the Sandscripti came from. Nobody ever said for sure where the Sandscripti called home. It didn't seem to translate, except as "the other side of the universe." There was a lot about the Sandscripti that didn't translate. I wondered how I was going to make them understand I wanted to join. I wondered how I was going to make them understand I wanted to see Theshei. I wondered what I was going to do when I saw him again. I wondered why he tried to kill me. I wondered if he'd try it again.

Anybody going off to save the world ought to have a lot more than unanswered questions. But the only way to get any of them answered was to find Theshei. I crossed the road half expecting to get shot because even if Orwoz told them to hold their fire, fire was what the Defenders were trained to do, and it's real hard to get people not to do what they're trained for.

I wasn't entirely sure Orwoz wouldn't have me shot on purpose. I knew he was capable of it, but I didn't think he saw me as a threat to the Saltspeakers the way he saw Theshei. He might have been pretending he thought we were on the same side, but I doubted it. But then I realized that even if he did think I was Theshei's accomplice, he didn't have to have me killed. I was out of his way; I didn't have the Black Stick any more, and the Sandscripti would probably save him the trouble. If Theshei didn't.

I didn't think about it very long. There was nothing I could do anyway but trust and cross, and I did. Nothing happened. I didn't even see the Defender that should have been there, and I thought maybe Orwoz had the good sense to remove him entirely instead of trusting him to follow orders.

Still, I moved as quietly as I could through the trees on the far side of the road. It wasn't easy. The moon wasn't up, and there was a lot of underbrush that I couldn't tell from shadows until I was in it. I kept getting tangled up and thrashing around, and if anybody wanted to find me, it wouldn't have been very hard. I kept having to go around things, and the ground was uneven, and I fell down into gullies and got tangled up in the bushes a couple times before I finally started putting the Old Wiseguy's stick out in front of me when I wasn't sure what the footing was.

I fell less, but before long, I wasn't even sure I was heading in the right direction. I was scratched and bruised, and I began to think maybe it would've been better to go along the road. Every time I tripped or a branch slashed me across the cheek, I asked myself what I thought I was doing there. I didn't have Theshei's gift for quiet movement; I didn't have his sense of direction; I didn't have his infallible feeling of being on the right road to wherever he was ultimately going. It seemed like I thrashed around out there all night before I finally broke into the clear.

When I did, I couldn't see all that far, but I could tell I was in a field and it was easier going. The ground was level, and I could see the stars again. The grass came up to my waist, and I waded through it like water, holding my elbows out above the tops of it and the staff in front of me like a tightrope walker's balance pole. I could feel where the air went through the field by the way the grass bunched and fell away like waves and the troughs in between them.

It made me think how many invisible things made tracks in the world. And when I looked up at the stars, I saw the same pattern, the clumps and voids that seemed like the marks of Goodguy's passage. It seemed to me that all of life was like that, strands of one kind of event or another, woods and fields, stars and spaces, good things and bad. Without in the least diminishing the fear that the end of everything was coming fast, I felt like everything was exactly as it should be and I was exactly where I should be in it.

So when I saw the treeline coming up again, I didn't feel depressed or annoyed that I was going to have to start fighting my way through again, I felt like that was the rhythm of things, and the trick was all in knowing when to swim and when to float and not feeling bad it wasn't all one or the other.

I was still in the open when the woods started to shine, and I thought at first it was the lights of some kind of patrol. It struck me that maybe I had gotten turned around and I was just coming right back to the compound and into a squad of Defenders looking for what had been causing all the racket earlier.

I thought of laying down in the grass, but the lights suddenly rushed forward at me, and I started to duck before I realized they were the Sandscripti.

In broad daylight, the glow of the Sandscripti was beautiful, but in the dark, it was nothing less than glorious. To see one of them was the sight of a lifetime; to see so many flooding out and surrounding me was a sight worth dying for. If they had been there to tear me to pieces, I would still have stood there admiring them. I could see why they were Theshei's Thunder.

They surrounded me and hovered there, lighting the whole field up with a golden glow. They seemed to float nearer and farther away like the breeze was moving them whenever they didn't concentrate on staying where they were. Then one of them raised his light wand and began tracing a filigree of fiery lines in the air until there was this big incandescent design floating between me and him. It was so amazing I just stood there openmouthed, staring at it.

I could feel he was trying to communicate with me, trying to tell me something he'd been trying to tell human beings ever since the Sandscripti came down, but I couldn't begin to comprehend what it was. All I could tell was that it was probably too good for human beings to know to begin with, and we wouldn't become spiritual enough to understand it for another thousand generations. It made me really sad to think of all that lost time.

But it was impossible to stay gloomy in the presence of that glow. It might be a dozen centuries before humans understood those swirls of burning light, but that wouldn't stop it from being beautiful to them until they did. I was glad that even our ignorance wouldn't keep that from us.

Even before he finished, the others started filling the air with blazing patterns of their own. Their light wands sparkled and swerved, and sparkled again, and the tracings seemed to burn permanent holes in the darkness until I was surrounded with a glowing curtain of lacy light backed by the golden glow of the Sandscripti themselves. It seemed to me that if I was a follower of one of the Traditional Theological Alternatives, I would have been certain I was in the presence of angels. But I wasn't, so it just seemed to me that they were physical proof of the persistence of Goodguy in the rough ugliness of Badguy's stuff.

I couldn't have made as much as an outline of even one of their drawings, but I could tell they were all different, even if were saying the same thing. It made me feel very empty inside that I couldn't even begin to understand what they were so anxious to tell me. I ached to know what anything that beautiful could mean, and when I thought of how ugly and deformed what I wanted to tell them was, it made me ashamed to be human.

And the moment I felt that, I knew exactly why Orwoz hated and feared them so much. It struck me that he said, "I've seen Ghosts," not "I've seen a Ghost." And I knew he must've seen a whole host of them just like I was seeing and he must've felt the same thing I felt when he saw them, that they were better than we were going to be for a long, long time.

He hated them for making him feel so insignificant, and he feared them because he could see that if human beings started seeing them the way he saw them, we'd all just give up and die of shame. I believed that he wanted to be one of them, and since he couldn't, he wanted them destroyed.

But I didn't think that was what was going to happen. I thought seeing them like that was going to make us want to be like them so much we'd do anything to pull ourselves up to their level. I thought, a lot quicker than we would get there otherwise, we were going to become just like them because what they were was already inside us. We were like loathsome caterpillars looking at the butterflies we were going to become. It didn't occur to me then that that would mean the end of being what we were.

And if it had occurred to me, I don't think it would have mattered very much. Standing in the middle of that amazing glow, I thought nothing I would ever see again would equal it. But I was as wrong, as painfully wrong as I could be. And I found out how wrong almost immediately.

CHAPTER 18

THE Sandscripti bobbed and floated behind the incandescent lines of their messages, and I stared at them in awe, like an illiterate savage looking at his name written in neon. I didn't even remember why I was there. And when I did, it didn't seem possible to me that they could be responsible for ending the world. If they were going to destroy us, I was sure, it was going to be by accident. But that didn't make me feel any better because I couldn't warn them about it, and I could see how hard it was going to be to make Theshei leave.

The messages began to fade gradually out of the air, and when they were all gone, the Sandscripti began again. I could see from the beginning that the patterns were different, even though I couldn't remember the old ones. And yet they felt the same. I wondered how many thousand ways they had tried to tell us whatever it was they wanted so desperately to tell us. I wondered if they were trying to warn us about the same impending doom the Old Wiseguy foresaw and what they wanted us to do to prevent it.

But the messages seemed too beautiful for warnings. They didn't make me at all afraid. They didn't make me want to do something immediately, before it was too late. They just made me want to stand there and look at them. I wondered for a minute if I wasn't like some

halfwit standing in the middle of the railroad tracks
fascinated with the blinking warning lights and if I
wouldn't turn into the face of the oncoming train with
absolute delight at the brightness of its light.

It reminded me I had work to do. I had to get to
Theshei. I had to stop whatever disaster was coming,
however inadvertently, from the Sandscripti. I could see
that I had an added difficulty now. Whatever I did, I had
to preserve the Sandscripti as well. Their loss, even to
save us, would have been too great a price. But I didn't
have a clue as to how to go about it. I didn't even know
how to say hello.

I probably would have stayed there staring at them for
the rest of the night if the most beautiful woman I ever
saw didn't step out of the woods, waving a light wand
and shouting at them as she did. What she was shouting
wasn't very flattering. "Stop!" she said. "Don't waste
your time. He's as deaf, dumb, and blind as the rest of
them!"

I assumed she was saying the same thing with her light
wand, like a child reading out loud as it labored over its
first letters. Her wand moved so slowly compared to
theirs that the beginning of her pattern was fading before
she got to the end. Her drawing was a stick figure
compared to a mural, and she labored at it while they
flew through theirs with so much grace and ease it took
your breath away.

But it didn't matter. For a thing of flesh and blood, she
was as magnificent as any Sandscripti, and the instant I
saw her, it was like all those luminous ghosts disappeared. I had seen gorgeous women before, at least at a
distance, and I had seen some of my own class and kind
that stirred desires that left me helpless and aching. But I
never felt anything remotely like what I felt when I saw
that woman. It was like seeing the Sandscripti for the
first time. All I could do was stare at her.

But the moment I saw her two things were unmistakably clear to me: I wanted her more than anything in the world—more than I wanted to find Theshei, more than I wanted to know the Sandscripti, more than I wanted to stop the end of the world—and I would never have her.

Nothing before or since made me feel that good and that bad at the same time. She made me ache with something I never felt before. It was too complex for mere lust. I'd been through that kind of yearning before, and I knew the ache of leaving those cravings unfulfilled through no intention of my own. It was no simple physical ache like that. It was like what I felt for the Salt except that there was a dimension to it that the Salt never stirred.

I believe if Badguy had appeared and told me I could have her totally and completely for one hour and the world would be ashes when we were finished, I would have said, "Done" without a second thought. I understood the beginning of the Salt in a way Orwoz would never understand it. I knew exactly what Whatzername felt when she looked at Whatzisname and realized, thanks to Badguy, what she'd been feeling, guilt-free, all along, "I need this person more than I need Goodguy." I knew exactly how she caught her case of Death: when she looked at Whatzisname and Badguy said in her ear, "This can't last."

When I looked at her, I knew someday I was going to die, and when I did, without her, Goodguy wouldn't be enough and annihilation wouldn't mean a thing.

She was wearing one of those wraparound things made of that new clingy synthetic that got popular a little while before the Sandscripti came down, and the light made it look like golden skin. The glow of the Sandscripti made the green of her eyes seem shot through with scattered gold. The light was behind her hair, and it was flowing out from her head like the wind was blowing it back because she was striding ahead and it looked like golden flames.

I thought, "This is what I've been waiting for all my life." And Badguy whispered in my ear, "And you'll die waiting."

She walked right through one of the Sandscripti to get to me, and it looked dull compared to her. She pointed her light wand at me and said, "Another idiot! What are you doing here?"

CHAPTER
19

I was tempted to tell her I was there to save the world, but I didn't think she'd believe it. I didn't think it would impress her much if she did believe it. She didn't even look at the Sandscripti the way I looked at her, and I knew she was never going to look at me that way. I felt lucky she looked at me at all, even if she looked like I was a personal insult. So I just stood there staring at her like she was one of the Sandscripti, forever beyond my reach or understanding.

I thought, "Theshei has a better chance with his Sandscripti than I have with her."

She looked at me like she could read my mind, and there was nothing in it that didn't disgust her at best. "Well!" she said. "What are you doing here?" But she didn't give me a chance to answer. "Don't you know who these creatures are? This is their land. You're trespassing." She looked at me like she thought I'd be trespassing anywhere on the planet. It gave me a hollow feeling.

I said, "I want . . . uh . . . I want . . ."

She said, "I know you want." She shook her head in utter contempt. "That's all human beings do is want."

I said, "Aren't you a human being?" It was stupid, but she confused me. Maybe she wasn't a Sandscripti, but I never met a human being like her. It seemed perfectly

145

plausible that she was something between the two. For all I knew, being around the Sandscripti turned you into something better.

She looked like I'd slapped her. I guess it wasn't something she thought about very often or wanted to. I could see one of those moments of doubt and self-loathing go across her face, and I began to wonder if Orwoz wasn't right. If being around the Sandscripti made somebody like her feel bad about herself, what would it do to the rest of us.

But it didn't set her back for long. "Is that what you came here for," she said, "to ask me that?" She didn't let me answer. "Why didn't you just hit me with your stick?" She didn't let me answer that either. "What is it you want, want, want?"

I couldn't even formulate what I really wanted from her, and it wouldn't have done any good even if I could, so I told her what the Saltspeaker part of me wanted. "I want to join the Sandscripti," I said.

She looked at me like I was a child. "You don't have any idea what that means!" she said.

Unrequited lust used to make me mean; it used to fill me up with this rage I didn't even know I had. This was worse. I had nothing to lose, so I went on the offensive. "All right, Queen of the Ghosts, you tell me what it means."

It took her back for a second. I suppose she was so used to bowling people over, she wasn't used to any kind of resistance. I could see why; standing in the middle of a circle of Sandscripti, even Theshei would have been easy to intimidate. "It means you have to learn how to use the light wand," she said. She raised her own and slowly scrawled a simple figure in the air between us. Her hand shook, and the muscles of her arm stood out like she was lifting herself off the ground with one hand. The lines were scraggly and uneven, they had none of the flair the Sandscripti patterns had, and they weren't a millionth as complex.

When she finished, she said, "It's taken me every waking minute for a year to learn how to do that." She wasn't bragging; there was a despair in her voice at how little she'd accomplished.

I would've pitied her, but I knew she'd hate me for it, and maybe it was just that there was so much rejection in her voice that it brought back parts of me I thought I'd left behind when I found the Salt, hurts I hadn't thought about since Theshei and I were in school together. I regretted it as soon as I said it, but I said it just the same. "Maybe you're a slow learner."

"Slow learner? Slow learner?" I thought she was going to punch me. "I'm the best they've ever seen!" she said. "And *that's* all I can do!" She shook her finger in my face. "You know what happens to slow learners?" I knew she was going to tell me. *"Poof!"* she said. "One big flash and there's nothing left of them! Nothing! Not even ash."

I'd heard that. It was what everybody was afraid of. Whatever energy ran the light wand was unstable, and if you couldn't control it, you got vaporized. "I know what a flare-out is," I said. I knew theoretically; she'd actually seen it. It made all the difference, and I knew it.

"You don't know anything!" she said. "It crackles," she said, "right before it happens." She looked like somebody from the bomb disposal unit who's heard the ticking stop once too often. "But it crackles every time you use it, so you never know when you've gone too far." She sounded like she'd been on the edge so long she wanted to flare out just to get it over with. "You know what it's like to be standing next to somebody you know and there's this *pop!* and the smell of mountain air and singed hair, and the light wand just drops to the ground and clatters there, and they're *gone?* Just like that?"

It wasn't really a question, and there wasn't anything I could say to it even if it was. She looked frantic for a moment, and then that tough fiery front came back up. "If that's what you want," she said, "why don't you just turn around and go blow your brains out somewhere?"

I felt her pain the way the Old Wiseguy felt the pain of all the Saltspeakers. I don't whether I felt sorrier for him, her, or me. But I didn't let it stop me. "I'm looking for a friend of mine," I said. "His name's Theshei." For a minute I was afraid it was him she was talking about.

The Sandscripti started filling the air with fiery figures, and they glided around like a stiff wind had suddenly come up and started blowing them into and through one another. They mixed with the sizzling lines of their drawings, and the designs stood out within them as they passed through. They overlapped one another and glided through one another until it was hard to tell where they began and ended. Their light wands flew so fast they were a blur, trailing flaming, intricate designs.

She threw her hands up in the air and shouted, "Not so fast! Not so fast!" but the Sandscripti kept tracing their icons in the air until they were almost a wall of slowly fading patterns. It was like we were in the middle of a maze made up of light. She looked at me like I was responsible for it. "You think you can keep up with that?" she said.

I shrugged. "If I can't," I said, "*poof!* You won't be bothered by me anymore."

It didn't make her laugh; it just made her madder. "It's not funny," she said. "You wait till you lose somebody like that, and then you laugh!" Her voice cracked, and I knew it was either somebody very close or somebody very recent.

"I'm sorry," I said. "I just want to see my friend."

"They don't take visitors," she said.

"Then I'll join," I said.

She looked at my robe. "Like you joined the Salt-speakers?"

I let it pass. "I'm asking for sanctuary," I said.

"So did your friend," she said. "You might as well take

sanctuary in a bomb plant." She held up her light wand. "This is a lot more likely to kill you than your friends the Saltspeakers," she said. "Go back. We're filled up."

I knew she was lying. I just didn't know why. I said, "Yeah, well, if it's as dangerous as you say, you won't be full for long. I'll wait."

The Sandscripti were shifting like sheets of light. Their new patterns were showing through the fading old patterns. Then they all made the same simple design at the same time. It was much brighter than the others and burned through everything they'd drawn before.

"All right," she said. "They'll give you sanctuary. But don't say I didn't warn you."

"I won't," I said. "And don't worry, I'm not going to flare out."

"Don't worry?" she said. "If I worried, I wouldn't be here."

"Can I see Theshei now?" I said.

She gave an exasperated sigh. "Follow me," she said, and I did. The Sandscripti hovered around us all the way through the woods, passing through trees and tangles of undergrowth like they weren't there. The walk seemed to mellow her a little. She said her name was Sandi. I had the feeling it wasn't her original name, but it *was* her real one.

CHAPTER 20

I followed her through the woods and out onto the Sandscripti grounds. Their Great Hall looked a lot bigger than the Saltspeakers', but otherwise it looked the same. It was like somebody developed a modular line of theological architecture, and all they did was change the symbols from one building to another. About the only difference besides the enormous size was that the dome roof was translucent and the shifting glow of Sandscripti moving around inside made it seem to flare and glow. I'd run out of things to say to her, so I said the obvious, "Big dome."

"You need a lot of space to practice with the light wand," she said. "Somebody too close to you flares out, you can go too. It's like a chain reaction."

She made it sound like it happened every day. When we went inside, it was all flat stone floor with no furnishing. It was maybe midnight, but it was still filled with people trying to force a line or two out of the light wand. A few got a flash or a few short bright dashes, but most weren't getting anything out of it at all. Sandscripti floated among them setting an example nobody could begin to follow.

She pointed to piles of what looked like mats stacked around the outside. "Just grab one of those and sleep where you can," she said. "The Sandscripti aren't much for accommodations. Everybody's here for one thing: to learn the light wand. Nothing else matters." She gave me that suspicious look again. "If you're not here for that, you won't last long. Either you'll flare out or the Sand-scripti will throw you out."

I said, "I thought they gave me sanctuary."

She said, "They don't have to give you anything. You learn the light wand; they'll put you up for as long as it takes. You don't learn, you're gone. One way or another."

I looked around at all the would-be Sandscripti; some of them looked like they'd been at it for hours. People at the far end of the dome looked so small all you could see of them was motion and the occasional flash. "That's all you do," I said, "practice with the light wand?"

She looked at me like I was an idiot. "There's nothing worth saying that can be said without the light wand," she said. "You have to learn the wand before you can even begin to learn anything else." Everything I said seemed to annoy her. She looked at me like she hated me.

"You'll like me better once you get to know me," I said.

"I don't want to get to know you. You're going to die here," she said. "You pretenders come in here, running away from something, and all you do is get yourself killed."

"Theshei apparently didn't," I said.

She looked like I'd touched a sore spot. "He's been lucky," she said. "And besides, he's serious. You're just a flare-out waiting to happen."

I took a wild guess. "He's better at it than you are," I said.

She flushed. There was bitter disappointment in her voice but grudging admiration. "It took me nine months to learn what he's learned in two weeks."

I said, "Yeah, I could never beat him at anything either." It was like I had a gift for saying whatever would annoy her most.

"It's not about beating anybody!" she said. "This is not a game!" She strode away across the floor, and I had to run to catch up with her. Just when I did, she turned on me and said, "And stop looking at me like that! I thought you Saltspeakers were supposed to be celibate."

I knew I was looking at her, but I had no control over how I was looking. I wasn't even aware of it. I didn't know what to say, so I denied it. "You've been working your light wand too much," I said. "You don't even interest me."

"Well, you certainly don't interest me," she said. "So you can stop making an idiot of yourself."

"What?" I said. "What am I doing?"

"You're leering," she said. "You've been leering ever since we met, and you're still doing it."

I denied it categorically. I swore it was my normal look. I swore I had no interest in her except to get to Theshei. "I'm sworn to celibacy," I said. "Saltspeakers have no interest in anything but the Salt." I didn't even sound convincing to myself. Up until I saw her, it had been the absolute truth. Now I couldn't look at her without aching for her and aching more because I knew it was absolutely impossible.

She didn't look like she believed me. "I have no interest except learning the light wand!" she said. "I have no time for anything else! I have no desire for anything else! I have no interest in anything else!"

We were like bickering children. I said, "Then what were you doing in the woods?"

She came right back at me. "Translating for idiots like you. That's what I do for the Sandscripti."

I said, "Fine! Just show me where my friend is, and you can get back to practicing your scribbling."

She pointed to a kind of arc welder's flash at the far end of the dome. "Over there," she said. Then she turned her back and began working her light wand, but nothing was coming out.

I made my way through the crowd. There was plenty

of space between them, but I still startled whenever one of their wands flashed to light near me. I expected one or another of them to flare out at any second and take me with them. I didn't even look back toward Sandi. I didn't want to give her the satisfaction. But it wasn't easy.

Occasionally, I'd have to step over a body curled up on the floor with its light wand beside it. At first I thought they were dead, but they were only dead asleep. When they couldn't do it anymore, they just lay down where they were and fell asleep, and as soon as their eyes opened, they were at it again. Probably for a lot of them, staying under the protection of the Sandscripti was a matter of life and death, but I think for most of them, it was the same as it was for Sandi: They just wanted desperately to know what the Sandscripti wanted to tell them.

Theshei was facing me, but he didn't see me. He didn't see anything but the tortured arcs he was making at the end of his light wand. They weren't much better than Sandi's, and I knew they were the best he could do. Concentration seemed to draw his face to a point. There were beads of sweat on his forehead, and he wrestled with the light wand like it weighed fifty pounds.

I waited five minutes for him to be finished, but I could see he was like everybody else: He'd be finished when he couldn't stand up anymore. So I moved a couple steps closer until I was standing just beyond the dying lines of light he was cutting in the air. He still didn't see me, and I didn't know how dangerous it was to interrupt him.

But then it occurred to me that maybe Theshei's flare-out started some kind of chain reaction that destroyed the planet and I had better stop him before he did it. But just as I went to wave a hand in front of his face, I thought maybe I was the one who triggered the final flare-out by distracting him. There was no way to know which was the right thing to do.

So I took a step back and put the tip of the my staff

just beyond his lines and followed the tip of his light wand wherever it went. I don't think he even saw that for a while, and when he did, he didn't look beyond the point of my stick. He just seemed amused by the way it followed the tip of his wand like a solid shadow. Maybe he thought it was some sort of natural effect. It wasn't until the first half of what he was drawing faded before he could finish the second half that he shut down his wand and looked up.

He didn't look happy to see me, but he didn't try to kill me either. "What are you doing here?" he said.

I was never very good at lying to him, so I told him the truth. "I came to kill you."

Theshei laughed and held up his light wand. "Wait a bit," he said. "I might save you the trouble."

"I'm in no hurry," I said.

"Orwoz send you?" he said. I think he really believed I was there to kill him, but it didn't bother him. I didn't know why.

"No," I said, "it was my idea."

"How come?" he said.

"How come you tried to kill me?" I said. It was something I really wanted to know. If I had to kill him, I hoped it wouldn't be before we got that straight.

He looked like I'd lost touch with reality. "What are you talking about?" he said.

I pointed to my head. "You tried to kill me!" There was a lot more anger in my voice than I expected. I didn't even know I was mad about it. I thought I was puzzled, hurt, surprised, betrayed, anything but enraged.

Theshei just shook his head. "I didn't try to kill you, you idiot," he said.

"Yes, you did," I said. "You tried to kill me because I was trying to protect Orwoz."

That made him laugh. "Listen to yourself," he said. "You tried to protect Orwoz. Does that sound likely to you?"

"Maybe I thought I was protecting the Salt?" I said.

That made him laugh even more. "I can't believe you've become that stupid in two weeks," he said. "At this rate, you'll be brain dead in another month." He turned the light wand on again like he didn't have any more time for foolishness. Then he turned it off again. "I danced you around between me and Orwoz and made it look like you tried to save him so you could stay there with your precious Salt when I left." He shook his head. "How dumb can you be that I have to explain that to you?"

I pointed to my head again. "I almost died from this!" It was the only evidence I had.

Theshei sighed like he was the Old Wiseguy trying to deal with the Rhinettes. "Almost!" he said. "Almost. You think Orwoz would have believed anything less? You think you could've stayed there any other way?"

I knew he was right, but I just didn't want to believe him because I was afraid I was going to have to kill him.

"How could you think I'd really try to kill you?" he said.

I could think it because I was really going to try to kill him, but I couldn't bring myself to tell him that. So I said nothing.

"All right," he said. "You still believe I tried to kill you?" He waited for an answer I couldn't give him. "OK," he said. "I didn't hurt you. You didn't hurt me. Badguy did it."

I knew he didn't believe the Salt, but he was right just the same. If I was true to what I believed, I couldn't hold it against him. "Do what you have to do," he said and turned the light wand on again. This time he started making his figures in the air. He labored over them like he was cutting them into stone, and in no time, he'd forgotten I was there.

If I wanted to kill him, it was the perfect opportunity. He was completely defenseless. But I didn't. I knew he didn't try to kill me. I wasn't sure I could kill him even to stop the end of everything. I certainly wasn't going to do it without trying some other way first, however unlikely. I said, "You have to put that light wand down and come away with me."

He didn't even hear me. I could see from the thin lines he was making that it was going to be a long intricate drawing, and I knew there was nothing I could do but wait. There was nothing, as far as he was concerned, but him and those lines in the entire room. I didn't exist. The other light-writers didn't exist. The Saltspeakers didn't exist. He was carving a doorway into the world of the Sandscripti, and that was all that mattered to him.

I didn't know what to do. Every sweep he made with that light wand might be the one that sent him flaring into eternity and the rest of the world with him. Without Theshei, that wouldn't happen. But I couldn't kill him. I wasn't sure I ever would be able to.

I leaned on my staff and waited for him to finish. It was an hour before the last thin line hung glowing between us, and most of the rest of it was already gone by then. He watched the last lines fade with a frown. Even I could tell it was too slow, and he was afraid he'd never get good enough at it to make any sense of the Sandscripti. I thought maybe it was an opening.

"You have to give this up and come with me," I said.

He looked up at me first like he was surprised that I was there and then that I was *still* there. "I don't have time for this," he said. He lifted the light wand to begin again. "You want revenge, take it. If not, stop distracting me."

"Look," I said. "Don't you ever take a break?"

He gave a sigh of exasperation. "Yeah," he said. "When it's not going good, sometimes I put down my wand and take a walk."

"Is it going good now?" I said.

He looked at the wand like he hated it, but he didn't say no. I said, "Take a walk with me. Outside. Fifteen minutes."

"Then you'll leave me alone?" he said. "You won't interrupt me again?" I nodded. "By the Salt?" he said.

I said, "By the Salt." I was ready to walk the whole way back across the floor, but he motioned me to a closer door. We walked past another dozen light-writers; not one of them even noticed we were there.

Outside, he was different. Some of the intensity drained away. "I'm sorry," he said. "I just get so wrapped up in it." He shook his head at his own pigheadedness. Then he said, "What am I apologizing to you for? I didn't accuse *you* of attempted murder." I never thought that would bother him as much as it seemed to.

"You should," I said. "It might be what I'm really here for."

"Might be?" he said.

I said, "What if you believed it was kill me or the world would end? What would you do?"

He didn't answer me right away. I was glad of that; it meant he was taking it seriously. Finally, he said, "Take the chance I was wrong." And I knew he meant it. But it didn't take me off the hook. I still had to make my own decision. "Who says I'm going to end the world?" he said.

"Me," I said. "And the Old Wiseguy."

"Well, I'd definitely take a chance that he's wrong," he said. He smiled when he said it, and it was like it was just me and him again, like before we joined the Salt-speakers.

I said, "There's going to be a big flash, and everything we know is going to be destroyed. You cause the flash. I think it's this light wand. I think you flare out and start some kind of chain reaction that destroys the world."

Theshei looked like I was reading his mind. He said, "Let me tell you what I believe. The end is coming. I feel it too. And the big flash, I dream about that every time I go to sleep." He didn't look like he did much sleeping.

"But these beings have something to tell us that can stop it, something that will make everything perfect. Only there isn't much time, and they can only say it through the light wand." There was a kind of desperation in his voice I'd never heard before. "I have to learn how to use the light wand so I can find out what it is before it's too late."

I looked up at the stars. The Milky Way was out. I wondered if that was going to perish in the big flash too. I didn't know what to do. Theshei at least seemed sure he was right. All I had was a secondhand premonition. "What if you're wrong?" I said.

"What if I'm right?" he said.

I could see his point. If I killed Theshei and the world didn't explode, we still had the same old world full of fallible human beings tormenting themselves and each other over things that were too stupid to even discuss. If Theshei was right, the world wouldn't end and we'd have perfection. His bet was better than mine.

Theshei put a hand on my shoulder. "I gotta go back," he said. "Every minute counts. You do what you have to." He smiled. "All choices are right," he said.

I smiled too. "You still know the Salt," I said.

He shrugged. "Who knows?" he said. "Maybe the Salt's what the Sandscripti want to tell us." Then he went inside and left me out there, looking up at the stars.

CHAPTER 21

I fell asleep looking up at the stars, and when I woke up, they were gone. I woke out of one of those dreams you never get to finish, the ones that end at the crucial moment. I hadn't had a dream like that since I first joined the Saltspeakers. I couldn't remember it in detail, but Sandi was in it, and all that was left of it was Badguy's horn.

The sky was just turning from gray to blue, and there were still streaks of pink just over the treeline. The grass was wet with dew, and the birds were waking each other up like a line of shops opening for business. I almost forgot where I was for a moment. But wherever I was, it was beautiful.

It made me think Theshei was right, or that I at least ought to wait and see. Somehow I thought there would be some kind of warning just before it happened. I didn't think a change like that could occur without the universe screaming some kind of alarm, and if I didn't hear it, at least the Sandscripti would. I didn't decide to forget killing Theshei, I just decided to forget it for the moment. The decision made me feel good. I wanted to go in and tell Theshei, but I remembered my promise not to distract him, and I knew he'd hold me to it. I decided to wait until I saw him come outside for a break and talk to him then.

All my plans went down the drain in the next minute. I

heard Sandi before I saw her. "There you are," she said. And she didn't say it happily. She was shouting at me from the curve of the building. I think if she was closer, she would have been hitting me with each word. "You know how much time you've cost me already?" I knew she didn't expect an answer. "Every time some idiot decides to hide out here, I have to stop practicing."

It was like watching a storm rolling in; you're afraid of what it's going to do, but it's too miraculous not to watch. "I don't have time to go hunting you down," she shouted. She was standing over me by then, but she was still shouting. "This is your light wand," she said. She tossed it in my lap. "It's an interface for the will. Just hold it in your hand and concentrate. One of the Sandscripti will come along and show you what to trace if you ever get it going." It was amazing: She glowed even in the daylight. And she was just as beautiful as the Sandscripti. And just as unreachable. "Try not to get yourself killed," she said. Then she turned and walked away.

I jumped up and tried to follow her. She never looked back. I called after her. "Where do we get breakfast around here?"

She answered over her shoulder without breaking stride. "Practice with the light wand and you won't be hungry." I liked her stride, it pulled the fabric tight across her as she moved. I could have caught up with her, but I kept walking behind her to watch her walk. "You won't need much sleep either," she said.

"Isn't there some kind of orientation or something?" I said.

"You want rules?" she said. "Make your own." She didn't even turn her head. I didn't mind. The back of her head was also gorgeous. "And stop leering," she said. She opened one of the doors to the dome and disappeared. She pulled it shut behind her, and I couldn't get it open again. I thought about knocking, but I knew I could knock the door down without any of the light-writers even noticing. So I went on around the building and in the front door.

There weren't as many of the would-be light-writers standing, but the place was still crowded. A lot of them were curled up pretty much where they were standing the night before, and a lot more were laying around near the walls. There were still flashes and sparks from everywhere, but the only steady glow other than the Sandscripti themselves was from Theshei's part of the dome.

I looked around to see if I could spot any of Orwoz's secret agents and picked out five of them without trying. They weren't wearing their robes, but they had the look. Watching their eyes led me to a dozen more in the next ten minutes or so. If one of them looked in the direction of another, he immediately dropped his eyes so nobody would think they knew each other. They spread themselves out as much as possible so it was almost impossible for one of them to look anywhere without almost making eye contact with another. Most of them usually dropped their heads as well as their eyes when they did, and the sudden jerky movements made them look like they had some sort of nervous affliction. They seemed to spend most of their time correcting accidental eye violations so it was no wonder they were doing as poorly with the wands as they were.

Only two of them had even the faintest glow from their light wands, and they were two who had apparently solved the eye contact problem by shutting their eyes completely. I had no idea what Sandi meant by "an interface for the will," but apparently concentration had something to do with getting the light wands to work, and few of Orwoz's spies could stop being aware of themselves as spies long enough to concentrate on anything else.

I assumed there were a few competent Saltspeaker

agents scattered throughout the crowd, but if "critical number" was more than a half dozen, I doubted Orwoz's master plan would ever be put into effect. The idea of a gang of Saltspeakers getting their light wands going at the same time seemed unlikely and the odds against a band of kamikaze Saltspeakers pushing the light wands past their limits simultaneously looked astronomical. Still, some of them must have gotten the light wands going because Orwoz was always losing agents, and I made a mental note to find out if there was some way of reversing a chain reaction if they ever did get one started.

The world seemed in no immediate danger of annihilation from Saltspeaker stupidity, so I decided to go over near Theshei and start doing what Sandi had said. My stomach was empty, and I was a bit stiff from sitting out all night. I passed her on the way and stopped to watch her. Her lines died out of the air almost as soon as I stopped. She glared at me. "Go away," she said. "Go far away." She started forcing the wand through a series of complex arcs like I'd already gone. Before she was well into them, I was already gone as far as she was concerned. I wasn't even a memory. It was a lot easier to be abused than ignored, but I took it for a little while longer just because I liked to look at her so much. Eventually though, I went on my way.

Theshei was deep into some complex pattern that was almost still intact when he finished it and launched into another. I had the feeling that two icons still visible at the same time was a minor breakthrough for him, but I didn't congratulate him. I'd promised not to distract him, and a promise was a promise.

It left me nothing to do but try the light wand myself. I took up a position opposite Theshei but a little off to the side so I wouldn't distract him. Of course, I could have set myself on fire directly in front of him, and it wouldn't have broken his concentration. I watched him and then I watched some of the others, but there didn't seem to be one technique other than absolute concentration. Some of them accompanied what little they drew with intricate body English and facial expressions that ranged from terrifying to ecstatic to ridiculous.

One of the Sandscripti came floating toward me, and I thought I'd better get started before they decided I was just a hanger-on and threw me out. In the back of my mind, I thought that maybe if I got good at it, Sandi might lighten up on me a little. Even though I'd seen Theshei struggle, I just assumed it was going to be easy. The wand was light, barely an ounce, and even after hours of movement, I couldn't imagine it getting heavy. It hardly even felt like it was real.

I held it in my left hand and held my staff like a walking stick with my right. I thought about trying it sitting down, but Theshei made swoops and sudden changes of direction that I could see you needed to stand up for. The first thing I tried was circles, and I moved my arm in a big one, drawing it out in front of me. Nothing happened.

Fifteen minutes later, I was still drawing invisible circles in the air. I was still hungry. I was still stiff. I was still sleepy. And I was getting nowhere. I tried to concentrate, but my mind kept wandering. I was surprised that nothing worked. When I first held the wand, it had felt familiar somehow, and I expected it to come to life the minute I started to move it, but it didn't. It was just a very light stick, like a band leader's baton, except there was no band and whatever music was in the wand wasn't going to come out for me.

I wanted to put it down and wander around for a while, but I could see the Sandscripti out of the corner of my eye, and I imagined he was watching me. I knew I was watching him. Even in the dim daylight of the dome, they were still spectacular. I wondered how anybody could fail to pay absolute attention to them, and yet they glided through the mob without anybody noticing them except me.

It took me a while before I figured out that when they came near, they weren't in the least interested in my progress or the lack of it; they were checking on Theshei. None of them came and showed me any elementary figures to draw. I suppose there was no point if I couldn't get any light out of the wand, but nobody came and showed me how to use that either.

I went through the motions, waiting for Theshei to get tired and stop for a minute so I could talk to him, but he was focused in completely on the shapes he was making in the air. There was a different quality to the light he made too. He wasn't just better than anybody else, he was different. It might have been the Sandscripti's light, but Theshei made it his own.

When he finished one really intricate design, a Sandscripti glided up and drew the same pattern over the top of it in about half a minute. Then he touched the points where they differed, and they lit up more brightly than the rest. Theshei took the correction with a grateful smile. In an image about three feet high, three lines about as thick as a hair curved left instead of right. Theshei began the whole thing over again, trying to slide through the lines the way the Sandscripti did. Two hours into the morning, he still didn't know I was there.

It was awkward. I wanted him to notice me, but at the same time I wanted the Sandscripti to overlook me, so I was trying to look highly visible and invisible at the same time. It just didn't work. Finally a Sandscripti stopped in front of me and watched me for a second. Then he held his light wand up and touched one end with a fingertip. It seemed to sparkle. Then he pointed to mine, and I could see why nothing was working.

Both ends of the wand looked pretty much the same to me, but when the Sandscripti showed me the wand, I could see instantly that one end was tapered more than the other. When I looked at my own wand, I could see I was holding it backward. At first I thought it was funny, but then I wondered what would have happened if the thing had suddenly flashed to light while I was holding it backward. Would it have burned a pattern into me? Set fire to my robe? Singed all my hair off? I wasn't anxious to find out, and I twirled the wand around. The Sand-scripti smiled and drifted away.

I pointed the right end of the wand in the air and began to draw circles again. Nothing happened. I began to think I had a defective wand, and I wanted to go get a good one. But I didn't want to leave Theshei long enough to go find Sandi, and I had to keep reminding myself that I wasn't there to learn the light wand, I was there to stop Armageddon.

After another hour of lightless circles, arcs, ovals, squares, and triangles, I got lucky. Sandi passed on her way somewhere with one of the Sandscripti. She looked at me and then at the point of my wand and shook her head. "Pretender," she said.

I wanted to make that wand work so bad I could taste it. But all it did was get heavier than my staff. Then it got to weigh about ten pounds, and I concentrated on it and wished it, imagined it, flaring to light before she was gone past entirely. Sandi was already past me, and she wasn't looking back. I was filled with anguish, with longing, I wanted her to notice me without contempt. I imagined her turning around, and just as she turned her head to look back as if I called her, there was a blinding flash and the light wand came to life.

It jerked my arm toward the ground like I was trying to hold up the building. I couldn't believe how heavy it was. I dropped my staff and grabbed it with two hands like some deep-sea fisherman landing a marlin before they went extinct.

I scraped it through the air. It took all the strength I had just to get it over the first hump, and when it shot down the first curved side of the figure, it was all I could do to keep it from hitting the ground. I stopped it just short of the floor, and then I bent my knees and swung it back up the arc of the other side with all my strength. It didn't leave me much to swing it over the second hump, and I leaned to my left and let my body serve as a kind of axle for its momentum to turn around. When it dropped into the start of the first hump, I let it go out.

It didn't last long, and it was fiery red instead of gold, it was misshapen as a kindergarten drawing, and the lines were shaky and bent and lumpy, but it didn't take much imagination to see that it was a heart.

The Sandscripti raised an eyebrow. I thought Sandi would melt at least a little, but all she did was scowl at it and say, "Damned Saltspeakers," and stalk away without waiting for the Sandscripti.

CHAPTER 22

SANDI stalked away, but the Sandscripti stayed. They were remarkably human when you looked *at* them instead of through them. The one in front of me reminded me of the Old Wiseguy, or at least what he'd have looked like if he got to an age he liked and stopped aging. He wasn't quite as transparent as other Sandscripti either.

When I noticed that, I began to look at the Sandscripti more closely, and I realized two things. First, they didn't seem to carry their light wands anywhere on them; the wands just seemed to appear in their hands out of nowhere. But when you watched closely, it was like the wands gradually became visible and then more visible and finally solid. At least they looked solid, but the more I watched, the more it seemed like the wands were extensions of the Sandscripti and were no more solid than the Sandscripti themselves. The light wand they had given me was as solid as I was, but I suspected that theirs, if anybody ever had the foolhardy courage to reach for one, would turn out to be as impossible to touch as they were.

That made me notice something else: They didn't just have unique features like human beings; they varied in their density as well. They even had little personal quirks in how they moved and how they stood. Later, when I got better at the light wand, I could see that there were even differences in the way they moved the light wand, a kind of handwriting except it involved changes in brightness and color and staying power.

Everybody had a style, even my heart. Clumsy and irregular as it was, it lasted a lot longer than anybody expected, and it had an intensity that turned people's heads. I was amazed myself at how bright it was. When any of the Sandscripti drew, it was like music; my heart was like a shout. The color was anything but subtle too; it was a deep blood red with silver highlights that made it look like red metal. Everybody's lines were thick when they first started, but mine were thick and deep, and the whole heart looked like it weighed more than I did, even if it *was* made out of light.

I watched everybody's style after that. It fascinated me, and I got so I could tell personality from it. I never thought of the Sandscripti having personalities before that. They were just natural phenomena, remarkable events; even knowing there were males and females didn't change that way of looking at them. It was like thinking of lightning strokes as having individual characters, but when I watched them moving their light wands, I could tell them apart as easily as people.

If they had names, they could only reproduce them with the light wand, but I had my own names for them based on how they drew their figures. The one who stayed to examine my heart was Slip, because every time he made a downstroke, it seemed to have slipped out of control. Then at the last instant, he would turn it in another direction like somebody pulling a slip knot tight. I thought he must have a mind like that, one that went sliding down an idea and then turned it in on itself to everybody's surprise. If the Sandscripti were capable of underestimating each other, I imagined he got underestimated a lot.

He stood and watched my heart until it finally faded away. He smiled at it, and every time it shifted another phase toward dissolving, he smiled more. That was something else about my style: It didn't decay gradually from the first drawn line to the last, like almost everybody else's did. Different parts of it would wane and then come back and wane again without any consistent order, until at the end it would seem to break apart and dissolve all at once. Slip was fascinated with that.

He put his own light wand up to it and made an almost instantaneous copy of it right behind it and then he watched the differences between them in the way they dissolved. I had no idea what he saw in them, but I suspected from his eyes that it was some kind of truth. The way he kept experimenting with it for as long as it lasted made me think the truth was scientific, that he was deriving some set of natural laws from it and that it fit somehow into a larger understanding that he was working out.

The fact that the Sandscripti didn't know everything there was to know about the light wand surprised me a little. It worried me too. If there were things about the behavior of that light they didn't fully understand, then an accident they couldn't foresee was entirely possible.

I comforted myself with the idea that it was just me that puzzled them. No matter what I did after that, Slip seemed interested in it, and he usually showed whatever it was to Slide, a female Sandscripti whose light wand moved like a child sliding on the ice. It never knotted itself, and whenever it changed directions, it never lost speed. No matter how convoluted the design, it looked like one long slide when she did it.

They had a lot to look at, because I became as fanatical about light-writing as Sandi and Theshei. But that first icon took a lot out of me. Slip kept drawing it over and over again in front of me and then waiting for me to do it again, but I couldn't lift my arms. And a lot of the heart had gone out of me as well when Sandi walked away in disgust.

Tired as my arms felt, the rest of me was full of energy. I didn't notice it right away, but I wasn't hungry either.

Gradually, I realized I wasn't stiff or sore, and the scratches and bruises from coming through the woods didn't bother me anymore. Slip kept smiling and encouraging me to pick up my wand again, and I rubbed the tiredness out of my arms and tried again.

I was afraid it was a fluke because at first nothing happened, and then Slip drew this short line that kept reversing itself as it dropped, and I followed it with my wand even though nothing was coming out of it. Slip kept renewing his line, and I kept following it until finally, without my realizing it, there were two lines zigging and zagging out behind my wand. The two lines didn't match exactly; in fact, they matched less often than they didn't, but it was a beginning.

Slip beamed and went gliding off, and I watched him drawing the most amazing flourishes to another Sandscripti. Slide drew some equally amazing flourishes back, and then she glided back over with him. Slip's line was pretty much gone by then, but mine was still phasing in and out on its way to final breakup.

Slide seemed to fold into herself to get down close to it, and she watched it that way until it finally broke up and dissolved. Then she and Slip exchanged a flurry of icons that made me sick with envy. I knew they were talking about me, and I felt proud of that in a strange kind of way, but I knew they were like people whose parrot just said its first words. I was never going to be able to make the patterns they took for granted, and I suddenly wanted to make them very much.

When they were finished, Slide drew a simple curve and reverse in front of me, but I didn't really want to copy it. It seemed pointless. I was never going to be as good as they were, even at the simple stuff, and it made me feel clumsy and stupid in a way I hadn't felt since childhood. But Slide looked disappointed, and Slip looked like he was apologizing, so I finally lifted the wand and tried to copy it.

The wand was heavy enough in the curve, but when it

came time to reverse it, it was like trying to stop a rolling truck. I clapped my right hand over my left wrist and wrenched the wand back, but it felt like it was sliding out of control. Just at that moment, my eye went out over the point of the wand, and I could see Sandi standing over beyond Theshei watching me with a smile on her face that said, "Not as easy as it looks is it, smart guy?"

She was right, of course. I was in over my head, and I'd gotten too cocky too soon. My hand was dropping in a long parabola toward the floor, and there was no way I could turn it back up again. It was going to go crashing to the floor and break up in a shower of sparks. It felt like metal being scragged over metal, and I did the only thing I could to save it: I twisted my wrist with all my might and tried to turn it into a curlicue toward my body. I almost had it when I thought I heard Sandi laugh, and that snapped it. I made a sound like somebody trying to lift a house and wrenched my wrist so sharp the tip of the wand turned in place.

All of a sudden, the wand tip weighed a thousand pounds, and the figure was being swallowed by this expanding ball of brilliant white light. I could see the expression on Slide's face just beyond it, and it wasn't good. It was a mixture of horror and remorse and shock all at once, and Slip didn't look any happier. The ball seemed to be expanding in slow motion, but everything else seemed to be going even slower.

It dawned on me suddenly that I was flaring out.

CHAPTER 23

MY stomach dropped out of me. I'd come within touching distance of death before, but I was halfway down its throat this time, and I didn't know what to do. I looked at Slip, but he didn't seem to have any suggestions. He just looked very sad for me and disappointed that I wasn't going to be around anymore after such a promising start. And Slide wasn't any better. I don't think there was anything they could do except watch; it was my wand and I was the only one who could do anything about it.

The ball was about three feet wide and swelling. I didn't know how long I had before it vaporized me, but I took one last look over its edge at Sandi. She looked angry, like I was doing it on purpose just to show off. I looked to Theshei, but he was just starting to look up from his own design, and I knew he didn't know what to do either.

I was going up in a flash of light, and nobody knew how to stop it. For a minute, I thought maybe that was what my premonition was: not that the universe was going to dissolve in a flash of light, but that *my* universe was going inevitably into the void. It was the first time I really thought about the certainty of my own annihilation. It made me want to scream.

But then right behind that wave of panic, I could hear the Salt. "Nobody dies, not even Badguy." And I could have let the flash keep growing if there wasn't so much of interest I didn't want to miss out on. The Salt told me what to do. "In the grip of the Inevitable, do not resist."

I stopped trying to stop the widening ball of light. Instead, I pushed my light wand deeper into its center and focused everything I could into making more light. The center of the flash got brighter and brighter and the wand became so heavy I didn't think I could hold it even to stay alive. At the tip, a small glob of light, thick and sticky and immensely dense, continued to grow. It didn't get bigger, only denser, and just as the flare-out was about to envelope me, it started to shrink.

And it kept on shrinking, down into the thick lump of light at the tip of my wand. I watched it dwindle until the last diffuse fringes of it shrank into the mass of incredibly dense light, and as soon as the last of it disappeared, I twirled the wand and withdrew it, leaving the glob with a tail of wiry light. And it was done.

It was two days before that knot of light finally dissipated in a shower of tiny sparks.

For the moment though, we all stood there waiting to see what it would do. I felt giddy. I almost started to laugh for pure joy, and then I had a horrible thought. What if, in the process of reversing my flare-out, I had just made the bomb of light whose explosion would destroy the universe. I watched it for signs that it was going to continue shrinking inward until it sucked everything in after it. But after a minute, the knot seemed just as solid and stable as ever. Slip and Slide looked satisfied that it was over, and everybody human heaved a sigh of relief and started breathing again.

For a moment I thought the flare-out was still expanding beyond me, but I realized that it was just the glow of so many of the Sandscripti all in one place. They came sailing in from all over the dome, hovering above me, gathering around on the floor and above it until they formed a kind of dome of their own. One by one they sailed in close to the core of light and either examined it or marveled at it. They didn't seem in the least worried about it now, and some of them got close and studied me as intensely as they did the knot of light.

I was just happy to be there. I thought it was going to be a long time before I ever touched a light wand again, but I was wrong. Theshei walked through the Sandscripti, shaking his head. "That was close," he said. "I thought you were a dead man." He looked at the knot of light and shook his head admiringly. "Nobody ever reversed a flare-out before," he said.

The Sandscripti were drawing up icons so thick and fast it was beginning to hurt my eyes, and I put a hand up to shield them. For a second I could see through my hand, and then it was back to normal. I looked at my hand and then at Theshei. "Did you see that?" I said.

"What?" he said. "Your hand coming back? You were transparent as the Sandscripti for a while there. We thought you were gone."

"So did I," I said. The Sandscripti were still drawing away, and about half of it seemed to be flashes and bursts of light. I figured they were talking about the flare-out, and then I realized I had recognized my first word in Sandscripti. I wasn't crazy about the fact that it was *flare-out*. It didn't seem like a very good omen.

"They want to know how you did it," Theshei said.

"I stopped resisting it and pushed out all the light I could," I said.

"No, no," Theshei said. "They know what you did. They want to know how you knew to do it."

I laid my light wand down and picked up my staff. "The Salt," I said. Theshei looked like he wondered what part. "In the grip of the Inevitable . . ." I said.

Theshei smiled. ". . . do not resist." He shrugged. "I don't know how to tell them that," he said.

"Draw them a heart," I said.

And he did. It was the first word any human ever intentionally added to the language of the Sandscripti.

Of course, most of what was human wasn't worth talking about with a light wand. They had a kind of open-ended sign language for that. When I looked over at Sandi, she was going through a dance of gestures and expressions trying to tell the Sandscripti what Theshei was telling them. There was probably a lot of it that didn't translate at all. We had no idea how much then.

Surrounded by so many Sandscripti and bathed in their reflected light, she looked like one of them. She made me think of Theshei's woman, and I wondered why I hadn't seen her. I wondered why Theshei was still here if she wasn't. I hoped I'd get a chance to ask him. But for the moment, I was just happy to watch Sandi move.

When she finished, she came over to me. I hoped she would at least say she was glad I didn't destroy myself. I thought she'd say, "I told you so." But all she said was "Asshole," and she stormed away.

Theshei started to laugh, caught himself, and forced a straight face. I shrugged. "Why does she hate me so much?" I said.

Theshei said, "Cheer up, she hates me too." He pointed to the door and said, "Let's take a walk."

I was surprised at how bright it was outside. Everything seemed to shine, like after a rain, but it hadn't rained. Even the few clouds in the sky had a glossiness to them. It made me realize how beautiful ordinary things are, and that made me realize how close I came to being dead. It made the back of my knees weak, and I sat down with my back against the wall again and let everything go slack. Theshei sat down beside me. Neither of us said anything for a while.

Sandi came out the door, saw us, and went back in again. "What's wrong with her?" I said.

"You probably remind her of her brother," he said. That didn't seem like a bad thing to me. "They came here together." I knew the rest without his telling me.

"Flare-out?" I said.

Theshei nodded. "Less than a week after I came," he said. "She was right next to him. Almost went up too."

I said, "You remind her of her brother too?"

Theshei smiled. "No," he said, "she thinks I keep showing her up." He shook his head at the way people are. "She wants to learn the light wand so bad, but she just doesn't have the talent."

I was surprised. "She said she was the best they ever saw," I said.

Theshei looked at me like I would never reach the limit of my gullibility. "If she was that good, would they keep taking her away from the wand to translate?" he said.

"She looked good to me," I said. I knew I wasn't exactly objective.

Theshei said, "Didn't you take a vow of chastity?"

"We," I said, "*we* took a vow of chastity."

Theshei shook his head. "Oh no," he said, "when people try to kill me, all vows are off."

"That reminds me," I said. "I meant to tell you, I'm not going to kill you." I was going to say, not for a while, but I knew after what happened with the light wand I was probably a bigger danger than Theshei.

Theshei nodded. "I don't owe you any vows, do I?"

I said, "No."

He said, "Good." Then he smiled. "Of course, it doesn't get *you* off the hook."

"Well," I said, "there's no chance of my breaking it anyway."

"But you're thinking of it," Theshei said.

"It's more than that," I said. "You remember asking me if I was ever in love?"

He nodded. I could tell by the pain on his face he remembered everything about that day.

"I didn't even know what you were talking about then," I said.

"Everybody's got a bad case of Death. Stop screwing

around, and it'll go away," he said. Theshei never missed a chance to quote the Salt to me, especially when there was nothing I could say in return.

"What ever happened to your true love," I said.

Theshei shook his head ruefully. "Talk about your doomed love affairs," he said. "I saw her once. The day I got here. I don't think she saw me at all." I could hear the same tone in his voice as I heard in mine: agony and irony.

"I feel like an idiot most of the time," I said. "I can't believe I'm acting like a teenager."

Theshei laughed. "You?" he said. "The first icon I learned to draw in Sandscripti is the one for Scry's name. Scry's the nearest I can come to it in less than twenty syllables." He drew a small intricate icon in the air in blue and silver. It was beautiful enough to be her name. "That's the short Sandscripti version of it," he said. He smiled at it.

"And I just almost got myself killed trying to show off for somebody who hates the sight of me," I said. It made us both laugh.

"I thought we were supposed to outgrow stuff like that," he said.

"It's a hard life for an idiot," I told him. It paid him back for sticking me with his quote from the Salt earlier.

"Well," he said, "you start working the light wand, and it'll help get your mind off it."

"Is that what you do?" I said.

Theshei smiled, but it was like the way you grit your teeth when you're in too much pain to smile for real. He was worse off than I was, and I felt sorry for him. At least what I wanted was theoretically possible; there was no possibility of a future for him and Scry.

There wasn't anything else to say about that, and we sat quietly for a little while. Finally, he got up. "Well," he said, "I can't talk to her unless I can work the light wand." I could see why he focused on that. There was nothing beyond it.

"Not to mention saving the world," I said.

Theshei smiled, but it was a thin smile. "You be careful," he said.

"You too," I said. I knew neither of us would. And I knew if either of us flared out, that was what the other would remember: "You be careful." I watched him walk away toward the door, and I wondered how long it would be before one or the other of us weren't there. It wasn't something you could think about for very long. I got up. There were a lot of things that didn't bear thinking about. That was the best thing about the light wand: All you thought about was those glowing lines. I had an urge to go in and use it.

CHAPTER 24

THE door opened just as I reached for it, and Sandi came out. She was scowling. It looked good on her. Besides it was as close as I was going to get to a smile. I scowled myself. I thought it might stop me from leering.

"The Sandscripti want me to teach you some things," she said. She made it sound like her punishment for unspecified crimes. I figured whatever I said she'd take as an insult so I just nodded. "I don't like this any more than you do," she said. I couldn't imagine where she got the idea I wouldn't like it, but I didn't say so. It didn't matter; she knew what I wasn't saying. "All right," she said, "don't look smug. I don't think this is funny." I tried to keep a straight face. I really did. "I don't know what you're laughing about," she said. "I don't know why they're wasting my time with you. You'll do it again, and next time you won't be so lucky!"

"You have me confused with somebody else," I said.

"What's that supposed to mean?" she said.

I thought the best thing was to get it out in the open. Besides, she hated me already, so it wasn't like I was going to lose any ground. "I'm not your brother," I said.

When she cocked her arm, I thought she was going to slap me, but when her hand came forward, it was balled in a fist. I could've gotten out of the way even then, but I knew she had to hit something, so I took the shot. It's a hard life for an idiot. She punched me right where the Black Stick hit me. I went down like I was shot. I thought my head was pretty much healed; she showed me different. The pain was so intense I couldn't open my eyes. I just sat there on the ground holding my head, trying to figure out how to put the pieces back together.

She probably would've kicked me as well if I didn't look so helpless. Truth was, I *was* helpless. I couldn't have fought back if I wanted to. "What's the matter with you?" she said. I'd have given her a smart answer, but I couldn't talk. It even hurt to listen. "I thought you Saltspeakers were supposed to be tough guys," she said.

I kept waiting for the wave of pain to wash over me and subside, but it was a tidal wave. The pain just kept coming and coming. It was like the ball of the flare-out growing and growing. The little part of my brain that wasn't already consumed by the pain started worrying that something serious was wrong. It was like part of me was sitting there with a stopwatch saying, "This is too long; this is way too long!"

"Are you all right?" she said. There was fear in her voice and concern, but I wasn't sure it was for me. More likely she was worried about what the Sandscripti were going to say about her killing their rookie sensation. It was certainly going to be hard for her to explain, and I was half tempted to die just to put her on the spot. But I didn't even have the power to do that, and the pain didn't seem like it was ever going to subside.

She crouched down beside me and pulled my hand away from my head. "Let me look," she said. "I used to be a nurse." My hand went right back to where it was. She pulled it away again. "Where'd you get that scar?" she said. "That's fresh. It's barely formed."

I could feel just the slightest weakening of the pain. If she shut up, it might even go away. I wanted to tell her that, but it took everything I had to keep from passing out. At least I thought it did. The next thing I knew I was leaning up against the wall without any recollection of getting up or moving. I kept lurching into awareness, like I was dozing off and jerking awake when I started to fall over. I kept hearing sentences from the middle on. None of them made sense anyway.

I was still holding my head with my right hand when she put something in my left. It was the light wand. It seemed to me that, short of a loaded gun, it was the last thing I'd put in the hands of a semiconscious man. I still couldn't talk, so I dropped it. She picked it up and put it back in my hand. I opened my hand and let it fall again. "It'll help you," she said. I had my doubts, ex-nurse or not.

"Try!" she said. Her voice was frantic. It sounded like she thought she'd killed me and she wanted to undo it. She put her hand over mine and held it shut so I couldn't drop the wand. The pain was a dark room, and I pictured light spilling in from everywhere. The wand got heavy in my hand. But the pain started to go away. The more light I pictured flowing in, the more pain got washed out. In a little while, my head was clear, and the pain was gone. When I opened my eyes, the light wand was shooting out light like a fountain.

"How does it feel now?" she said.

"It's fine," I said. I was amazed. There was no pain and no hangover of pain. My head felt a little light, a little fragile, but it didn't hurt.

"Let me look at your pupils again," she said.

I said, "Again?" I didn't remember the first time. But I let her lean close and look again. There was a kind of heat that passed between us with her that close. I couldn't believe she couldn't feel it.

"You're clear now," she said. "How'd you get the concussion?"

"Friend hit me with a stick," I said.

She shook her head. "He must've had a running start," she said. "How do you feel?"

"Like somebody who's been punched in their broken head," I said.

"I'm sorry," she said. But she took it back right away. "But you asked for it."

I said, "Yeah, well, somebody told me you might have us confused because I look like him."

"You don't look like him at all," she said. "You act like him. He was an asshole too."

"Did you beat him up too?" I said.

She ignored it, but her voice cracked when she talked again. "Who told you you looked like him?" she said.

I didn't see any reason to lie. "Theshei," I said.

"Oh," she said, "that Saltspeaker scum." I was going to defend him, but she didn't give me a chance. "Did he tell you how my brother died?" she said. It was like an accusation.

"Flare-out," I said.

"Yeah," she said, "but he didn't tell you he pushed my brother into it, did he?" It didn't sound like the Theshei I knew, and I said so. She said, "Right from the moment he came here, he kept trying to outdo Terry."

"Terry kept trying to outdo *him*," I said. I got ready for another punch. I knew I was right. He would have had to be competitive just to survive as her brother.

"He kept it up," she said. "He was the one taking all the chances. Making Terry take more."

I said, "You keep telling yourself that lie; you'll never get over it."

"What do you know about it?" she shouted. She seemed close to tears, but it was no time to let her hide from it again.

"Might as well blame yourself as Theshei," I said. "Younger brother. Tomboy older sister. You tell me who he was competing against." I knew she was really thinking *she* killed him, not Theshei. She cocked her fist back to hit me again, but she started to cry instead. Really cry. Two weeks of grief came spilling out all at once. She put her head against my chest. She was in so much pain, I felt like the Old Wiseguy. So much pain and nothing I could do about it. I cried along with her. It seemed like the right thing to do. I was surprised I remembered how.

When her sobbing got quiet enough, I said, "You helped make him who he was; you didn't kill him."

"I did!" she said. "I did!" The big sobs were back, choking her.

"You act like death's the end of everything," I said.

"How do you know it isn't?" she said.

I asked her, "How do you know it is?" She didn't have an answer.

I put the light wand in her hand. If it was good for one kind of pain, I thought it might be good for another. I put my hand around hers and moved it. The light that came out was gray and brown. I moved her hand through the shape again. The color shifted toward white. It took five more times to work it through to gold. She wiped her eyes. I let her hand go, and she moved the wand around the outline of the heart one last time. It hung there, shining brighter than the sun. Every day after that, when we came out, it would still be there, and we would renew it. She looked at it and then at me.

"That's how I know," I said. "Nothing dies."

CHAPTER
25

IF there was a high point in my life before the Change other than when I found the Salt, it was the moment when Sandi looked at the heart and then at me. It was like the glaze of grief washed from her eyes and she saw me suddenly the way I had always seen her: filled with the transcendent beauty of the light. I knew in that instant without a word ever needing to be said that she loved me as much as I loved her, and we had been streaming toward that moment for the whole of our lives.

I had been in love with Sandi since the first moment I saw her, and it wouldn't have surprised me that she was suddenly just as in love with me as I was with her if only I had remembered the Salt a little better. It's not hate that's the opposite of love; it's indifference. "Hate is just love gone bad or spoiled in the making." Badguy did it. And like the Salt also says, "Bad is just Good misunderstood." In the end, even Badguy is good.

"I thought I hated you," she said. It seemed to amaze her that she could have been so wrong.

"Hate's just love misunderstood," I said. It was from the Salt, but I didn't say so.

"I'm sorry," she said. "I was taking Terry's death out on you."

"I didn't hurt you. You didn't hurt me. Badguy did it," I said.

It made her laugh. I doubt she had laughed since her brother died and maybe not for quite a while before. It made her even more beautiful. I didn't even mind that she was laughing at the Salt. "It's only the Salt," I thought, and the instant I did, I remembered what the Wiseguy had said to me just before I left: "Don't take the Salt too seriously." And when I'd asked him which part, he'd said, "You'll know when you come to it." And I thought I had.

I would have told her that, but at that exact moment, she leaned toward me and kissed me.

I don't know what it was that kept us from trotting off to the woodline right then so we could be alone. That's what most people our age would have done, FastAIDS or not. But it never even occurred to us. And the truth was, I don't think I would have gone if I had the chance. As long as there was no real chance of breaking my vow, I could think about it. Once it became a possibility, that was another story.

It wasn't that I was afraid of some divine retribution, or punishment by the Saltspeakers. It certainly wasn't that I didn't want her. It was just that I believed that I had made a commitment and it couldn't be broken, and I think she understood that even without my saying it. I know there are women who would have found an oath like that an irresistible challenge, but Sandi wasn't one of them. Sex just never came up between us.

But love, love was always there. We were always together after that. And always practicing. And when we were too exhausted to practice anymore, we lay down on one of the mats, nestled together like spoons, and slept. We lost all sense of time; days seemed to go by three at a time, and at the same time each one seemed to last a decade. Sometimes when we came outside, we would be astounded to see that it was night, and other times, we were amazed that it was sunrise or late afternoon or that we hadn't been out of the dome for more than a day.

Sometimes when we came out, we just stood silently and watched the world, and sometimes we talked. It was more than a week before she talked about her brother.

"Terry used to make me laugh so much," she said, "before we came here. And even after for a while. But it all got so serious. We wanted to know so badly. And we were trying so hard." She got tears in her eyes when she said it, and I held her a little tighter. "It was his idea to come here," she said. "He saw one of the Sandscripti on the road in front of our house, and after that, all he talked about was coming here." She smiled at the memory. "I asked him why, and he said, 'Everybody has to go somewhere.'"

"It sounds like the Salt," I said. I'd told her a lot about the Salt by then, but it didn't mean to her what it did to me. The Sandscripti were her Thunder, and your Thunder drowns out everything else. When she had the light wand in her hand, she couldn't hear even me. I didn't mind. I disappeared into the wand myself, although even when I did, I did it as part of the Salt.

"You would have liked him," she said sadly. Even when she couldn't see the heart, I think she believed me that nothing dies, but dead or not, he was gone and that never stopped hurting her. When it hurt her too much, she would stop talking and just cry softly. And when the crying didn't help, we would go back inside and she would lose herself in the wand.

It was easier when we talked about the Sandscripti. She probably knew more about them than anybody else would until somebody mastered the light wand, and she liked to talk about them. But even *she* had more questions than answers. "I come closer to talking to them than anybody here," she said once, "and I don't even know where they come from, except the Ribbonverse, whatever that is."

"They're worse than the light wand," I said.

"They are," she said. "They drive me nuts. They have

so much to tell us and they can only do it one way. You ask them how they got here, and they show you the wand. You ask them why they came, and they show you the wand. You ask them what made them come here now of all times, and they show you the wand. I don't even think they understand the questions, and if they do, they start drawing that huge icon for the Ribbonverse, and in half a minute they're spilling out icons so fast you can't even see them form."

It was true. "Things just pour out of them," I said. "It's like Sowing the Salt." I wished she could know what that felt like for me, but I could no more put it into words than the Sandscripti could.

She looked at me steadily for a minute. "You *are* just like that when you talk about the Salt," she said. She shook her head. "Maybe this really is a religion and they're some kind of missionaries." I thought she was serious, but she started to laugh.

"They might be," I said.

"If they are," she said, "they're missionaries of Science."

"You know what the Sandscripti would say to that," I said. She waited for me to tell her, and I held up the wand.

"An interface of the will," she said. She got up and took out her wand.

"Or the spirit," I said. She looked skeptical. "It's true," I said. "The wand works a lot better when you *let* it happen than when you try to force it to happen."

"Are you telling me how to use the wand?" she snapped. There was anger in her voice and a strong undertone of having been insulted. For a moment, she sounded like she did when I first came.

"I only meant . . ." I said.

She cut me off. "Meant what?"

But the truth was I didn't know what I meant, only that I hadn't meant to offend her. When I couldn't answer her, she let it drop, and we went inside. I tried to say something about it the next time we came out, but she just looked at me like she didn't know what I was talking about. I thought everything was all right again. I guess that's what Whatzisname must've thought.

But it really did seem like everything was all right, and by the next time we talked, even I had forgotten about it. The days flowed by, and I forgot even that I had forgotten. We were close when we talked, closer when we just sat together barely touching but touching more than with the deepest touch, and closest of all when we did the light wand. When she traced a figure, I would stand opposite her and trace it along with her. We both improved, and after a while, I was teaching her things about the light wand and about the icons of light we made. She had a much bigger vocabulary of images than I did at first, but whenever I wasn't working my own light wand, I watched the Sandscripti use theirs. Before long, I was showing her things the Sandscripti hadn't started to teach anybody yet.

And that was where the trouble started. I began to pull away from her. Theshei was right: She worked hard, but she had no natural gift for it, and everything she learned was a struggle. I was surprised at that; nobody had a better feel for the Sandscripti themselves, not even Theshei. But she never had a natural feeling for the light wand. I think she understood the meaning of what we were writing far better than I did, especially the nuances, but she just couldn't make the pictures.

When we worked together, she was always much better than when she was alone, and she could notice the difference. I could've made bigger strides, but I kept holding myself back because I didn't want to get too far ahead of her. I started spending more time "studying" the Sandscripti or just watching her than using the wand. She noticed that too.

She didn't say anything about it, but I could see the

frustration building in her and I could see an interminable sadness in her eyes whenever she realized there was always going to be a gulf in our abilities. When you have a gift like that, it's easy to accept that it has nothing to do with how smart you are, or how good a person you are, or anything else. It's just a part of you; you didn't do anything to earn it, you don't know why you have it; it's just there. That's not so easy to accept when you don't have the gift.

Sandi blamed herself for not being able to keep up with me. I didn't understand that then. I didn't blame myself for not being able to keep up with Theshei, so I couldn't imagine *her* doing it. I was making small strides forward; Theshei was making giant leaps. In another two weeks, he was beginning to talk with the Sandscripti. I wasn't jealous of him; I didn't feel inferior to him; I didn't even think he was "ahead" of me. He was where he was supposed to be; I was where I was supposed to be. I was content with that.

Sandi wasn't content. I don't think she'd ever been content. There were a couple hundred light-writers trying to learn the light wand, and almost all of them would have given whatever they had to have been as good at it as she was. But she wasn't the best, and that was all that mattered to her. I don't think she admitted that to herself, and she changed the subject whenever I tried to point it out to her.

I didn't pursue it like I should have. I should have made her talk about it. As it was, I let it fester, and little by little, it started to come between us. And by the time I couldn't ignore it anymore, it was too late.

I suppose I didn't want to notice it because it felt so good when I worked with her. Working the wand always pumped me full of energy just the way it did everybody else, and she was right: After a while, the wand was all you needed. You didn't eat; you didn't drink much; you rarely slept. But you never felt hungry, or thirsty, or empty. When you weren't working the wand, you were thinking about working the wand, and when you slept, you dreamed about it.

There was something to drawing that mirror image of what she was drawing that made me feel like we were sharing the same energy. It made us intimate in a way no other lovers had ever been intimate before. It was like we were one person. When she felt tired, I felt tired, and we always lay down exhausted together and slept curled together like children, there on the floor of the dome.

You didn't really get tired working the wand, but if you stayed at it too long without a break, your ability began to drop off and your mistakes went up. Flare-outs almost always occurred when somebody had been at it too long. It turned out that I hadn't invented the cure for flare-outs after all. There was something about the density of my strokes that made it possible for me to make that flare-absorbing knob of light. Nobody else could do it. Except Theshei.

Of course, nobody much tried. It was too dangerous starting a flare-out just to see if you could stop it, and panic usually took over when one started for real, and whoever was flaring out couldn't bring themselves to go with it and force more light out. The Sandscripti could probably do it, but they never had flare-outs.

I saw less and less of Theshei as time went by. When Sandi and I took a break, we took it together. Sometimes, Theshei would be between exercises as well, and he came over and talked or went outside with us, but even though Sandi was no longer blaming him for her brother, there was a coolness between them. I think also whenever Theshei saw us together, it made him feel like half of something that was never going to be made whole, and that made him start avoiding us.

I didn't really notice that right away. I didn't notice much of anything except Sandi. It amazed me how the more we were together, the less we talked or needed to.

The only thing that interested us outside of each other was the light wand and the Sandscripti, and when we talked, that was what we talked about.

We talked even less about our past. I still thought in terms of the Salt, and I still thought of myself as a Saltspeaker, but my mission was entirely forgotten. I didn't even remember most of the time that the Saltspeakers still expected me to assassinate Theshei. But the Saltspeakers hadn't forgotten.

I rarely thought of the Saltspeakers at all except when I saw Theshei, and that happened less and less often. The Sandscripti kept us at opposite ends of the dome because they were afraid we might flare out together or set up so much energy people around us might start flaring out. I suppose they would have separated Sandi and me for safety reasons as well, but they could see we wouldn't do it. We were together all the time, and I thought everything was fine between us. It wasn't.

The better I got, the bigger the distance between us got. It became harder and harder to make myself go as slow as she did on the figures. I had to concentrate more on keeping myself to her pace than on what I was doing. She could sense how much impatience I felt and tried to go faster, but it was dangerous, and she made more mistakes than she used to. I didn't make mistakes and that just frustrated her more.

It all came to a head when Slip and Slide gave us a new icon to copy. We were tracing a really intricate design together, and they came over and told us to stop. The design hung between us for a moment, and we looked through it at Slip and Slide with justifiable pride. We were stunned when Slide moved her wand over it from end to beginning and erased it. I watched the way the lines vanished almost as if they were being sucked back inside Slide's wand. We waited to see what we had done wrong, but instead of redrawing the icon correctly, she drew a simple icon instead.

When we looked at her without comprehension, she touched it and it brightened. I looked at Sandi, and her face was gray. "It's one of the first twenty figures," she said. There was a near absolute despair in her voice. "They're starting us over!"

I recognized the figure, but it seemed different somehow. I couldn't imagine why they would want us to start all over again. "Why would they want to do that?" I said. I felt a little deflated by it, but Sandi was crushed. I thought for a moment she was going to throw down her wand and walk out.

"Don't you see," she said. "We've been doing it wrong all along."

I couldn't believe that was true. "They would have told us if it was all wrong," I said.

"Not *all,*" she said. Her voice was frantic, and she was fighting for control. "Just little errors, but we must've been making them so often it's become habitual, and the only way to break the bad habits is to start over again from before you started making them. That's why it's not all the way back to the beginning."

"It can't be that," I said.

"What do you know!" she said. Her voice was bitter, angry, and brokenhearted all at once. "I've seen them make people start over before." It must have been what she was dreading all along. I knew she was thinking that all that work she had done in her brother's memory was in vain.

"Look at it," I said. "It's different somehow."

"How do *you* know?" she said. "All you ever look at is me. All I ever see is you. It's no wonder we keep making mistakes." She sounded like she wished she'd never seen me.

I looked at Slide, and she was smiling and I knew Sandi couldn't be right. "No, look," I said. "It's something new." And as I said it, Slide touched the figure and it began to change colors, as if each color were seeping out of the color before it, like a message within a message within a message.

I thought Sandi would be relieved, but she was only slightly less upset. It made me sad to see how close she always was to the brink of despair. Even her happiness was only a few degrees from it. Slide smiled at her and drew the figure again slowly. When we watched closely, there were intricate movements I thought might be making the difference, but when I tried it, I could see I was wrong. It was fundamentally different from anything we'd done. I looked at Slip for some guidance, but all he did was smile, and I could see we were going to have to figure it out for ourselves.

The two Sandscripti drew the icon in the air in multiple flowing colors over and over again with infinite patience. We watched them; we mimicked them; we traced it with them; and then we began to trace it alone. Sandi had regained her composure trying to follow Slide through the figure. It was just a new struggle, and she was used to struggle. I wanted to tell her she should be happy really, that it was an advance, that they wanted to take us to a new level, but she was too intent on what Slide was doing to be able to listen.

They showed us a few more times and then floated back away from us to observe. I moved next to Sandi and held my pen up to where the figure started. I looked over at her before I let it come to light, and she smiled sheepishly. "I'm sorry," she said. "I was afraid."

"You didn't hurt me. I didn't—"

She cut me off before I could finish. "Right," she said. "Badguy did it."

It made me laugh, and she laughed with me. If I had only kept my mouth shut, things might have been different, but I said, "Well, we're back to being rookies, but at least we're even again."

We had never really admitted out loud that I was better at it than she was, and when she hinted at it, I always denied it or made excuses for what seemed to be differences in our progress. I meant it as a joke, but she took it as a boast, and she scowled and looked away. It was silence between us after that, but in a few minutes, we had both forgotten everything but the struggle with the wand.

We went at it for two hours straight with only the occasional interruption by Slide or Slip to highlight some point on our figures as if that was where one or the other of us had come close to making the breakthrough. More and more often though, it was my figure they came and pointed to, and I could see her frustration growing. I could feel myself that I was on the brink of passing over into the new complexity, but I didn't want to get there before Sandi.

When I came to the end of a figure, I stopped and lowered my wand. When she finished her figure, I said, "I'm getting stale. I'm going to stop a while and watch the Sandscripti." It was what I always did when I felt like I was getting too far ahead of her. It didn't fool her, but she pretended it did, and I thought things were all right again between us and everything was forgotten.

I moved away from her a little so I wouldn't be a distraction and started watching Slip and Slide. They were watching Sandi, and they must have thought she was making progress because they were writing almost continually to each other with their light wands, stopping only occasionally to look at Sandi like she might be listening to them. I watched them as I always did, admiring the easy way they filled the air with light and meaning. I could never tell what the Sandscripti were saying, but sometimes I could at least pick up the tone of a discussion, and it seemed to me they were rising from mere discussion to intense excitement. The more passionate their discussion got, the brighter their images were, and then it struck me, the more they used their light wands, the more transparent they got.

I was stunned that I had never noticed it before. They didn't get dimmer, if anything they got brighter, which was probably why I hadn't noticed it in all the other times I had watched them, but they got more transparent. I could see the people beyond them more and more clearly the longer they continued. It fascinated me, and I couldn't take my eyes off them.

It was one of those amazing things you just have to share with somebody, and I said, "Sandi, look! They're getting more transparent!"

Normally I probably would have had to say it twice just to get her attention, but she was struggling so hard to finish the figure and to do it perfectly that it startled her. She was hurrying through it as if speed was going to help her make the breakthrough, and she was at a crucial point when I disturbed her. When I looked away from Slip and Slide, a ball of energy was swelling in front of her.

Slip came gliding toward us, but there was nothing he could do. She was flaring out, and if she didn't get it under control in the next second or so, it would go critical and so would she. She tried to connect it up with her icon, but the momentum of the wand was too powerful for her. I knew how heavy it was for her. I knew she wasn't going to be able to do it. The bubble just kept growing. It was out of control. There was fear in her eyes. She knew what was happening. Her brother must've looked the same way.

I kept shouting to her, "Force it out! Force the light out!" but she knew what to do, she just couldn't do it. She looked at me through the ball of light where it was thin and hazy around the edges. I knew it was good-bye. She looked so sad, like leaving me was worse than dying. She tried to smile as the ball swelled past her face.

I didn't think consciously that I would rather be dead with her than alive without her. I didn't think at all. I just stepped through the bubble of light. I had my hands out reaching for her, and they went through the ball first.

I was amazed. They were transparent. They looked like the hands of a Sandscripti. When I stepped fully into the ball, the rest of me went the same way. Sandi's mouth dropped open. I wasn't sure whether it was surprise or because she was saying "No!"

I didn't have time to think about what might be happening to me. Nobody knew what happened to somebody who stepped into somebody else's flare-out. I stepped out of the other side of the bubble and grabbed her hand. I forced my fingers in between hers around the wand and pressed one side of it against my palm.

It was like somebody dropped a cinder block in my hand. The wand dipped, and I thought it would go straight to the floor, but we pulled it back up. My muscles were shaking with the strain. I put every bit of will and imagination I had into the wand, trying to make the light at the tip dense enough to reverse the flare-out.

There was no reason to assume it could be done, and for a split second, it looked like it couldn't. I thought it was over for both of us, but I wasn't afraid. Dying wasn't the end, and I couldn't think of a better way to die. But I didn't give up. I tried to force the light out of the wand. But it wasn't until I felt *her* will flowing into the wand that I knew we were going to be all right.

It wasn't easy, and we were shuddering with exertion, but that thick glob of light squeezed out of the tip of the wand, and the bubble slowed, stopped, and began to contract. Her fingers were around the wand and digging into the back of my hand. Blood was dripping down where her nails dug in, but it didn't stop us. We forced a knot of light out of the wand and watched the flare-out shrink into it until it was all gone.

Slip and Slide were astounded. Two people had never tried to operate the same wand before; nobody even knew if it could be done. Certainly nobody had shared one during a flare-out. The Sandscripti were streaming toward us from all over the dome. I smiled at her. She was still a little transparent. "Was it good for you?" I said. I thought it would make her laugh. Instead she started to cry, pulled her hand out of mine, and ran out.

CHAPTER 26

I followed her outside, and she stood with her arm against the wall and across her eyes, crying. I figured everybody had their own way of almost dying, and I let her alone for a while. It must've been harder for her, having seen it happen to her brother. When I finally went up and put a hand on her shoulder, she shrugged it off. So I just stood there and waited.

Eventually she let me gather her in, and I held her and told her it was over, it was all right. But it wasn't, and we both knew it. "It's so easy for you," she said. "You don't know what it's like to have to work for it." It wasn't easy for me, but compared to what it was for her, it was easy. I'd have made it look harder if I could, but once you were working the wand, instinct took over, and you can't fake that.

And it was going to get worse. I could see it with Theshei; he made gains, then big gains, then revolutionary gains. There was a turning point, and once you went around it, things started going up geometrically. I was going to turn that corner before Sandi, and until she turned it, the distance between us was going to accelerate. She knew it as well as I did.

"I'm just holding you back," she said. I denied it, but we knew I was lying. "And you're holding me back," she said.

198

I couldn't understand that. "When I make a break-through," I said, "the first thing I do is share it with you. How can I be holding you back?"

"By making me just like you," she said. "I don't have your talent; I can't do the things you do."

"Sure you can," I said. "It just takes you a little longer. You can do things nobody else but Theshei and I can do." What worried me wasn't holding her back, it was forcing her forward too fast.

"I can't keep up with you!" she said. I couldn't understand what she was mad about.

"Sure you can!" I insisted. "You keep up with me every day." I'd have told her any lie to keep her from going where she was headed.

"You slow down," she said. "I hate that."

There was no good denying it. "I do it because I love you," I said.

She shook her head like I couldn't understand any-thing. "Don't you know how it makes me feel that you have to slow down for me?" she said. "I hate that you have to do it. I hate that it comes easy to you and I have to fight for everything. And I'm never going to get as good as you as long as I keep trying to follow. I have to find my own way."

I knew what she was driving at, but I didn't want to know. "What do you mean?" I said.

"I have to go at my own pace," she said. "I have to learn my own figures in my own way. I have to develop my own style." She looked at me sadly for a moment. "I can't do that with you. I'm going to have to start working by myself."

It was like a death sentence. "I can't do it without you," I said. "It's the only time I feel alive."

"I know," she said. "Don't you think I feel it too? But I have to do this my own way."

I knew she was right, but I just couldn't bring myself to let go of her. But it wasn't my choice. "When?" I said. It was like asking for an execution date.

"Now," she said.

I said, "You mean *now!*"

She nodded and reached up and kissed me and went back inside. I followed her in, but when she picked up her light wand, she said, "And don't stand around and watch me. Go way over there somewhere." I knew where she meant, an equal distance from both her and Theshei. I must've looked despondent, because she said, "All right, all right. When I break, I'll come and get you." She smiled. "This isn't going to be easy for me either, but it has to be done."

I knew she was right, but for the wrong reasons. The flare-out was a warning. The bigger the gap between us, the more she'd have to push it and the oftener things would get out of hand. If I kept working with her, sooner or later, it would kill her. I had no choice but to go and work by myself. But it wasn't easy.

The first couple hours, I regressed. I didn't even try the new icon. It was like I went back to where I was before we started working together and started over. I was making little mistakes I hadn't made in a week. A lot of the joy had gone out of it, and even when my icons were technically correct, they weren't alive. And they weren't even technically correct that often. I couldn't keep my mind on any of it. Everything seemed so incomplete without her.

Slip came over and watched me, but he wasn't smiling. I looked bad, and I knew it. He wasn't pretending otherwise. I put down the wand and sat down. I wasn't fatigued, but I was more tired than I got with Sandi.

In about half the time it would normally take us to reach the point of diminishing returns, Sandi came over and nodded toward the door. Outside, I asked her how it was going. She said, "We have to get used to it." I tried not to smile, but I had the hope she'd give it up if it wasn't working. She took the smile as an I-told-you-so and blew up. "I don't need you!" she said. "I was doing just fine before you came along. You and that other Saltspeaker." Then she turned on her heel and stormed away. At the door, she turned back and said, "Stay away from me, I mean it!"

That was the last thing she said to me for three days. If I stood around near her, she ignored me. If I was outside when she went out, she came back in. If I came out while she was there, she went back early. If she was making mistakes and she saw me stop, she kept going until I came back.

It was hard because, even apart, our rhythms were still the same. Neither of us were doing anything worthwhile. Slip started watching me from a distance like he didn't want to pressure me, and I could tell when he was talking to Slide about me because the brightness of his icons dimmed down. Slide's did the same when she was talking about Sandi.

I didn't notice it, but I'd turned a corner in picking up the language of the Sandscripti. It wasn't just the tone of their conversations anymore; I could tell what they were talking about even when I couldn't tell what words they were using. It was a breakthrough, like thinking in a foreign language or speaking one without translating from English first. If I had noticed, it wouldn't have made me happy. It only meant I was going to move further beyond Sandi.

I was worried about her. The color of her work was not good, and there were little knots in her lines that could have been flare-out points. I wanted to stay close to her in case one of them started to go critical. It wasn't easy. If I stayed where she could see me, she made more mistakes, or she got mad and poured too much energy into everything. So I moved around. We all liked to stay in the same spot day after day, but I started working in different places, always behind her somewhere or off to the side, out of her peripheral vision, so she wouldn't know I was there. I was always on the fringe of where I could get to her in time, and it drove me crazy. I didn't dare get fully into my own work because she might flare out and I wouldn't be able to stop it.

Twice I thought one of those knots of hers was starting to grow and I started toward her at a dead run, but I was wrong both times, and the second time, she saw me. I ran right past her and kept on going toward Theshei, but it was ridiculously obvious. When I thought I'd got some people between us, I stopped, but she came right after me and said, "Stop watching me! I know you're there. I can feel your eyes on me all the time."

"I can't stop watching you," I said. "I'm scared to death something will happen to you."

"You're doing more dangerous stuff than I am," she said.

There was nothing I could say to that but "Yeah, but I'm better at it," and I wasn't dumb enough to say that. I said, "All right, you give me one truthful answer, and I'll stop. Did you keep watching your brother after he told you to stop watching him?"

She looked like I had finally brought it home to her, but she tried to avoid it. "How do you know he asked me to stop?"

It was too obvious to explain. She must've seen him going beyond his limits to try to catch up to Theshei; she must've warned him to stop, she must've worried about what would happen if he didn't. And she must've watched him the way I watched her, with her heart in her mouth every time he tried something difficult, because she loved him. So all I said was "Well, did you?"

She couldn't meet my eyes, and she wouldn't answer.

"Would you have stopped watching him if you thought you could step in and save him if anything went wrong?" I said. She wouldn't answer that either, but we both knew she would've done the same thing I was doing. "Then how can you expect me to do it?"

She didn't have an answer for me, any more than I had an answer for how we could work together without my pushing her over the limit. "I have to do it!" she said. "We have to know what the Sandscripti have to tell us. We have to!"

It was such a bogus argument it infuriated me. I wasn't really mad at *her*. I knew she wanted it to be her that found out so her brother's death wouldn't have been for nothing. It was the whole situation; there just didn't seem to be any safe way to turn. It was like we were being swept up in these forces that carried us along no matter what, and we couldn't stop ourselves even if we knew we were headed for the falls. We couldn't even swim against the current.

I didn't mind that for myself. Being the event where Goodguy and Badguy come together was fine for me. But for her—I just couldn't stand that she was stuck in that collision of forces too. I tried to shout her out of it. "Who are you kidding?" I said. "You're not the one who's going to unravel all this. Theshei is light-years ahead of you! And he will be until he gets there." Somehow I thought if I could only make her see it was hopeless, she'd give it up.

She looked like I hit her, but she wouldn't give it up. "I have to try!" she said.

I was in too deep to go back. "You don't!" I said. "You're not going to beat out Theshei, and it wouldn't bring back your brother even if you did!" I felt like I was beating her up, but there are some truths you can't only half tell. "All you're going to do is get the both of us killed."

"Don't you think I said all this to Terry?" she said. It never dawned on me until that moment that she had. "Do you think he could stop?"

It was that same old agony. There was nowhere to go but destruction, and we couldn't stop going. And then I saw the solution. "All right," I said, "don't stop; work *with* me."

She looked disappointed. "We tried that!" she said.

"No, no," I said. "With me. Using the same wand!"

It stopped her short. "We'll hold each other back," she said finally, but she didn't say it with much conviction.

"Maybe we will," I said, "and maybe together, we'll jump past Theshei." It was a long shot, but it was the only shot she had and I knew she'd take it. I didn't even feel guilty that I didn't believe it. Deep down I knew Theshei was destined to make the breakthrough, and nothing either of us did was going to change that, but at least we'd survive, and that was all that mattered to me then.

CHAPTER 27

IT took a while to convince her, but finally she agreed. But not without reservations. She would work with me on one wand on a trial basis if it worked, but I had to let her work entirely on her own and not even be in the building. I agreed.

I was sure it would work, and even if it didn't, at least we'd be working the wand together again, for a while anyway. I thought we would make such great progress together after a while she wouldn't want to work apart. Besides, I figured we would be so far ahead jointly of where she would be singly, anything she could do alone would be pretty safe by comparison. The odds were that we were going to flare out together trying to work one wand anyway. It was the best deal I was going to get, and I took it.

The individual part wasn't easy, but I didn't mind working outside. The light wands seemed as unaffected by the elements as the Sandscripti, and I was surprised nobody had done it already. Besides, compared to working tandem, it was no great innovation. Even the Sandscripti seemed surprised that working tandem could be done.

When Sandi and I came back in that day and picked up the same wand, everybody within twenty yards of us suddenly decided it was a good idea to take a break. Even Theshei stopped what he was doing to watch. Slip and Slide came soaring over to us, and at first I thought they were going to try to stop us. They were drawing icons so fast they were overlapping one another, and Sandi was gesturing almost as fast. The last thing they drew looked like permutations of the infinity sign made in all the shades of green and gold imaginable.

She turned to me finally and started to tell me what they were saying, but I already knew.

"They're wishing us luck," I said.

"How did you know?!" she said.

"The same way you do," I said. "I just know. That sign language is just a backup; you know from the way they draw and the colors and brightness."

She looked like she hadn't ever thought about it before, and then her eyes lit up. "I already know Sandscripti!" she said.

"We know the meaning of what they're saying; we just don't know the words," I said.

She picked up on what that meant immediately. "Then Theshei isn't that far ahead of us," she said.

I nodded. "The breakthrough isn't knowing; it's knowing that you know." And as soon as I said it, I realized it was just like the Salt; I didn't know any of it; I was just remembering it.

I told her about the Salt and about remembering, and she said, "Yes! It is like I've known it all along." She laughed with delight. "Every time I would do something new, it was like I did it before, like I'd always known how to do it."

But our optimism was short-lived. We gripped the wand in our hands and began to make the simplest of designs, but we weren't anywhere near as fluent as we were alone. I was afraid she was going to change her mind, but when we finished the first erratic figure, she said, "We just have to get used to it." And laughed. It was a carefree, confident laugh, one I hadn't heard from her in a long while.

She was right. The second figure was better, and by the

tenth, we were anticipating each other, and there was no more wavering of the wand as one of us tried to slide it one way and the other pulled opposite. The lines were closer to my thick, stable lines than to her thinner, more fleeting ones, but they had a subtlety mine lacked, and the colors blended more. The icons often had more than one color in them, at least after the first twenty figures, but there was always a sharp distinction between one color and another for me, and even different shades had a clear division between them, but with Sandi, they flowed into one another through a series of in-between shades I couldn't make alone.

A lot of the more complex icons were like somebody had laid a big stencil of a letter over a full-scale oil painting and cut it out, only the "letters" were a lot more like Japanese picture/words than English letters. There was never enough of the picture, if it was one, to recognize, but it colored the lines of the icon in varied and unpredictable ways. Sometimes a pastel would shade gradually into a vivid Day-Glo version of the same color, and sometimes there would be two primary colors butted up against each other with a sharp demarcation between the two. But whatever the colors, they were single and distinct, even when they gradually shaded into one another. The icon Slip and Slide had showed us before Sandi flared out was completely different.

In the new icon, colors seeped out of other colors; they moved and changed but without leaving their place in the icon. It was like the icons we had learned were slides and the new icons were the videotapes the slides were taken from. As soon as I realized that, I knew we could make the new images. Sandi was skeptical.

"Think of it like a movie," I said. "Each of the old icons is a single frame, each one from a different movie. The new icons are the movies themselves."

"You mean a freeze-frame," she said, "like where the rock is moving toward the glass, and just as it hits, everything freezes."

"Exactly," I said, "and if you see a picture from a movie you know, you can run the whole movie forward from that point in your head."

"But we haven't seen these movies," she said.

"It doesn't matter," I said. "In these movies, the whole movie is contained in every frame. It's like a hologram: The smallest piece contains the whole picture, only these holograms move, and all you have to do is shine light through them."

She thought about it for a minute, and then she waved Slide over and gestured for her to make the icon. When Slide did, Sandi watched the colors expand out of the previous colors. She watched it over and over for five minutes, then she turned to me and shook her head. "It's too complex," she said. "We're never going to be able to remember how each of those colors moves into others."

"We don't have to," I said. "We just have to let them start."

"How are we going to make them do that," she said.

"Not make them," I said, "*let* them. It's like the Salt." It was useless. She knew about the Salt from what I'd told her, but it didn't flow for her. Theshei would have understood, but I didn't say so. Mentioning the Salt only emphasized our differences as it was, and I was afraid she would get mad again because she thought I was implying I had some important experience she didn't.

All she said was "Let them?" I nodded. "And it'll just happen?" She sounded skeptical, but then her eyes lit up. "Like the way we learned Sandscripti." I felt like an idiot for not saying it myself. "It will just happen," she said.

She put the wand in my hand and closed her hand over it. "You ready to start the movie?" she said. I nodded. "Then let's shine the light through this frame."

"What light?" I said.

She smiled and squeezed my hand around the wand. "Our light!" And the wand began to move.

I don't know who was more amazed, me or Slide. From the very beginning of the line, the colors didn't just seep out, they flowed out, and by the time we curved the wand into the last curlicue, the colors were streaming out. If the colors were a movie, we'd somehow skipped it into fast forward. Our colors were brighter and faster and more complex than even what Slide had shown us. It was like we had tried to take a step forward and had made a leap. It was a kind of ecstasy.

Slide was delighted. Slip came sailing up, and she practically buried him in the most vivid icons imaginable. He was sketching out icons, and she was pouring hers out over his, and for an instant it looked like somebody had dynamited a rainbow and the liquid colors of it were spreading out everywhere. It was the next step beyond what we had done, but I knew it was within reach. Our colors streamed out, theirs shot out and expanded, and it was like a million-color searchlight was playing out from them all over the inside of the dome. It was nothing short of miraculous.

But the great thing was that we didn't feel the least bit intimidated by it. We just felt happy, happy with our own joy and happy with theirs. What they did put our little show to shame, but we didn't feel any shame. Instead we felt tremendous accomplishment. We hadn't just turned a corner, we'd crossed a street, and there was going to be no stopping us now. We could feel it.

It was hard to say which delighted the Sandscripti more: that we had made our breakthrough or that we had done it together. The whole concept of working in tandem fascinated them, not that it was something they hadn't thought of and maybe done, but that we had discovered it was apparently something they had never expected. I had the suspicion that they were discovering that we were a lot brighter than they thought at first, and they were elated by it. Not only their icons, but they themselves were glossier. They seemed to glow more, the way they did when Theshei made some huge step forward, and I felt as if the timetable for real communication had just jumped ahead of schedule.

The longer Sandi and I worked, the better we got. There was a feeling of celebration whenever one of the Sandscripti floated over to watch us. But the best part was the way it felt. Once we got the basic mechanics down, it was like dancing but more intense, and after we'd been at it for a couple days, it was like we were one person. I didn't have to think about where she would be going with the wand; I didn't think at all. It was like the icons were writing themselves.

Sometimes I felt delighted with what we were doing, and I realized it wasn't me that felt that at all but Sandi. And we could keep at it hours longer than we could alone. Even Theshei had to break a lot oftener and a lot longer than we did, and I thought we really might overtake him. We just didn't get to that point of over-load we did by ourselves, and when we stopped, it was more from physical exhaustion than mental.

More and more often, we stopped because it felt *too* good. It was like the rapture was replacing us. There was a point when we would begin where there were two of us, moving perfectly in sync, but still two separate people. Then, after we were a few icons in, there was only one of us. And if we kept at it, without noticing it, we just stopped being there at all. The icons made themselves, they flowed through us, and we became them.

When an icon was finished, we were suddenly present again, aware of being separate from the language. Nobody had to tell us what each figure meant; the meaning was part of us once we had drawn one. But while we were drawing it, it was like we weren't even there. And that was what was frightening. Wonderful as it was, that vanishing was both magnificent and dreadful. It was too much like death to be totally comfortable, and it scared us, even though we wouldn't admit it.

Still, I could feel both of us pull back a little when we felt ourselves slipping over the line from ecstatic oneness to blissful nothingness. I think it frightened us more than we wanted to admit that that nothingness was so beautiful, so peaceful, so serene. It wasn't really nothingness; it was somethingness, but something so large that it engulfed us and made us part of itself. It was as if we became Everything, but Everything wasn't *us*.

We had worked individually all along, and I had kept my promise and gone outside where I wouldn't inhibit her, but I knew we were doing far more dangerous things together than either of us would be able to do separately so I wasn't afraid for her. In a week we were so far beyond where we had been before we started working the wand together that I stopped worrying about her getting into any situation by herself that she couldn't get out of alone. We were so at one with the wand it didn't seem a danger anymore.

It even got to where I liked working alone because I would discover things that we couldn't learn together, and when we got back together, Sandi would have new insights as well. It was like we would renew ourselves, so we had something to depart from when we became one. As long as we didn't work alone too often or for too long, I was content.

I liked working outside as well. I couldn't imagine why I hadn't gone out there to begin with. Whenever I finished an icon and looked at the world through it, the world changed. Clouds weren't entirely clouds anymore, and the trees shifted and became rooted in the sky as well as the land. When I looked at them through an image hanging luminous in the air, even the stars changed. There always seemed a wholeness to things that focused on the image, like the icon was interpreting and changing my experience of the world, the way language does. To do a thing and to think about doing that thing are separate experiences. The Salt says, "To Be is nothing, to be aware of being, everything."

It seemed like everything I knew about the Salt meant something much more after I joined the Sandscripti. It was hard to explain that to Sandi; we were one person when we held that wand, but she didn't know the Salt so she couldn't fully understand what I meant. It was good to be able to talk to Theshei about it, because skeptical as he was, he had a feeling for the Salt deep down that he didn't want to admit to, a feeling of its rightness despite the distortions of the Saltspeakers.

I shared my new insights into the Salt with Theshei; he shared what the Sandscripti said with me. Especially when they started talking to him about the universe. They called it the Ribbonverse, and it was what they always wanted to talk about.

"I wish I knew more physics," Theshei said. "I wish they taught us more in school."

"You didn't pay attention," I said.

He shrugged. "It might've sunk in anyway," he said. "It's just that I'd be able to follow this Ribbonverse stuff a lot better if I knew more about physics."

"Science is a deaf man with one eye," I said.

"More Commentaries on the Salt?" he said.

It made me smile. I knew I was never going to write them down, and there was even less chance that any Saltspeaker would ever read them, but I still thought of them as the New Commentaries. "I'm still the Wiseguy," I said.

Theshei laughed. "You don't have the Black Stick," he said.

I tapped my head where he'd hit me with it. "I have enough of it," I said.

Theshei held up his light wand. "That was the dark wand," he said. "This is the light."

"Oh, oh," I said, "another convert."

Theshei shook his head. "No," he said, "I don't think this is theology. That's why I wish I knew more physics. I think they're trying to tell us about the nature of the universe."

I said, "Well, it wouldn't surprise me if Science has it all wrong."

"Listen to this," he said. "What-Went-By went by.

Pop! What-Went-By went by. *Pop!* The Ribbonverse."
He didn't actually say *pop;* he made a loud popping
sound with his tongue and the roof of his mouth, and the
second time he made a louder one. He looked at me like
it was perfectly clear. Then he shrugged. "It's so simple
when you say it with the light wand."

"It sounds like the Salt to me," I said.

I knew he wanted to dismiss that idea out of hand, but
he didn't. "Maybe everything true sounds simple and
contradictory," he said. "It only gets complex when you
try to explain it."

"You can explain that?" I said.

Theshei nodded. "A gigantic ball of megamatter en-
ters local space, say a billion times bigger than the
universe. It's so big and so dense it bends space around
itself, like somebody pushing a finger into a balloon."

I could follow that. "Space stretches along the finger,"
I said, "making a long sack."

Theshei nodded. "But this finger has no hand. Once it
gets a certain distance inside, the space around the
opening all slams together trying to follow in its wake.
What happens?"

"Superdense space," I said. "Where the entrance was
becomes a black hole."

Theshei said, "Right. A black hole sealing off one end
of this closed column of inverted space. But not all the
matter around the opening gets closed off. Fragments of
it follow the finger on its path. And fragments of the
finger get pulled back toward the black hole."

I could see where he was going: It was the track I could
see in the sky. "A trail of cosmic debris following behind
it."

"Right," he said. "But it's debris being sucked backward by the black hole where the entrance was."

"So it strings out like a lot of little pebbles," I said. It
wouldn't have seemed obvious when all I knew was high
school physics, but it seemed everything he said was part

of what I was learning in each icon from the Sandscripti. "Only every pebble is a local universe, and inside each one is lighter debris clumping together into stars and planets and us."

"But that's not all," he said. "The moving finger pushes back out through space again like the other side of the balloon."

I knew exactly where he was going. "Space gets puckered shut there too. The debris trailing it crashes into the pucker, making another black hole, with a whole lot of debris strung out between the two."

"Exactly," Theshei said. "And because both black holes pull at the debris, it stays hung up in an equilibrium between them."

"They're both pulling on it equally, so it doesn't go into either of them," I said.

Theshei shook his head. "At either end it does. But in the middle, the cosmic debris is strung out in this zone of equilibrium. That's the Ribbonverse."

It was a great idea, but it didn't seem enough for all we'd been through. "That's what the Sandscripti wanted to tell us?" I said. "The universe is a long, thin balloon of inside-out space with a black hole at each end and the sun, the moon, and the galaxies hanging in equilibrium between them? That's *it*?"

"No!" he said. "That's just all they've been able to tell me so far." He smiled. "Except one thing you'll like."

"What's that?" I said.

Theshei said, "Everything dances."

It sent chills up my spine. The words were right out of the Salt. "That's their exact words?" I said.

Theshei nodded. "I don't know what the Sandscripti mean by it," he said, "but they *are* going to tell me."

I knew what the Salt said about it. The full quote was "Goodguy sings. Badguy sings. Everything dances." And I couldn't wait to hear what the Sandscripti meant by it.

"I just need to learn a couple hundred more icons," he

said, "and they'll be able to tell me the rest of it. Well, more of it anyway. I don't know if any of us could understand it all."

"Did they tell you anything else?" I said.

"Oh yeah," he said, "they told me all that's a lie. It's true, but it's a lie." He smiled slyly, and I didn't know whether he was just teasing me or if he was serious. Then he said, "That's how I translated it anyway. I don't think they really have a word for lying."

"They don't have a word for anything," I said. And it was true; the icons were less words than symbolic images of whatever they represented. Sandscripti didn't really have nouns or verbs; it just had discrete experiences captured in the icons we thought of as words. You strung them together, but their order meant less than the color and intensity and longevity of each image. Everything about the Sandscripti was so complex, so full of nuances, we were bound to misunderstand most of it. It might even be that we weren't capable of understanding anything they said, at least not in the way *they* understood it. "You think we're ever going to be able to understand all this?" I said.

Theshei shrugged. "I don't know," he said, "but the further we get into it, the more familiar it seems."

I knew exactly what he meant. "It's like I'm remembering it," I said, "just like the Salt."

Theshei nodded. He was the only one in the world who could understand that. "Even when you think you understand it," he said, "you can't explain it."

He was right; I knew there were shades of meaning even in what Theshei was telling me that I didn't understand in the way he did. Complete explanation, complete translation is impossible. It made what passed between Sandi and I so special. We shared the same experience; there was no reason to explain it, no reason to translate it into words. We even shared the same being.

Thinking about it made me anxious to begin again. I started to go in, but Theshei said, "How's this tandem light-writing working out?"

"It's like we're one being," I said. "Instead of longing, there's belonging." He nodded like he envied me. I don't think he thought about Scry while he was concentrating on the wand except in some indirect way. She went out of his attention, but she never went out of his mind. I'd brought that emptiness all back again. I didn't want to make him think about it, but I thought maybe it would do him some little good to talk about it. "Have you heard anything about . . ." I made a small part of the icon for her name.

Theshei smiled at it. "Scry?" he said. It seemed to make him happier mentioning her name. "They won't tell me anything about her or where she went," he said, "or they can't."

"You asked them?" I said.

"As soon as I had the icons for it," he said. "They just seemed puzzled that I asked. They told me something, but I don't know what it meant. It's one of those self-contained icons." He drew it in the air. He wasn't as fast as the Sandscripti, but he was getting there. I was amazed at how quickly he did it, especially because of how complex it was. I tried to follow it with my own light wand, but he was much too fast for me.

What it looked like was a simple series of nine concentric circles. They were different colors going from red through the spectrum to black. Each one had all the shades of one color in it. Theshei's colors were like mine, bright and separate, they didn't shade over into one another the way Sandi's did. Somehow I felt that was an important detail, one that changed the whole meaning. I said, "Is that exactly the way they draw it?"

Theshei shrugged. "Who knows?" he said. "They draw one thing; you see something else. They keep correcting me, but theirs look the same as mine to me."

Suddenly, the circles began to pulsate inward from the biggest into the middle of the smallest. And then one by one, they disintegrated until only the black one remained. Then it turned silvery white and disappeared as well.

"Is that the way it's supposed to go?" I said.

He nodded. "Yeah," he said, "except theirs pop when they go." He made that same loud popping sound with his tongue. "You have any idea what it means?" he said.

I shook my head. If he was drawing it right, I didn't think it was anything particularly good. I felt like it meant absence or yearning or loss or even death or maybe all of them together. But I wasn't sure; with the colors shading into one another it might have meant just the opposite, and I didn't want to say anything that would make him feel worse and then have it turn out I was totally wrong. I knew it meant infinitely more than any of us would ever be able to understand. "I'll try it a couple times with Sandi," I said, "and ask her what she feels." We could usually feel what the meaning of an icon was even when we couldn't draw it properly, but I was hoping what I felt was wrong and that I was missing something important.

Theshei must've read what I thought it meant in my face, because he looked sadder than ever. I tried to get his mind away from what I thought. "What did you think it meant?" I said.

Theshei shrugged helplessly. "I don't know," he said. "Gone to lunch; on vacation; gone dancing; return to sender, address unknown." He forced a smile and shrugged again. "Deceased?"

"Can't be that," I said. "I don't think they die."

That seemed to cheer him a little. "They don't have an icon for death," he said. "Unless that's it."

I hated to leave him like that, but I wanted to get back to Sandi. It was past time for her to take a break. I knew she'd be completely engrossed in the icons, but I liked to believe she'd be wondering where I was. Besides, Theshei's heartache made me think of what it would be like to be without Sandi, and I didn't like thinking about that.

"Nothing else seems to affect them," he said. He smiled. "Besides, if they're Ghosts, they're already dead." I don't think it reassured him much. Even if she was alive, it didn't mean he'd ever see her again. There wasn't much even the Salt could help him with there. But I knew the light wand would.

"Time to get back to work," I said.

Theshei gave a little smile and nodded. "Sandi will be waiting for you. You go in. I'm going to work out here for a while." He started to make the icon for Scry, and in a little while, he had lost himself in it. I felt a little better for him, but when I finally turned to go, I had a real bad feeling. In my mind, all I could see was Theshei's vanishing circles going *pop! pop! POP!* out of existence. It made me think of Sandi. It made me run.

I burst through the door at a dead run and stopped almost immediately. Sandi was where she was supposed to be; Slide was near her. And they were talking!

It was halting and full of mispronunciations on Sandi's part. Her icons were drawn so slowly compared with Slide's, and there were mistakes in the way she drew them, but it was clear that there was an exchange going on.

I didn't know what it was about, but I knew it wasn't about the Ribbonverse. I heard Sandi laugh, and for all I know, Slide was telling her that even for Sandscripti women, males were intolerable and invaluable. It didn't really matter what it was; the fact that they were communicating was enough. She'd made her breakthrough.

I was glad that she had made it before me. I was even happy that she'd made it without me. When she moved forward, I moved forward. I still believed Theshei would get the Big Message, but what would link us to the Sandscripti would be what came out of Sandi. Theshei might learn the scientific and philosophic principles the Sandscripti wanted us to learn so badly, but the exchange between our cultures would follow *her* lines, not Theshei's. We might learn the best of them through Theshei, but they would learn the best of us through Sandi.

I was as proud of her as I was happy for her, and I couldn't wait to tell her that. But I didn't want to intrude so I stayed where I was and waited for her conversation with Slide to finish. I watched her icons, and they were radiant. They blazed with happiness. They might have been about the everyday things that make up the bulk of existence, but they were as profound in their way as the Salt. Slide was a thousand times more fluent, but Sandi had an intensity that could only come from being human. It made me certain that in the long run the Sandscripti were going to get back as much from us as they gave.

There was a new connectedness to her images; they seemed to flow into one another even when they didn't quite fit. Even Theshei looked half mute talking to the Sandscripti, so she seemed a little awkward, but everything she did had a special grace that seemed to delight Slide. She seemed as animated and enthusiastic as Sandi.

It was clear that something special was going on, and the light-writers all around her had stopped their drawing to watch. Then outward from her like a ripple, in twos and threes, they put down their wands and watched. I was glad that so many of them were seeing her moment of triumph, and I knew they were thinking that she was as far ahead of the rest of them as Slide was ahead of her.

Some of them were envious no doubt, but most of them felt honored to be there at that turning point between us and the Sandscripti. In the whole history of the human race, that was one of the most important moments, and you could feel it. I thought someday there would be a big picture of that moment exactly as it was, with Sandi and Slide standing there on opposite sides of this elaborate set of icons, the lines burning with significance, the colors blazing with shades never seen before. Slide luminous with satisfaction, Sandi radiant with achievement.

She looked across the crowd and saw me and smiled. I didn't think it was possible that she could be more beautiful than before, but she was. The tension that strained her face even at the best of moments was gone, and she seemed relaxed for the first time in all the time I had known her. I believe it was the only time in her life that she was at peace with herself. Her serenity made me think of Theshei's Scry; it made her that beautiful.

She was exuberant, and when she saw me, she pointed to the new icon still hanging in the air between her and Slide. It was more complex than anything we'd done together and more elegant. It had shades and nuances it would've taken me days to fully appreciate. It was a marvel, and it hadn't even begun to dissipate. I didn't know what it meant, but I felt it was the word for *everlasting.*

Her delight with it made her even more beautiful than her serenity, and I didn't think anything we did together for the rest of our lives would touch that moment for perfection. I believe she thought it too, because she raised her wand toward me and started to talk to me in Sandscripti. I think she did it because she wanted us to be the first humans to talk to one another that way, and the images flowed out of her wand, and as I raised my wand to answer her, she made a flourish that sparkled like a lightning flash. At the center of it was the heart, the first human word in Sandscripti, and the light flashed out from it like a searchlight. I thought for a minute that in a thousand years, human beings would say with pride that the first thing two human beings said to one another in Sandscripti was I love you.

I rejoiced for her and for myself, and because I did, I did not realize until it was too late that the glow spreading from that first human icon was a flare-out.

The ball of light was so bright, people near her were shielding their eyes, and it was spreading so fast that even if I was standing next to her, even if we had been holding the wand together, there was nothing I could have done to reverse it. She put everything she felt into that icon, every ounce of joy flowed through it.

But it was too much. You can't take the high point of your life and turn it into light without it getting away from you. I ran toward her screaming, "No!" but I wasn't even halfway there before she was gone.

The last I saw of her, she was more transparent than Slide. She looked stunned, and sad, and astounded, and a half-dozen other things, without diminishing in the least the joy from which she had drawn the icon that was destroying her. There was no time for her to have thought of much. Out of the flash, I heard a small laugh, as if she was so startled in the middle of that ecstasy, that it seemed the only thing she could do. It was almost as if she had opened a present and found in the box a treasure so valuable she could not have imagined it there. I will never forget that tone of surprise and delight.

When I got to where she had been, there was nothing left of her. The flare-out had swollen so much that it filled the entire dome, but it was so thin, it was harmless. Slide was so transparent, I could hardly see her. The dozen people nearest to her had been knocked to the floor, two were holding their eyes and screaming that they were blind. People further out were starting to cry. Someone behind me was screaming, a long haunted wail that would have served as a summary of human grief. Then I realized it was me.

There wasn't any word for what I felt. Agony is too light. Devastation too trivial. Sorrow is too momentary. I knew there was no word for it in Sandscripti, and I wanted there to be one, I wanted there to be an icon for the grief that comes from being human, from being mortal, so the Sandscripti would know the other half of what we were.

I knew what I wanted. The heart still hung in the air, solid as the stone floor and just as permanent. It is there still. I raised my wand to split it in two.

Theshei knocked the wand from my hand.

He was right to do it. If I had forced what I felt through that wand, all the Sandscripti together wouldn't have been able to stop the flare-out. Nobody would have left that building alive. No wands were active when Sandi had flared out, or there would have been a cascade of flare-outs triggered by hers. All wands were silent still. It wouldn't have mattered. My lines were always so thick, any icon I made would have saturated the room and set off every wand under the dome. There would have been a chain reaction of flare-outs. Maybe not even the building would have been there when it was all over.

I looked at Theshei. I looked at Sandi's heart. I kept trying to say something, but all that would come out were these little cries that were all we had for speech when we were still a million years short of being human.

Theshei looked like he knew what I was feeling. He put a hand around the back of my neck and pressed his head against mine. There were tears in his eyes, but even then I didn't know if they were for Sandi or Scry, for me or for himself. "Badguy does his worst . . ." he said.

I knew what he meant to do. I knew he was trying to put me in touch with the Salt, which was the only thing that would stop me from going with her. I knew what he wanted me to say. But I couldn't say it.

"Badguy does his worst . . ." he said. He kept saying it over and over, waiting in between for me to finish it. I don't know how long we stood like that before the cries finally evolved into words.

"Badguy does his worst . . ." he said.

I answered finally, "Goodguy laughs."

There was only one more thing to say, what Salt-speakers always said over their dead. I didn't want to say it, because once I did, she would be irrevocably dead, even for me. But Theshei began it, and began it, and began it again, until finally I said it with him. "Nothing lost. Nothing gained. Everything that goes remains. No good-byes."

CHAPTER 29

I couldn't bear to lift a light wand after that. I didn't want to be in the dome, and Theshei practiced outside just to be with me. I didn't even carry my wand around, so it wasn't entirely that he was afraid I'd commit suicide. I don't think I had the will for it anyway. I had no desire to do anything, even that. I had no energy. I had no aspirations. I had no needs.

It wasn't any state of enlightenment; I wasn't free of material things. I just didn't care about anything. I couldn't care. I wanted to go on, I knew I owed her that much, the way she owed it to her brother, not because she didn't save him but because if it all failed, his death was for nothing. But I also knew it was Theshei's breakthrough to make. I wasn't going to be the one to get the Big Message from the Sandscripti. It made no difference what I did. So I did nothing.

I felt nothing. Not even grief. I was numb. Theshei would harass me off my mat in the entryway to the dome and out into the sunshine, and I would pull myself up my staff and go, but it was a matter of indifference to me whether I stayed or went. That seemed to be all my staff was for: pulling me up. Everywhere I went was uphill and I leaned on it. But I couldn't lean on the Salt. I couldn't even remember it. And I didn't know why that was.

Nothing interested me. Nothing moved me. Theshei

was talking regularly with the Sandscripti, but I wasn't even curious about what they were telling him. He told me anyway. I didn't listen.

I don't know how many weeks it was before Slip came up to him, and they started talking in a flourish of icons. Theshei was almost as fast as any of them now, and his colors were beginning to flow through gradations into one another in a way that reminded me of Sandi. His whole style was becoming more Sandscripti than human. I watched his light wand spray them out and Slip answer them almost simultaneously, often before Theshei even stopped drawing one of the icons.

Slide was never with him, and the few times I was inside the dome, I didn't see her. I just didn't have enough interest in anything to ask where she was. Besides, only Slip would know, and asking him would mean I had to use a light wand. I wasn't even curious the way any normal person would have been about a loose end like that involving somebody they knew. I knew the only thing I needed to know: Sandi was dead. Beyond that, nothing mattered. When Theshei told me Slip said Slide had "gone dancing," it hardly even registered.

Theshei tried to jar me out of it, coax me out of it, talk me out of it. Eventually, he just dragged me around like some sort of stuffed animal with sentimental value. He'd even talk to me the way somebody might talk to a stuffed animal, without expecting any response, just to organize his thoughts. And he had plenty of thoughts. The Sandscripti were telling him more every day, but even the Sandscripti seemed to feel time was running out. He told me that.

As he talked, he drew out the same ideas in Sandscripti. The icons were mind-bogglingly convoluted, and the colors and brightness were just as incredible. If I had felt anything, it would have been amazement at how he could comprehend anything that complex. "You know," he said, "I think there's stuff about this Ribbonverse thing even the Sandscripti don't comprehend." He thought it over. "No," he said, "*can't* comprehend. Not because they're not smart enough, just because of the way they are."

He stopped and looked at me like I was talking. "So what?" he said. "I'll tell you so what. That's why they need us. They're a lot like us, but they're different just the same. They see things different. And they can't see how to stop whatever's coming. They hope *we* can."

Then he sat there quietly like he was listening to my comments. "You could be right," he said. "I just think there's more to this Ribbonverse thing than physics. Here's the thing, everything dances. I think I know what that means."

I thought, "It means they haven't lost anything." But it would have taken more energy than I had to say it.

"The black holes are not exactly the same size," he said. He smiled as if it explained everything and he was waiting for applause. "So everything is drawn toward the slightly larger one. But the place where their fields come into contact is way out in the middle of the Ribbonverse, and that means that as any part of the mass of the Ribbonverse shifts one way or the other, it becomes part of the mass of that black hole."

He looked at me like I was making an objection. "Yes, that's true," he said. "Everything ought to go into the larger black hole until it gets so big it pulls the other black hole across the whole column of inverted space and swallows it, eliminating the bubble What-Went-By created when it came through that space. *Pop!*"

He raised a finger of exception. "But," he said, "everything dances!"

I waited for his explanation of that with complete indifference. It wasn't going to bring Sandi back.

"The equilibrium between the competing black holes is dynamic. It shifts back and forth continually," he said. "All the scattering of matter in the Ribbonverse is pulled first one way and then the other. The entire elongated droplet of matter fluctuates back and forth at tremendous speeds as the black holes align and realign their perimeters."

Even his enthusiasm didn't have any effect on me. The words were just words. I sat there drawing in the dirt with the end of my staff.

"You can see what that means," he said. I couldn't. I didn't care to. I couldn't care to. "Look," he said. "The only difference between light and lead is how often they fluctuate."

He looked like he expected me to leap to some conclusion. I didn't. "Everything dances!" he said. He gave me that expectant look again. I disappointed him. "It's the key to the light wand!" he said. "It's the key to everything!"

I sat there looking at him, and in a flash he went from joy to rage. He reached down and grabbed me by the front of my robe and jerked me to my feet. The stick clattered to the ground. Then he started shaking me. "How can you sit there feeling sorry for yourself when everything in the universe is about to change?" he shouted. He slammed me up against the wall; I hung there from his hands. "You're a disgrace!" he said. "When Sandi comes back, she shouldn't have anything to do with you!"

"She's not coming back," I said.

"You hypocrite!" he said. "What was all that stuff from the Salt you told her? Lies! You didn't even believe it yourself?" He started shaking me again. "Nothing *dies*, you idiot!" He held me up in front of him and shouted in my face. "Don't you understand what I just told you? Everything dances! Nothing dies!"

I don't know whether I couldn't understand him or couldn't believe him. He didn't care. He shoved me back against the wall and threw his light wand at me. I caught it and then dropped it. He picked up my staff. "Pick it up!" he said. I didn't move. He smacked me in the head with the knobbed end right where he'd hit me before. My head exploded in pain. It was the first thing I'd felt since Sandi died.

"Pick it up!" he said. "I'll hit you again, and I'll keep hitting you."

My head hurt, but it was better than feeling nothing. I knelt and picked up the wand. I almost blacked out when I put my head down. Theshei tapped me with the end of the staff on the arm hard enough to warn me. "Stand up!" he said. And I stood. I didn't mind the pain; it was like waking to a loud noise out of a bad dream. "Use it!" he said. I hesitated. He raised the staff. My head throbbed. "You want to flare out, do it! But you're not going to keep making yourself miserable for nothing!"

I concentrated, and the light began to flow out of it. I began to cry.

I drew the icon for Sandi. I drew the icon for myself. I drew what I could remember of the last icon she had drawn with Slide. The longer I drew, the less pain I felt. I went through the icons we did together. It made my heart hurt, but it didn't kill me, and it didn't make me want to die. My energy came back, not all of it or all at once, but it was a beginning. I knew every time I picked the wand up after that I would be stronger.

When I was done, Theshei smiled and said, "There isn't much time left. You're going to have to do the rest of this on your own."

"Why?" I said. I could imagine putting things back together. I couldn't imagine doing it alone. I knew there would be days when I wouldn't want to pick that wand up again, days when I would need Theshei to make me do it or at least to help me do it.

"That's what I'm going to find out," he said. "Wait for me."

"Where are you going?" I said.

Theshei laughed. "Dancing," he said.

CHAPTER
30

IF Theshei was going dancing, he didn't seem to be going just then, and when he didn't do anything except stand there smiling at me, I gave him his wand back and started to go back inside to get my own. But as I reached the door to the dome, it flew open and a dozen light-writers streamed out. I wondered what was happening inside that could drive them out so fast. The only thing I could think of was a chain of flare-outs. I rushed inside to see if I could reverse some of them. Theshei stayed where he was, still holding my staff.

I ducked through the door and scanned the room to see which way to run. There was nothing out of the ordinary. No panic. No cluster of Sandscripti trying to figure out what went wrong. Just the usual motion of the light wands and the spread of icons that went with it. I had the bad feeling I was in the wrong place at the wrong time. I bolted back through the door.

Theshei was backed against the wall, and the light-writers were packed two deep in a semicircle around him, just beyond the reach of my staff. One of them was lying on the ground behind the mob face down with his wand laying next to him, so I knew at least one of them had gotten too close.

I always thought I would know Orwoz's undercover agents on sight, but it never occurred to me that I would forget to look. Once I had decided they would never be able to pull off their plan, I stopped thinking about them. I thought Orwoz would go on trying to get enough competent Saltspeakers inside to reach critical number and never get close to it, and I assumed he'd leave Theshei alone until he did rather than jeopardize his grand scheme. I never even thought about what Orwoz would do when he found out I apparently wasn't even going to try to assassinate Theshei. I guess I just thought he'd wait and take me out when the whole Sandscripti sanctuary went up, which I knew was going to be never, but which Orwoz was probably always telling himself would be any day now.

I was sure they still weren't anywhere near critical number even though another of Orwoz's would-be assassins had probably been showing up at the front door, begging sanctuary every couple days since I'd gotten there. New recruits weren't anything to worry about; it would be months before they could even begin to become dangerous, and I had never given them a second thought. Orwoz might have had enough Saltspeakers inside, but he didn't have enough who could get their wands going, let alone force a flare-out. But I hadn't given a thought to the fact that they might improve, and I never thought to watch their progress once I started making my own.

Besides, I couldn't see anything but Sandi most of the time I was there anyway. At first it made no sense; all attacking Theshei would do was expose them and make it impossible to carry out Orwoz's master plan. But even before I got close to them, I figured it out.

Either Orwoz had lied to me about how difficult it was to contact his spies or they had improved their communications as well as their skill with the light wand. Somebody must have told Orwoz about Theshei's progress, that he was talking daily with the Sandscripti, and that must have forced Orwoz's hand.

They had been around us all the time, but it was no wonder they were easy to forget. If there was anything that made them stand out, it was their sheer ordinariness. Only when their faces shone with purpose, as they did when they looked at Theshei, did they look different from anybody else.

I wasn't very worried about Theshei; he was hard to hit, and I had no doubt he could break out of their circle whenever he wanted, even without the staff. I couldn't understand why he waited. Unless it was for me to come back out so we could hit them from both sides. I guessed he wanted to take them without killing any of them, just disarm them and throw them out. We both had better things to do than fight a war against the Saltspeakers, and we were too close to the end to spend the time.

I looked at them the way Theshei did, as a minor annoyance, and I wasn't worried until they all lifted their light wands toward him at the same time. After that, it was a nightmare coming true. I knew exactly what they planned: all of them flaring out at once and taking Theshei with them, but I never thought until that instant that they would ever be able to do it. I realized Orwoz must have taken all of the best he had in there, the ones who had been practicing since he first started sending spies inside and was throwing them all against Theshei at once. That many flare-outs all in the same place wouldn't start a chain reaction that would end the world or even vaporize the entire sanctuary, but it would probably take out a sizable piece of the dome. It was Orwoz's kind of a plan: subtle, treacherous, meant to succeed in a lot of different ways.

It would certainly destroy Theshei, and even the newest spy would have reported that killing Theshei was a way to cripple Sandscripti efforts. It would set the Sandscripti back and make them look bad as well. No doubt the Saltspeakers were already spreading rumors that using the light wand turned ordinary people into homicidal maniacs.

Killing Theshei with their light wands had another purpose besides making it look like the Sandscripti were running a factory for madmen. It was meant to repulse the Sandscripti, and it might have worked. Any species that could turn a thing like the light wand into a weapon was clearly not worth trying to civilize or save.

And even if it didn't turn the Sandscripti against us, news of a new kind of explosion was bound to create a furor. People would imagine all kinds of radiation and side effects. There'd be a demand for controlling the Sandscripti, for putting restrictions on their use of the light wand. The Government wouldn't have been able to do anything about it, but even the Government's helplessness would generate widespread fear and the hatred fear creates, and all of it would be directed toward the Sandscripti.

I didn't understand why the Saltspeakers had let me get by them when they came out, unless there was another team of assassins for me, but it was a mistake I intended to capitalize on. I rushed them from behind, knocking some of them down, throwing some out of the way, shouting for Theshei to make a break for it.

Balls of flaring light were already spreading in front of five of them. I picked a wand up off the ground and jammed it into one of the flare-outs, trying to reverse it. When I had it stopped, I moved on to the next one. But the rest were already surging beyond the possibility of control. It was like one of those dreams where you're falling behind, and the harder you struggle, the further behind you get. As soon as I reversed one, it would only start back up again. In a few seconds, half a dozen of them were past the point of no return, and the rest were not far behind.

I looked to Theshei for help, but he just stood against the wall. His own light wand was glowing. There was a small brilliant drop of incredibly bright light at its tip, and then there was a flash that knocked us all back, and Theshei was gone.

I knew he was gone even though I couldn't see him. I couldn't see anything except a uniform field of red that kept shifting into other colors and finally settled into black. I stumbled over somebody and fell. Some of the Saltspeakers were screaming that they couldn't see. There were other flashes from the Saltspeaker kamikazes, but none of us could see them. I thought there would be a chain reaction and I would be gone too, but Theshei's flare-out seemed to have swallowed the others and the backwash had blown out the rest.

I got up and tried to feel my way to where Theshei had been. All I found was the wall. It was hot, very hot. Then my foot touched part of my stick, and I bent down and felt for it. It was shortened by half, and one end was smoldering. I stood there holding it like a candle until some of the people pouring out of the dome came to help me.

They rounded all of us up, tried to treat us, reassured us the blindness was only temporary. Somebody put a wet towel over my eyes and sat me down. They asked me what went on, and I told them. Somebody else asked me, and I told them again that Saltspeakers trying to discredit the Sandscripti tried to assassinate Theshei by flaring out around him. In order to stop the chain reaction that would happen if all twenty flared out in the same spot, he sacrificed himself. His flare-out overwhelmed theirs and stopped the chain reaction.

I couldn't believe he could have flared out that fast, not even intentionally. And the force of it was beyond anything anyone could have expected, even including the seven Saltspeaker flare-outs. But I was obsessed with the brightness of the flash. I kept telling anybody who would listen over and over, "It was so bright! It was so bright!" They thought I was in shock, and they were probably right. But I kept thinking it was the flash at the end of the world, and I couldn't figure out why we were still there.

It was two days before my eyesight came back. That's a long time to think in the dark. But I didn't give way to despair. They let me have a light wand, and even though

I couldn't see what I was doing, I could still trace
rudimentary figures. It felt good, it kept my spirits up,
and it was a way of reminding myself that I was not
going to give up this time. I had Theshei's work to carry
out. I had Sandi's as well. I wanted to be ready to go
when my eyesight came back.

There were still blobs of iridescent color in my vision
when Slip came to see me. He seemed oddly at peace, as
if some resolution had been reached. I assumed, since we
were still there, that something Theshei had done had
put off the End of Everything. The icons I drew him were
simple and flawed, the color blotches kept interfering
with what I saw, but he understood. When he answered,
he had to redraw his own icons a couple times so that I
could see them right. But we managed.

I asked him if the End of Everything was still coming.
He made the same image Sandi had copied from Slide. It
was so beautiful I assumed it meant everything was all
right. I knew the explanation of how was beyond me, but
I asked anyway. Slip filled the air with icons; I recognized a lot of them as the ones Theshei drew when he
talked about the Ribbonverse, but even human physics
was beyond me right then, so all I could do was try to
remember them for some future time when they made
sense to me.

I knew there was no deadline anymore, but I was still
anxious to learn, and when my eyes cleared almost
completely, I was back in the dome working with the
light wand. Slide worked with me constantly, and I
became more and more fluent until he could draw me
the same icons he had drawn Theshei and I could
understand them.

I don't know why, but I was oddly content. There were
pangs of grief for Sandi almost every time I saw some
icon she would know, and there were moments every day
when I missed Theshei and missed having someone who
knew the Salt. Sometimes I quoted it to Slide, but it

must've lost something in the translation because he almost always misunderstood and thought I was talking about the Ribbonverse or What-Went-By.

About the only thing I was fairly sure he understood was what it was like to lose somebody, even if they weren't really lost. How even when you know the grief is for yourself and not for them, you still keep grieving. But we didn't talk about that much.

I asked him where Slide was once, and he made a magnificent image full of color and delicate lines that vibrated on and off faster and faster until it vanished. I knew it was what Theshei must've seen when he said Slip told him Slide had gone "dancing." I knew I couldn't begin to understand all that it meant; every Sandscripti icon was a library of meaning, but it made me feel good to see it anyway.

A lot of the images I didn't understand made me feel good anyway, not only when I drew them, but when I saw them drawn by Sandscripti. It seemed every moment I didn't spend talking with the Sandscripti, I spent watching the Sandscripti talk. The more I watched, the more I understood, and the more I was surprised to find that what I thought I knew about an image was often completely wrong, except for the general feeling.

It was more than a month before I found out that the End of Everything hadn't been stopped at all.

CHAPTER
31

WHAT I liked most about the Sandscripti, especially Slip, was that they simultaneously enlightened and bewildered me. And nothing baffled me more than how the End of Everything could have occurred and we could still be sitting around discussing it. Or how the Sandscripti could be so unconcerned about it when they were so intent on preventing it before Theshei flared out.

What Slide couldn't understand was why I kept insisting that opposites were necessarily contradictory. Everything that is true somewhere is false somewhere else, it was all in the "framework." The framework apparently had to do with who was looking at a particular experience and where. But like everything else Sandscripti, what was true in general disintegrated in a series of contradictory particulars.

I had figured out early on that the Sandscripti had only a vague concept of time. Instead of past, present, and future, they had only the-moment-as-experienced-here/now and the-moment-not-being-experienced-here/now, which seemed to include the past, the future, and all things that were possible but didn't happen, or did happen but at least weren't happening here and now. Slide explained that the End of Everything was occurring but not here/now and not to us.

I didn't know whether that meant the universe was slowly and irreversibly dissolving but just hadn't evaporated this far yet, or that we were already dead and just didn't know it. I was pretty clear that they weren't very concerned about it in any case. They had an infinite tolerance of contradiction. He told me the most important thing about everything I had learned was that it was absolutely true and at the same time absolutely a lie.

I remembered Theshei telling me the Sandscripti had told him the same thing, but it didn't seem to bother him to leave it unresolved. It bothered me. At least when I wasn't working the wand. I would sit outside, leaning against the wall and drawing in the dirt with the half a staff Theshei had left me with, or making the icons I didn't understand over and over again in the air, and trying to make it all make sense.

I was sitting there, trying to resolve Slide's latest contradiction. I had asked him, "What was What-Went-By that made the Ribbonverse?"

And he had said, "Us."

I was sitting there trying to figure out exactly what it was that wasn't translating about his answer when I saw two Sandscripti coming across the field from the trees. There were always Sandscripti around, and it struck me that I had fallen into the trap I thought I never would of taking them for granted. I still admired them, but I didn't have that awe of them I used to have. Just seeing them didn't leave me speechless.

I thought of that because something about the Sandscripti coming across the field brought back that same feeling. There was something special about them, something about the way they moved that was remarkable even at a distance. I thought about that day in the woods when we looked out onto the road at Scry and Theshei found his Thunder. I thought about how that was as near as I would ever come to the miraculous.

I had gotten into the habit of drawing the icons for everything I was thinking about, which was the equivalent of talking to myself as far as the Sandscripti were concerned. So without thinking about it, I made the icon for Scry.

And as soon as I did, the closer Sandscripti raised its light wand and wrote "Yes?"

I thought for a minute that I had drawn it wrong and said something aloud I didn't intend to. So I drew the icon for Scry again, but this time I made it linger and pulse, the way you do with a question in Sandscripti.

And the same answer came back, "Yes."

The first Sandscripti was close enough that I could see it was a woman, but I couldn't see her clearly. The one behind her was edge on and distorted a little by being behind the first, and I couldn't see if it was male or female. I got up and started moving toward the female, and when I got about fifty yards closer, I could see it was Scry! I was astounded. She'd never come back while Theshei was there. And she hadn't come back when he was gone, and I'd assumed she was dead or whatever the Sandscripti equivalent of that was. I was amazed that she was here and alive, and I ran toward her. I'd never really met her; I'd only seen her for that brief moment on the road beyond the woods, but it was as if I knew her. I wanted to tell her about Theshei. I thought she probably wouldn't know who he was, but I wanted to tell her about him anyway, and I ran toward her.

Just as I got close, the second Sandscripti came around from behind her, and I stopped dead. He looked just like Theshei except that he was a Sandscripti. It was like finding and losing him all over again, and it was all I could do not to break down.

Then he raised his light wand and icons of incredible grace and brightness flowed out of it. They were so beautiful, I didn't even translate them, I just stared at their color and the swift sure way they were made and thought that if someday I could speak Sandscripti as fluently as that, everything that had happened to me would have been worth it.

But the most startling thing of all was that he ended everything he had to say with the icon for my name. The icons before it still lingered in the air, and I flashed back over them. They said, "Badguy does his worst . . ."

I couldn't believe my eyes. It was definitely a Sandscripti, I could see through him, he was three times as big as Theshei, and yet I knew it was him. I was afraid to let myself believe it, and I said, in icons so intense they seemed too heavy to hang in the air, "Theshei! Theshei!"

He touched his icons, and they glowed again as if he had just rewritten them. "Badguy does his worst . . ."

And my light wand swirled in the air, making images that said, "Goodguy laughs."

And the Sandscripti who looked like Theshei, who had to *be* Theshei, laughed soundlessly. Scry smiled at me as if she knew me, had known me for a long time. And I said, "You're a Sandscripti! How?" in icons that seemed to be on fire.

And Theshei, with his elegant intricate images, said, "We're all Sandscripti."

After that, I could hear the sound of his voice in my head every time he made an icon, just the way he would have said it if he were still flesh and blood. He wasn't putting the sounds there, it was just that the icons had become so second nature to me that I could hear them. I said, "How? How? How?"

Theshei smiled. I could see through him to the treeline beyond the field, but it looked transformed. "Everything dances," he said. "Human beings are just Sandscripti dancing slow."

Since the Change, nobody would believe I didn't entirely understand that. But I was still human then, and I thought in terms of the little Science I knew from high school. What Theshei meant was that everything in the universe vibrates, some things fast, some things slow. The slower, the more solid. In our part of the Ribbonverse, everything vibrated slowly, that made the world of solid things. In the Sandscripti's part of the Ribbonverse, things vibrated faster and were, to us, thinner, less material, even invisible, and therefore to Science, unreal. When a Sandscripti comes here, they start to gradually vibrate more slowly and become more physical, more matter and less light. That was why some seemed more transparent than others. It depended on how long they were here.

We humans, of course, were just Sandscripti who had been here too long, gotten too dense, and forgot not only how to get back, but forgot we'd ever been anywhere but here, ever been anything but human. The Salt was right again: "Death is just Remembering. There is no dying." The Sandscripti we could see in their bodies of light never slowed down long enough to become completely material beings, and if they did, they would have suffered the same forgetting we did. That was why Slide and Scry had left: They were slipping into the forgetfulness that would have slowed them down into being human.

They wouldn't have been the first trapped here, mired in the slow stagnant end of the Ribbonverse. Too many Sandscripti to count had forgotten themselves into human form and had had to die to become Sandscripti again and return to the world of light. Most of them never wanted to get trapped here again. But a few who had compassion on those still trapped and those who would be trapped intentionally slowed their dancing down until they solidified into human form once again to tell us we were all Sandscripti. But they couldn't because the very slowing down of their vibrations made them forget what they had come to tell us.

Deep down they knew, just as we all know, it just couldn't be put into words, not even enough to remember except as a small vague insistence on believing that we never die. That belief was never snuffed out completely in any of us, no matter how deep our forgetting. That was why the Salt was always remembered instead of learned. The Salt was as close as the truth ever got in human words, maybe as close as it could be said without the light wand. And the light wand, which made it all possible, was just the recognition, after so many failed attempts, that you could come back a little at a time, that you could control the rate of your dancing. It was what the Saltspeaker Commentaries would have called a physical manifestation of a spiritual fact.

Of course, everybody knows now that the Sandscripti don't actually come from somewhere else at all. There is no distance between us; they exist here simultaneously with us, vibrating at different frequencies, turning off and on too fast for us to see most of the time and too fast to see us. In our level of vibration, all matter, all things, all stuff dances toward one black hole and then the other, back & forth, back & forth, back & forth. For the Sandscripti, except when they come here and slow down as near they can to our level, none of this exists. Here the material world is true; vibrating at the Sandscripti rate, it's a lie, a dream.

"How did you get here?" I asked him.

Theshei shook his head as if I should know the answer to that. He held up his light wand. "This is the music," he said. "This determines how fast we dance."

He began to write with it again, drawing his own physical shape in the air, and as he did, the Sandscripti faded and Theshei the human being took form. The huge sail of light just got denser and denser and smaller and smaller until it fit into the outline Theshei had drawn in the air. When he was finished, he stood in front of me in the flesh. I stared at him openmouthed. "I told you it was all in the light wand," he said. "It changes your frequency, makes you vibrate faster or slower, once you know how to use it."

Like all the great truths, it was also a lie. All the light wand really was was a focus, a way of fixing our attention on the fact that we vibrated at all, that matter and energy were one, something even Science knew. It was just what the Sandscripti said it was, "an interface of the will"; it was the focal point of our desire to return to our true selves. Here in the solid world, it was an interface between matter and energy. But everything solid is untrue in the world of Light.

"You're you!" I said.

Theshei laughed. "I never stopped being me. You just couldn't see me. I wasn't dancing this slow." He took a step forward and hugged me. "I told you nothing dies," he said.

It was him. It was really him. I was so happy I didn't know what to do. "You flared out!" I said.

Theshei nodded. "Instant change of frequencies. You go from slow to superfast in an instant. All your slow-moving matter changes instantly to light. It doesn't kill you; it just changes your form." He raised the light wand. "And this changes you back."

"But what about the End of Everything," I said.

"This is it," he said. "The End of Everything as we knew it, the beginning of Everything Else."

"Then it wasn't the end of the world?" I said.

"Not the annihilation of the material world," he said. "But the end, yes; nothing's ever going to be the same again."

I could see that he was right. It was only a matter of time before even the Saltspeakers would be transforming themselves back and forth between the human and the Sandscripti universe. And that, of course, would change everything.

"Nothing," Scry said, "will ever be the same again anywhere." When I looked at her, I was stunned. She was as real and solid as Theshei. And she was just as beautiful in human form as she was as a Sandscripti. She smiled. "It's a great trick once you learn it," she said. Her laughter reminded me of Sandi. It must've showed in my face because Theshei turned and pointed toward the field. Just beyond where we stood another Sand-scripti was forming. I knew it would be her, and I ran toward her. By the time I reached her, she was slowing herself down to human form. I threw my arms around her. They went right through her, and I almost fell. I stepped back and waited with tears in my eyes. I had never hoped to see her again in this life.

Even when I couldn't see through her anymore, I waited, unsure if she was fully physical again. She shook her head and laughed. "You never did do anything right," she said. Then she threw her arms around me and kissed me. Nothing ever felt so good.

Theshei looked at Scry and said, "There are some things you're going to like about occasionally being human."

Back across the field another Sandscripti was taking shape. We watched it come toward us and Sandi's face filled with delight. Even in Sandscripti form, I could see it looked too much like her to be anybody but her brother. As I watched him slow himself down into the material world and human form, I knew that soon, all over the world, so many we thought were dead would be coming back from the world of Light.

CHAPTER 32

AND that, of course, was the beginning of the Change, which has transformed all of us human beings back into what we always were: spiritual beings. Once we weren't trapped by our forgetfulness in the material world, we could make it a park, a nice place to visit, and we visit it often, but we don't stay long enough to forget who we are. It's no more beautiful than it ever was at its best, but it *is* beautiful.

Theshei was right; nothing is the same as it was. I believe at the root of all the trouble we had caused ourselves, from war to pollution to greed, was the fact that we were going to die. We had come to believe that, and it poisoned everything we did. Afraid of leaving the physical world, we tried to hoard as much of it as we could. So we stole and lied and betrayed one another; we killed and destroyed; we corrupted everything we touched with our fear. We caught a bad case of Death, and we gave it to everybody we touched, our friends, our family, our children. It took Theshei to show us how to cure ourselves.

Earth is a wonderful place now, but no better than it could always have been if we hadn't forgotten who we were. Nobody fouls its air, nobody contaminates its water, nobody poisons its land. Nobody lives in cars anymore or dies in the street. All that old greed is gone. And the violence it made. And the fear that made it. We can't even remember it now. We can't even believe it wasn't just a bad dream we had a long time ago when we were frightened children.

I come to the Old Wiseguy's clearing from time to time. The Old Wiseguy was right: It isn't the same. It's better but not the same. I see him a lot as a Sandscripti, but he rarely becomes human now, so I never did see him again here in his clearing. Even Orwoz and the Rhinettes are Sandscripti now, though they do come back from time to time just to speak the Salt and marvel at how true it all was and how much we all misunderstood it. I get together with them when they do, and we laugh about old times. Occasionally, even Theshei comes back for a laugh.

I was the one, of course, who, in my Sandscripti form, brought the truth back to the Saltspeakers, and I couldn't resist bringing Morzon along. He looked so much more impressive as a Sandscripti than he had as a gawky Saltspeaker rookie that I was surprised Orwoz recognized him. I wasn't surprised when Orwoz ran around hooting that Badguy was bringing the dead back to haunt him and trying to hide himself behind the newest bunch of Saltspeaker rookies any more than I was to see the Rhinettes take off in all directions like a flock of startled birds.

The Saltspeakers didn't want to hear the truth at first, but after they threw, shot, or swung everything they had through us, and after Orwoz had been subdued and tranquilized; and the Rhinettes had been rounded up, they stopped and listened. But I don't think it was merely Morzon and I transforming from ourselves from Sandscripti to human that convinced them. It was what Slip told me about What-Went-By. He told me, "What-Went-By is us." And that's what I told the Saltspeakers.

As long as you exist at this physical level, there *is* an inside-out balloon universe with a black hole at each end making us dance back and forth like excited neon in a tube. And the light wand is a mechanism for changing vibrations by slowing down and speeding up the dance of your atoms. The Ribbonverse really is the end result of an enormous chunk of megamatter distorting space and setting up a self-contained plane of existence with its own rules. Here, the Sandscripti are made of light, we're made of denser light, and the world itself is made of light so dense it takes eons to dissolve itself. But even in the world as Science knew it, everything is dancing, atoms are shifting and recombining in new and different forms, and every form is in the process of disintegrating. Here, time is a reality, and events flow out of previous events and into later ones. But even here, they flow, the moment moves, and all we have that is real is our awareness of the moment.

But every great truth is a great lie as well. From the level of the Sandscripti, all this is a dream. Space, time, the material world, are all constructs with no more reality than our belief allows them. On the level where the Sandscripti exist, where *we* exist, even without our bodies of light, there was no space, there was no chunk of megamatter, there was only Goodguy. The world of seeming things, the world of matter and light and time is made of Goodguy. The black holes are Goodguy, the long closed bubble of space that constitutes the Ribbonverse is Goodguy, and the trail of debris from one end of the Ribbonverse to the other are droplets of Goodguy. And this is the great miracle and the great paradox, Goodguy is indivisible. Each tiny droplet of Goodguy, just the way a hologram contains the complete three-dimensional picture of the whole, contains Goodguy complete in every detail. Small as we are, light as we may be, vibrating fast or slow, within the illusion of the Ribbonverse or without, we contain the complete totality of Goodguy. Inside the smallest portion of each of us is the Whole.

Goodguy is just another name for What-Went-By. Badguy is just another name for our forgetfulness. In the end, everything remembers it is Goodguy again. That's where we are now. What Theshei missed at first was that What-Went-By wasn't only some physical object that created twin black holes that keep trying to swallow the universe, it was a *spiritual* object, it was us. We're Goodguy. We just forgot that. The Sandscripti are Salt-speakers after all, and everything the Salt said was true, once we understood it. "Everything dances. Nothing lost. Nothing gained. Everything that goes remains. No good-byes.

"And nothing dies."

AVONOVA PRESENTS
AWARD-WINNING NOVELS
FROM MASTERS OF SCIENCE FICTION

A DEEPER SEA
by Alexander Jablokov　　　71709-3/ $4.99 US/ $5.99 Can

BEGGARS IN SPAIN
by Nancy Kress　　　71877-4/ $5.99 US/ $7.99 Can

FLYING TO VALHALLA
by Charles Pellegrino　　　71881-2/ $4.99 US/ $5.99 Can

ETERNAL LIGHT
by Paul J. McAuley　　　76623-X/ $4.99 US/ $5.99 Can

DAUGHTER OF ELYSIUM
by Joan Slonczewski　　　77027-X/ $5.99 US/ $6.99 Can

NIMBUS
by Alexander Jablokov　　　71710-7/ $4.99 US/ $5.99 Can

THE HACKER AND THE ANTS
by Rudy Rucker　　　71844-8/ $4.99 US/ $6.99 Can

GENETIC SOLDIER
by George Turner　　　72189-9/ $5.50 US/ $7.50 Can

THE CONTINUATION
OF THE FABULOUS
INCARNATIONS OF IMMORTALITY
SERIES

FOR LOVE OF EVIL
75285-9/ $5.99 US/ $7.99 Can

AND ETERNITY
75286-7/ $5.99 US/ $7.99 Can